NO CORNER
TO HIDE

Mark E. Becker

NEW
N
G
GENRE

No Corner To Hide by Mark E. Becker

Library of Congress Case# 1-3021607001

Published by New Genre Publishing

First Traditional Printing 2016

ISBN: 978-0-9853500-1-7

Book Design: GKS Creative, Nashville

Printed in the United States of America

Disclaimer: This is a work of fiction. The characters, incidents, plot, and dialogue are products of the author's creativity and are not intended to be interpreted as true. Any resemblance to actual persons, alive or deceased, is entirely coincidental.

Dedication/Acknowledgment

I want to thank my many friends and family who
first encouraged me to write, and who read the manuscript.
The brutally honest critics made me a better writer,
and the rest gave me the support I needed to take
the story that was rattling around inside of my head
and give it release.
I have no investment in the words.
I do have an investment in the story.

Now, let me tell you about a guy who is not a politician
who just happens to be the President of the United States...

PROLOGUE

S am? Are you home?" Nikola Tesla paid a visit to his friend and occasional mentor, Samuel Clemens, known to the world as Mark Twain. The humorist and writer sat on a wicker glider in his undershirt and ever-present suspenders. He was barefoot and smoking his favorite pipe. After a pause that made Tesla fidget, Clemens exhaled a cloud of rum-scented tobacco and sighed.

"I'm in plain view, you mad scientist. If it wasn't me, I'd make a damnable ghost of me, and if you make me lose my place, I'll ... Oh, tarnation!" He laid the section of the New York Times on the previously-read stack at his side, and turned his attention to the source of the disturbance.

"Well, I come for a purpose," Tesla responded quickly in his Croatian accent. He was immaculately dressed, even though the temperature suggested casual. The inventor-genius clutched a large file under his arm. The word, **GOVERNMENT** was boldly inked onto the cover. Clemens drew on his pipe and languidly exhaled a cloud of smoke as he surveyed his visitor's appearance and obvious state of agitation. "Well . . . come on in and sit awhile, and we can talk about it," he croaked. He shooed his spaniel, Blue, off the wingback chair at his side with a soft whack of the thick Sunday version of the *New York Times* still rolled up in his lap.

Tesla chose a stiff straight-backed chair and pulled it close to Clemens' bare feet, causing his friend to peer at him between his toes. "You are the most peculiar man I have ever met. I know you're smart and all, but peculiar just the same. I like that in a person." Tesla smiled. Clemens had broken the ice in the most disarming of ways, a talent he had developed from years of public speaking. *If you can get them to laugh, your audience of one or one hundred will relax, and they will like you for it. Call it entertainment. I got him to relax, but I'll be damned if I know what this is all about.*

"You want a cigar or something to drink? How 'bout some lemonade?"

"No, I can't stay long," Tesla said nervously. His eyes shifted. The dark circles beneath his eyes betrayed a lack of sleep. *I wonder how long it's been since that head touched a pillow.* Clemens was concerned, but he had known his young friend to forego sleep for days when his mind was working on a project. It seemed to be his way of living.

"Well, then spit it out. What you got in that suspicious folder with **Government** written on it? If you have come here to tell me that you have invented something that will take the place of politicians, it might cause me to get up from this chair and vigorously shake your hand . . ."

Tesla interrupted, not one to banter. "I have here a cure for some of the ills of mankind, and I want you to give it to him next week."

"Who? Who do you want me to give it to, and what is this danged thing?"

"You are meeting next week, with our young president, this Mr. Roosevelt . . . I read it in the paper. My invention. I want you to give it to him."

"Now Nick, you need to slow down. I need to figure out what we're dealing with here," said Clemens, more accustomed to moseying than engaging in direct discourse. "What I'm saying is, Son, you gotta start at the beginning, because it's early in the day, and I haven't had my first drink, and I don't know what the hell you're talking about." He raised in his chair, but in his present state of comfort, he wasn't going anywhere.

"Sam, I'm good at making things. I think big thoughts. I dream in colors. I plan things in my mind. I think things that other people don't. I don't explain things very well." Tesla was quickly becoming exasperated.

Clemens saw that his guest was nervous. He believed the words, as his experience with geniuses had led him to the conclusion that they were incapable of deception, and had no concept of it. They were awful communicators, socially inept, and honest to a fault. They had an intense need to get their thoughts known, without the capitalist concept of making money from their ideas. Their satisfaction was the creation part. What happened beyond that was for others to exploit, and Tesla had experienced more than his share of that.

"Sam."

Nikola Tesla stood, and extended the folder.

"This is my gift to our country."

"What is it, Son, and why do you want me to give it to Theodore Roosevelt, for God's sakes? I have heard that he's crazy as a bedbug, and that he likes to go around doing these feats of strength and . . ."

"My friend, this is my life's accomplishment, and I entrust it to you." Tesla waited for Clemens to accept the folder. He pulled out the contents and perused them. After many minutes, he looked at Tesla with a stern gaze. "I write books. I have no idea of what this is."

"The papers in your hands describe free energy."

"What does that mean?" Clemens broke his gaze to reach for his lemonade, and took a big gulp.

"You will never need to rely upon coal to heat your house or oil to supply power to light Mr. Edison's lamps, or Mr. Westinghouse's generators. The energy comes from the earth."

Clemens gave a sigh, resigning himself to the idea that he would have to raise himself from his lounging chair to properly deal with Tesla's dilemma. "What I think you're telling me is that I hold in my hands an invention that will change the world for the better, but there's no money in it."

"Yes, I have learned that unless I can show my investors a profit, they are not interested. Just yesterday, Pierpont Morgan refused more funds for my Wardencyffe project on Long Island. . . . You know, my project to transmit power over long distances without the use of wires. I did not understand why, until he told me the reason. He has the monopoly on the copper that they put in the wires, and he would lose money . . ." Tesla stood and advanced toward the pitcher of lemonade. He poured himself a glass and drank it all, not pausing to take a breath until he had finished.

"I was on the verge of making the project a success, and he shut it down. He told all of his friends, Westinghouse is one of them, to refuse to fund my projects. He owns all of them, and they own me." Tesla hung his head in frustration. "By doing good, I have made many enemies."

"So what makes you think that Theodore Roosevelt, that upstart from New York, won't just steal your idea and dole it out to the highest bidder? He's as much a silver spoon as the rest of them." The conversation had struck a chord with the famous author, who had failed at every financial enterprise he had attempted in his long career.

"I don't know where to turn. This is a gift to my adopted country, and I want people to be the better from it. I read that this man believes that the president is the steward of the people and he should take any action necessary for the public good. If I cannot trust him, I cannot trust anyone." The sorrow and frustration was reflected in Tesla's dark eyes.

"I'm kinda soured on inventions myself, but I'll do your bidding. I got roped into going down to Washington next week to meet our Theodore Roosevelt, like they do whenever they take office. I'll make sure he gets it. One thing, though. Nick, why don't you just go down there and give it to him yourself?"

"I was not invited, but you were. Even though I am an American, I remain a foreigner to these rich and powerful men, and they are watching me."

❖　❖　❖

At the end of his life, long after Clemens had passed, Nikola Tesla laid on his deathbed. Within minutes of his arrival at the emergency room, Tesla's condition had been diagnosed: *Heart failure.* He was summarily dispatched to a hospital room by gurney, clutching a box of his beloved Ritz crackers. In his latter years, the crackers were the mainstay of his diet, when he took time from his experiments to eat.

If the contents of the box had been analyzed, the chemical testing would never reveal that the crackers were laced with a tincture derived from the root of a common plant that grew in the northern forests north of New York, a plant known by the locals as Monkshood. Modern laboratory testing in 1943 lacked the sophistication to detect it: The symptoms, sweating, dizziness, breathing difficulty, and tingling up the left arm into the shoulder, all were the same as a heart attack.

There was one unique characteristic that Monkshood possessed; it caused mouth numbness and rendered the victim mute. Even if Tesla knew he had been poisoned, he would have been unable to communicate his condition to his doctors. He would die there by the end of the day, never to return to his New York hotel room.

Within minutes of Tesla's departure by ambulance, the Nazi spies converged in a well-coordinated effort and picked the simple lock with practiced and expert swiftness. Once inside, they began sorting through Tesla's files in a desperate effort to find the plans to the weapon that had the potential to change the course of the war and ensure world dominance for Adolf Hitler and the Nazi regime. It was not the first attempt, and they were not alone. Previous efforts to obtain the plans for the death ray had been fruitless. The last break-in at Tesla's laboratory had resulted in a confrontation with another team of intruders in the darkness, but they all left empty-handed. There were no plans.

The Germans wanted the project the press had named the "Death Ray", an invention that Tesla claimed would end all wars. The rest of the technology became irrelevant to their desperate quest, and it would be left behind for the vultures who were employed by industrialists intent upon making another fortune from his brilliance. This time, the Nazi spies had an advantage over the rest. They had poisoned him, and all they had to do was watch from the hotel across the street for the ambulance to arrive to take the great inventor away.

The most recent spying was political and military in nature, but there were others. There had always been someone who watched and waited. It was a long-term stalking, always waiting for the next invention. The last project to fail for lack of funding, the project to wirelessly transmit electricity, had the potential to surpass the profits derived from all of the other projects combined, but he had perfected it without the support of the Robber Barons. Tesla's lifelong experience of creating inventions and making them work only to have his ideas stolen, had made him wary. Of more than two hundred patents Tesla had obtained over his lifetime, the most profitable inventions were stolen. While they made millions from his brilliance, he had struggled. Out of frustration, he began keeping his ideas organized in his head in intricate detail, where he could protect and revise them. His brilliant mind became a safe which no intruder could crack. He had never drawn a schematic or put notes on paper. The death ray lived in intricate detail inside his mind, but when he was gone, his creations would go with him.

Within minutes of the news of Tesla's rush to the hospital by ambulance, they were all there, clamoring to get into the apartment and fighting with each other like Christmas shoppers at a fifty-percent-off sale. A gunshot stopped the commotion as uniformed officers emerged from a large truck. Without a word, they produced hand trucks and brandished guns. The crowd became silent, and parted. One officer produced a badge and announced, "We are from the Alien Property Office. You are ordered to disperse. We are seizing the contents of this room on behalf of the United States government."

❖ ❖ ❖

As he drew his last breaths, Tesla smiled with private satisfaction. His best invention, the Tesla Generator, had never been patented. He had seen many others disappear from the patent office over the years. Radio. Radar. Alternating current. They were all his inventions, and they had all been patented and promptly stolen by the scavengers who could envision how to make a profit. They made fortunes from his genius, but he would die broke.

This time, he retained that cherished idea in his head. Every detail was there for him to see; his synesthetic memory kept it in extreme detail. The only plans for the generator that would remain, after death had extinguished his thoughts forever, had been given in trust to the president of the United States many years before. The vultures could pick over what they wanted, but the invention that would be his ultimate legacy would remain entrusted to the American people.

They must build it. My generator will make the world a better place.

CHAPTER 1

Max Masterson stood on the balcony on the brisk, clear, November night. It was the kind of evening that made you think about how big the universe is, and how insignificant we are: tiny fleas on a small planet somewhere in the vastness of it all. The day before he had hope, but now he *knew* how the presidential election would end.

Only a week before, the babbling incumbent had been dragged out of the debate feet first, and Max was left standing at the podium without an opponent. Then there was the pitiful assassination attempt which left the nation laughing. The final factor made winning inevitable: To the voters, Max Masterson was not the lesser of two evils. He was the only choice of a desperate nation. He went to bed at 9:30, when it had become a sure thing.

He was the President-Elect of the United States of America.

CHAPTER 2

He was elected on the first Tuesday in November of that year, in a landslide that would have been even bigger if the undecideds hadn't simply voted the party line. It got everyone's attention. He was an Independent, and Independents weren't supposed to win. But Max Masterson had won the popular vote, and with it the hearts and minds of the people of the United States of America. That development had smacked "the powers that be" from behind, and they were determined to thwart the new administration's efforts to disturb the status quo. To do nothing would threaten their privileged status.

He remembered the words of his father many years before, and the responsibility of it all washed over him like a cold wave. *"On election day, the voters will turn out and start to roll a massive, invisible boulder toward you. With every vote that is cast, that boulder will roll closer, until at the end of the day, it will be firmly nestled in your lap. You'll feel the weight of it every day for the rest of your life, and it will be your job to carry it."*

He was going to be president; the boulder had been rolled into his lap. Hope had become responsibility, and the weight of that responsibility was already becoming an ever-present burden. It went with the territory.

Max was acutely aware of the responsibilities of being president. He had been trained since early childhood for the position, spending his summers at a secret camp in the Adirondacks under the tutelage of his father's best friend, Luke Postlewaite. When he and the other children weren't playing, they were being trained for a life in politics. The rich and powerful families sent their most promising offspring there in the hope that one day their children would become the politicians of the future, occupying positions of great prestige and honor. Max's training continued from infancy through to the date he announced that he was running for president. First, from the wisdom and teachings of his father, Senator John Masterson, and by Postlewaite, who continued the training long after the senator's death.

The most-coveted position was a private goal that few would attain, but Max was single-minded in his approach: He would not hold any public office before running for president, and he would follow a path to the presidency that had never been tried before. He was not a politician. He believed that politics prevented the presidents of the past from accomplishing great things. To conceal their motives for voting a certain way, his modern predecessors hid behind the badges of conservative and liberal, and those of party loyalty. He would have none of that. The presidency of Max Masterson would transcend politics.

CHAPTER 3

I have come to the point in my life where I realize that I can't make anyone do anything, and now they want me to be the head manipulator," said Max, fresh from his morning swim and speaking to the only person within earshot, his Vice-President, Scarlett Conroy.

"You are not expected to be a manipulator," she responded. "You are the dream-maker, remember? That's what you told me when you asked me to be your running-mate, and I believed you. When I saw the size of the crowds that turned out for you—rallies that you never bothered to attend in person—I knew you were at risk of winning."

Max stood in the kitchen of Fairlane, his home on the banks of the Potomac. The water from his morning swim dripped onto the terrazzo floor. He was oblivious to his casual status: standing in front of the Vice-President barefoot, clad only in his swimming trunks. "You can have all of the speech-making, except the State of the Union, and you can sit in meetings while I'm out doing important stuff. You can even do most of the big parties, except the ones I'm attending. I've already been informed that the President and Vice-President don't appear together in public. Something about if terrorists get to one of us, the other one has to take over to prevent chaos, or something like that." Max was rambling, and Scarlett was ignoring him. She was intent on sipping her morning tea while she scanned the news and an intelligence report on her iPad.

Scarlett didn't like Max—sometimes her disdain bordered on contempt—but she respected him more than she would admit. From their childhood days in training for future political office, she secretly bore a crush for the brash, handsome son of a retired senator. She watched as Max grew into adulthood, and she saw his easy way with women. For Scarlett, her relationships were more of a distraction from her core purpose.

Women in politics are the serious pursuers of perfection and principle, and she simply did not have time to pursue him or any other man. She was single-minded in her quest to become the first female president of the United States, and she ran for every elected position that she considered to be another rung on the ladder that led to her goal. She had done well.

Elected to the House of Representatives at the age of 25 from by her home state of South Carolina, she defeated long-time congressman Dempsey "Bubba" Chambers after he was caught up in a scandal caused by his sleeping with a string of buxom prostitutes. His long-suffering wife and five children back in Charleston had no clue about his philandering until Bubba was the feature of a five-part video expose. The salacious report showed him out on the town with a different woman each time he was in Washington, seemingly oblivious to the fact that he had been married to the same woman for 28 years.

All Scarlett had to do to score her first win in national politics was to run campaign ads before and after each report. She used a clip of her speech to the League of Women Voters. She was seen dressed in a conservative blue dress, her red hair standing out against a white blouse, with the American flag proudly displayed on her lapel. Her words were succinct, and her message clearly contrasted with the public image that Bubba's indiscretions had created. She calmly announced, in her best Charleston accent, "Now is the time for a woman to take back South Carolina and restore dignity to our state and all of our citizens. Women in politics simply don't do those sorts of shameful things."

When Scarlett was 30 she was elevated to the Senate by default. Senator Terrell Parks, an icon in the South for having been the first African-American to be elected to the Senate in the former confederate state, quietly passed away in his sleep at the age of 77. He was the victim of too many years on the campaign trail, eating fried food and being waited on hand and foot. He had been a talented linebacker at Clemson and played for the Chicago Bears for six years before blowing out both of his knees. Reel footage of the pileup that ended his professional football career was continually played more than 50 years later, a painful image of the fragility of a human body destroyed by a mountain of muscle.

He never exercised again, and the senator's waist grew ten inches in the time he held public office. When the senator was in the room, he occupied more than his share of space, but that worked for him. He was always the center of attention. At the time of his death, Senator Parks was morbidly obese, and his doctors had long-since given up any effort to diminish the acceleration of his demise.

The image of a petite, red-haired woman as the successor of the formidable senator was striking. Scarlett wasted no time in proving what she was made of, and she took on the Washington political establishment at its core. The party had appointed her to finish out the term of her predecessor, but it was a decision that was not well-received by the men's club within the United States Senate. No woman had dared to enter the Washington headquarters of Skull and Cross or to demand membership, but Scarlett did just that. She entered the male refuge accompanied by three film crews and a contingent of woman politicians carrying signs.

The doorman had been trained to deny any female access to the male sanctuary, and members used their special status to enter the building from a private underground entrance using an electronic key that only Senate males possessed. Although a complete investigation was later conducted by a committee of enraged members during the year after the "intrusion", Scarlett's possession of a duplicate key was never satisfactorily explained.

"I'm here to apply for membership," announced Senator Scarlett Conroy to the desk clerk, who was startled to see a woman inside the traditionally male refuge, no less the film crew that was memorializing the encounter. While her female followers launched a diversion from the front of the building, Scarlett had slipped away and gained access by way of the parking garage next door.

Scarlett's foray into the exclusive lives of her male counterparts never resulted in the first female membership in Skull and Cross. The day after she entered the building, the club filed an action for an emergency injunction to prevent her from being considered as a member. Scarlett counter-sued as a matter of principle, but joining a male club was not a goal. Publicity and fame were her only goals, and she reveled in the way the public reacted. She now could command an audience at will, usually just by showing up.

It became sport for her to appear at an event, make a short speech about the issues of the day, and then do a few press interviews from prepared statements. These statements were prerecorded and copied to flash drives, which she would then palm in her hand and deliver during a handshake. Each evening, her message—misquoted—ran on every major network, and she soon began to develop a national persona.

Scarlett's fellow statesman in Washington was long-time Senator Hamilton Simpson, the king of Washington earmarks. He had earned the adoration of fellow South Carolinians by his ability to bring federal funds and jobs to his home district. He was an old

Southern gentleman, and he looked the part. Ham was known as an accomplished orator, and when he spoke, words would slide out of his mouth like butter on a hot biscuit.

In public, the senator took on the personality of everyone's jovial old uncle, telling jokes and amusing stories at every opportunity. He could work a room like nobody else. In public, Ham referred to his junior senator as "Little Lady," much to Scarlett's eternal embarrassment. In private though, he referred to her as "that manipulating, scene-stealin' bitch."

As the oldest living member of Skull and Cross, Senator Simpson treated Scarlett with polite disdain in public and with vituperous contempt over bourbon and cigars among his peers. Their relationship was cordial in public, as that was expected of elected officials in South Carolina. In private, the cotillion-like atmosphere had quickly dissolved into mutual disdain for the remainder of Scarlett's Senate career. Scarlett was denied access to Simpson's private world of back room deals and the privileges of his male world.

While Scarlett was the prototypical female politician, Max didn't fit any of the molds that had shaped the political careers of any of his male counterparts. He had no political career, and he held the deeply ingrained view that the President of the United States should not be a politician.

The election wasn't much of a contest. The incumbent president, Warren Blythe, had been carried from the final debate, raving like a madman. In a moment, there was only one person to be president. The popular vote of the citizens had voted Max Masterson into office, and Scarlett was his surprise running mate. He had literally stolen her from a probable third-place finish after being rejected by her party's elite, and she was the best choice to balance the ticket. A man who had never held political office had been elected to the presidency for the first time since Dwight Eisenhower. At least Eisenhower had been a general. Scarlett had been a United States Senator.

Max wasn't even a politician.

He had only been trained to be one thing in life; President of the United States of America. Scarlett was the Vice-President-elect of the United State of America, and she was a diligent public servant without peer. She was the first woman to reach that pinnacle, and she was better-qualified than Max to be President. He knew that, too, and it had become a private joke between them. Scarlett had done everything right, but her gender was a God-given impediment in politics. Politics is, and has always been, a boy's club.

Max, on the opposite end of the political barometer, was a renegade, and that made the political establishment perch on the edge of incontinence. He was the President-elect whether they liked it or not, and in his irreverent way, the political world of Washington, DC, was about to be turned on its ego-swelled head. Max and Scarlett had the potential to transform the executive branch in ways that would become the new standard that America would follow for generations, but for now, they were just President-elect and Vice-President elect.

CHAPTER 4

For the moment, the control center of the presidency consisted of the kitchen and den of the Masterson estate, Fairlane. The large, antique, oak table was strewn with laptops, iPads, and file folders. The paper files had been delivered by courier from some nameless government department that presides over the transition from one administration to the next, and they were marked with time-worn labels of the past.

Max thumbed through one 300 page binder marked "Ambassadorships," but he rapidly lost interest when he realized that the protocol for choosing ambassadors was directly linked to the size of the contributions that were made to political campaigns. His philosophy was fresh and untried, but he knew it would work: The ambassadors of the United States would be visible negotiators, who had been trained as mediators and excelled at their craft. They would represent what is right about America, and they would be charged with the responsibility of providing the world with what they craved most: to be American. The goods and styles, music and movie stars, cars and planes, technology and ideas—all crafted with quality and innovation—were the products that Americans would sell to the world.

"Our friends and trading partners will benefit from peaceful alliances with the United States of America, and our enemies will be deprived of the benefits of doing business with us. During my time in office, I believe that I can transform the country from a consumer society to a productive economy. We will restore our standard of living," said Max.

"For now, we are bound to debt through dependence on foreign oil and products built with technology stolen from our ingenuity. I believe this. I see it happening, and I don't like it. There are others who don't share that belief." He shifted impatiently, bouncing on the balls of his feet.

"I can't sit idly by and watch as America gets lazy and soft, while the rest of the world out-competes us," Max continued, still fidgeting. He had sat still for as long as he could without doing something. It made for short meetings, but it was annoying to Scarlett, who thrived on committee hearings that went on for hours. She didn't fidget. Max was at his best when he could dive into a problem, devise a course of action, and go for it without prolonged deliberation.

In Max's campaign, he only owed allegiance to the legacy of his long-departed father, Senator John Masterson, who had left him more money than he could ever spend, and to the American people, who had given him their votes. Masterson and Conroy had won the presidency with 80% of the popular vote, a landslide by anyone's account.

Setting the folder aside, he turned his attention to his iPad, and he accessed the confidential information that had been prepared for his transition team from the nameless bureaucrats that had provided invisible support for previous incoming administrations.

Like most social gatherings, people tended to congregate in the kitchen. Various staffers sauntered in and out, but they left Max and Scarlett deep in conversation without interruption, assuming that the affairs of government were being crafted by the two individuals who were best suited for the job. After all, the people did elect them.

"You know that we aren't supposed to be together," Max said. "What if some psychotic terrorist is evil enough to predict when we're in the same spot, and they make history? We are going to have to be really sneaky."

Scarlett Conroy was unphased. Unlike Max, she was a politician first and foremost, and her years in public office had taught her to be cautious. Cautious meant safe, but she was not one to obsess about the unknown.

"That's why we have the Secret Service, the CIA, the NSA, three branches of the military, and Homeland Security to protect us," she countered. "With you in office, they may as well paint a bullseye on your forehead and toss you out on the street for target practice, but I am not going to sit around worrying about it. We have a country to run." Scarlett had shifted from the news to an online search centered on the duties of the Vice-President.

"You know, Max, at the start of our nation's history, vice-presidents weren't running mates, they were runners-up. So the president and the vice-president were political enemies from rival parties who probably hated each other. My *friends* would have been gunning for you, not some terrorist." She chuckled at the thought. "Here's a quote from Will Rogers that I know you'll like," she teased. *"The man with the best job in this country is the vice-president. All he has to do is get up every morning and say, 'How is the president?'"*

Max smiled at the thought and responded. "Scarlett, if you want to be the first woman in the Oval Office to legitimately sit behind Jack Kennedy's desk, I respectfully request that you wait until the voters put you there...after I have completed my second term." He smirked, and both of them broke out in laughter. Scarlett was content, for the moment, being vice-president, and Max had delegated to her most of the politicking and social functions of the presidency, which she enjoyed.

"Okay, Mr. President, if you think you'll last that long," she answered. "But let's get back to work. We have cabinet members to pick and calls to make."

They retreated to the conference room at Fairlane, created by his father. Called "the den" all of his life, the room was modeled after the Jefferson Library at Monticello. Senator Masterson had studied and emulated Thomas Jefferson during his political career. He was most comfortable here, and most of his best thoughts were created in this room, recorded for posterity for Max to review after his death. He had not only devised the schematic Max had used in the campaign for president ten years after his death, but also the Maxims that his son had revised to address the issues of the presidency: a code of conduct that would govern his approach to the challenges ahead of him.

Max leaned back and admired Scarlett's ability to achieve the kind of intense focus that blocks out all distractions and allows creative people to achieve great things. He could do it sometimes, but she could do it at will, and that reason alone had her on the path to succeed him. She would become president after he had served his time.

"I won't be like the others," Max exclaimed.

"You aren't telling me anything I don't already know to the core of my being," Scarlett responded sarcastically. In time of need, she reverted to her best Charleston accent, delivered like honey pouring off a cliff.

"It's bigger than you can imagine," Max explained. "I'm not a politician, and I intend to be a non-political president." Scarlett began to protest, but Max raised his hands in a non-verbal *shush*. He needed to get his words out while they were clear in his mind.

"I know that's hard for you to understand, but hear me out. Congress is composed of politicians who believe that they have unlimited power. They don't. If they took the time to read the Constitution, which I have memorized down to the last word, they would realize that I can make treaties, appoint ambassadors, and take care that the laws are faithfully executed, but not much else."

"I'm basically the Commander in Chief of the whole country, not just the military, and people are going to look at me to lead. I can't do that by being a politician, worried about getting elected to another term. If I fail to lead, I won't get re-elected. I won't even run if I fail, but I'm not going to tell them that. I'm going to be the big idea guy, the nation's cheerleader, and you are going to be the big explainer, making speeches that expound on those ideas. I know how you like to make speeches."

Scarlett sat silently for as long as she could. She was used to being talked at, having sat through endless hours of hearings and meetings during her Senate career. In private conversation, though, the words couldn't stay bottled up for long. "I suppose that you're going to have me make your State of the Union speech, too, and maybe wipe your butt for you?"

Max ignored her, choosing instead to read over her shoulder, a habit that she found particularly annoying, especially when she wanted his focused attention. She was rapidly realizing that the president dreaded the political aspects of the office to which he had been elected three days earlier. "Since I'm going to be doing your job, what do you intend to do for the next four years, play golf while the country wallows in debt? I don't mind if I'm going to be your mouthpiece, but if you think—" Max cut her off.

"I don't do golf. It moves too slowly for me. Not my idea of exercise." He had enlisted her to be his running mate by a direct process of elimination: She possessed all of the traits of a leader that he lacked, and she resented that to her core. But still, she admired the way he could annoy and charm at the same moment, and the charm always won.

"That story about the oil spill in the gulf has a big hole in it. If that isn't espionage, I don't know what is…" He continued reading over Scarlett's shoulder while drying his head with an undersized hand towel. The effect was similar to sitting next to a drenched Labrador Retriever, and Max sprayed her proper clothing with vigor.

"Max, stop it! You're soaking me! If you mess up my hair, I'll…"

He was doing it on purpose, and she knew it.

"Rich buffoons are better qualified to be president," she added.

"Yeah, probably," he replied.

"How? Why?"

"Look. My Dad reared me to be president. I can think of about a thousand better jobs. He programmed me for a higher purpose. Higher than president." Max paused for the effect he intended. Scarlett's face told him what he needed to know. To her, there was no higher calling. Before she could properly express disagreement and launch into a debate on the subject, Max quickly changed the subject. He would never reveal to Scarlett his greater goals in life, and Scarlett would never understand. He may as well have been having a conversation with a mannequin.

Max continued, but his voice was more subdued. "I remember when he was almost gone. He was in pain for a long time. I think that after awhile, it makes a person hallucinate, and then they become profound." Scarlett realized that it was time to listen. "My dad died of a broken heart after my mom…when Adrianna… died." He took a deep breath. "She was my teacher. She was his girlfriend…they killed her." It hurt to look at his eyes, projecting the pain of his memories. For a brief moment, she felt sorry for him, but only for a moment. They had a country to run.

"Are you going to sit there and have a pity party, or are you going to do something?" Scarlett was determined to get Max on task. Tough love.

"What?"

"You need to get out there and show that you are in charge. You don't get a chance to think about the past. You need to build a future." She was hard on him, but right. He needed to be president. "Aren't you always yammering about how the image is more important than the candidate? You can't lead if you're stuck in reverse," Dwelling on the past, in her mind, was the equivalent of worrying about the future. Both activities were a waste of time. Her determination was unshakeable. Before he could protest, Scarlett took the initiative.

"Until you talked me into being your running-mate, and too soon before the election, I might add, I was your opponent." She stood, and grabbed the wet towel from his hands. "I already knew about your strange ways, and your strange ideas, and I signed on for this voyage despite my strongest instinct to turn and run. Don't you disappoint me, Max Masterson." She deftly snapped the towel at his bare midriff. Decorum kept her from aiming lower.

"Ow, that hurt!" Max retrieved the towel and prepared to retaliate, but Scarlett gave him a stern look that transformed his horseplay into seriousness. He had seen her employ it in several senate hearings he had viewed of her in action, and she was very adept at controlling an audience through nonverbal cues. *That's a talent that might come in handy. A politician who can get people to do something without saying a word. I wonder if she'll teach me.*

"Max, are you listening to me? "

CHAPTER 5

The report had riveted Scarlett's attention. It linked a recent oil spill in the Gulf of Mexico to the previous Deepwater Horizon spill that placed the blame on BP and Transocean, the contractor that supplied the equipment and engineers to do the drilling. The report implicated three employees who had reported for duty two weeks before the oil platform explosion, and were listed as missing or dead when the explosion illuminated the night and eventually sank the oil platform. Their bodies were never found. According to the article, they were not found because they were not dead. The three oil workers left the oil platform by speedboat in the late hours before the natural gas blowing to the surface ignited in a massive ball of flame.

The witnesses to their departure were two fishermen who had come to catch their limit of large grouper that were attracted to the lights of the structure. They had moved their boat away from the platform when huge gas bubbles began breaking on the surface, and became fearful when their shouts to the deck 90 feet overhead were disregarded. They were 200 yards away drifting in the darkness without their running lights on when the speedboat idled up to the platform and loaded three dark figures aboard.

It was espionage, or "industrial terrorism" as the press would soon call it. Whatever words they chose, the terms didn't describe the economic and environmental damage the perpetrators were capable of inflicting. They were a loose group of mercenaries funded by Chinese and North Korean interests, chosen for their ability to blend into the American work force without attracting attention. Their European ancestry and homegrown accents put them above suspicion on the oil platforms, where they were employed for weeks before the explosion. These men were trained to get in, place the charges in areas where nobody would find them, and get out long before detonation.

The terrorists performed their deadly tasks with precision and stealth, and were many miles away before the first charge soundlessly ignited the cloud of natural gas that enveloped the platform. The resulting explosions spread quickly, and when the heat of the fire ignited welding tanks stored on deck, the oil platform and many of its occupants were doomed. It was a miracle that more of the drilling team didn't perish in the ninety-foot plunge to the gulf waters after the life boats ran out.

The press was only able to report the accounts of eye-witnesses to the events surrounding the disaster. The investigation into the cause would proceed for many months after the spill had fouled the gulf, and their around the clock coverage had already shifted to the cleanup, with images of birds and aquatic life covered with oil. The official version of the disaster would come out long after the public's attention had moved on, and it would never contain the true facts: Espionage directed at the platform was meant to drive up the price of oil.

"This is turning into a bigger accident than anyone imagined," commented Scarlett.

"Well, it sure doesn't sound like an accident to me," exclaimed Max. "Who were those guys that were seen leaving just before the explosion, and who is behind this?"

"You don't expect us to do anything other than assume, do you? People are going to want to blame someone, and when they don't have anyone, they will probably blame you."

"I was afraid of that," replied Max. *It's the American way.*

CHAPTER 6

I need to go down to the Gulf Coast and see what's happening down there. People need to see my face and know that I'm still alive," Max announced. I would like you to stay here with the transition team and get us ready to hit the ground running. I want our cabinet members and agency heads to fire everyone from the Blythe administration immediately and have a report of replacements ready by the time I get back. I don't want anyone, and I mean anyone, that served under Blythe even to set foot in Washington, DC, again, unless they are elected to public office. We are going to replace them with acknowledged experts in each area of expertise, except for politics itself. That area is your baby, Madame Vice-President."

"But Max, you haven't even taken the oath of office. You need to wait another month before you begin to—"

"Scarlett, I never did anything like everyone else, and right now, this country is like a ship without a captain. These are the most dangerous times."

"But Max, the inauguration!"

"Oh yeah, I almost forgot. Swear me in," he replied.

"Swear you in?" Her shock at his breach of tradition was evident from her expression. "You need to have it done on Inauguration Day. You need to have the Chief Justice do it, I can't—"

"Oh yes you can. You're a United States senator. It will be kind of like when people go to a Justice of the Peace to get married and then have the big church wedding for all of the relatives later. We can do it in the den in front of all of our transition team. There's a Bible on the bookshelf in the den. Come on, it'll be fun," Max replied. He had that mischievous grin on his face. He knew she would do it.

Max's first oath of office took place in the den his father occupied continuously in the last days of his life, and Max had a pang of remorse that his father couldn't be there, perched in the big leather recliner, listening with pride. Max retrieved the family Bible from its exalted place in the center of the shelf above the fireplace and repeated the words that Scarlett had memorized:

"I, Maximum Masterson, do solemnly swear that I will faithfully execute the office of President of the United States, and will to the best of my ability, preserve, protect and defend the Constitution of the United States."

CHAPTER 7

E verything you know about anything is about to be thrown out the window," announced Roger Sinclair to Max as he settled into the soft leather seat on Air Force One. It wasn't his first journey with a new president, and it would likely be one of many he would take with Max. He had been the keeper of government secrets for many years, but due to his exceptional status outside of the public eye, nobody was quite sure how long he had been at it. He was a government official who survived presidential administrations to provide consistency, but his existence was an internal secret.

If he had chosen to accept a public position, he would be out of a job when the transition between administrations occurred. He liked the permanency that being the nation's unofficial Security Advisor provided, and his three children and two ex-wives enjoyed the benefit of his large, unofficial salary. Even his income was a government secret, and there was no record of him at the IRS.

Sinclair was, in a word, invisible. It was his job to brief the president on matters of public importance, supplying details derived from restricted databases and confidential sources. He worked independently from the FBI, CIA, and Homeland Security, but his access to the information compiled by those agencies allowed him to

Roger Sinclair had unrestricted access to any information, and to Max, he was indispensable. Two things were certain: nobody could keep a secret from him, and he wouldn't tell secrets to just anyone. That confidential information and access was reserved for high- ranking government officials, and Roger had sole discretion as to which members of this exclusive group were briefed.

Before Sinclair made his presence known, the intended recipient of his briefings was extensively and discretely screened. Max was duly screened, and Roger had approved him. He hadn't cleared the previous president, or his vice-president either. They served the previous four years in ignorant bliss, without the information that Roger was about to share. He didn't trust them.

Roger had one secret that that he would hold from Max and the rest of the world: he had no need to screen Scarlett for anything. He knew her better than anyone.

CHAPTER 8

Scarlett had been silent for longer than usual. Max looked at her face, and he saw her blush. She was staring at Roger, and her body language revealed her attraction for him better than a neon sign. She was smitten. The temperature in the room seemed to rise, and Max couldn't resist the opportunity to make his vice president feel as uncomfortable as possible. He caught her eye, and he turned quickly to see Roger winking.

"Is there something I don't know?" The arbitrariness of the question left it wide-open for interpretation. It was his way of finding out what was on their minds. Sometimes it worked, depending on their response.

"No," they said in unison.

Then, he knew.

Max was not one to let Scarlett conceal her secret love life, and he was tempted to prolong her discomfort by sitting and smiling impishly until she couldn't stand it any longer. But in a kind way, he was relieved. For years, the rumors and speculation about Scarlett's sexuality had ranged from non-sexual ice queen to closet lesbian with a masochistic bent. He knew that she had rejected his advances during their brief time together in their teens, but he had assumed that his vice-president wasn't ready. Even at the age of 17, Max knew that a man can have sex without emotional attachment, but a woman needed to feel love for the male she desired. It wasn't sport for her.

The press had been ruthless in the pursuit of her private life, and for that reason alone he knew the wall that she had created in her mind. It was a survival technique for her that he knew too well. Public figures who reveal too much soon live to regret, and his mystique had been the impetus for more intense scrutiny than anyone. It was a time for sharing, not teasing.

"I want you both to know that your secret is safe to me, and you don't know how good it feels to finally disbelieve all of that gossip about you, Madam Vice-President. I think I'll stop watching that mini-series they did about you and just give you a big hug." He launched himself in her direction, knowing that his attempt at causing her one last bit of embarrassment would produce his intended result.

"Stop it, Max," she squealed as he entered her zone of privacy, restrained from backing away by the thick carpet that held her chair in place. One kiss on the cheek and a look toward Roger for approval, and he was done with their shared moment of privacy.

"I'd give you a hug, too, Roger, but I'm not that kind of president," Max said. "I have to reserve myself for kissing babies and shaking hands, you know, and I don't want to wear myself out."

"I fully understand, Max. And if you keep our secret, I'll keep yours, whatever they may be," Sinclair replied.

"I don't have many secrets to keep. My life until now has been an open book."

"Nobody serves in the Oval Office without picking up a few secrets over time." Roger stood and turned toward the door, and Max took the nonverbal signal. It was time to leave.

"Scarlett, hold down the fort while we're gone. Are you sure you don't want to ride down to the coast with us? I'm sure Roger won't mind if you sit on his lap..."

"Shut up, Mr. President," she replied.

CHAPTER 9

The first time aboard Air Force One Max immediately realized that he wouldn't be having a relaxing trip. To avoid down time, the president's jet is a command center, boardroom, and office, equipped with state of the art technology. He had not been officially sworn into office, but the outgoing president was in rehab, and Blythe wouldn't be needing the jet for the remaining weeks of his term in office. Besides, there were two identical jets, and Blythe could have the other one for his personal use if he suddenly decided to leave Washington behind.

Two helicopters containing the bulk of the Secret Service security detail had flown in advance to New Orleans for Max's visit to the oil spill. To save time, he was also accompanied by a person assigned to brief him. The only person who possessed the full body of knowledge necessary to brief the president was Roger Sinclair, and due to the extreme secrecy of the matters to be discussed, his travel companion would not be seen exiting Air Force One.

"You're about to hear some things that I never shared with your predecessor," Sinclair offered. "He never bothered to ask any questions. Bright guy, but corrupt. Rotten to the core." Sinclair munched casually on a Braeburn apple, as if a meeting with the incoming president was just part of his typical day. "I checked him out before he got into the White House, but he got in anyway." Sinclair had a tendency to ramble, but he didn't mince words. "His running mate wasn't worth a bucket of spit. I lost a lot of sleep during those four years, thinking he was one heart attack away from the presidency." He tossed the half-eaten apple into a metal wastebasket, where it landed with a satisfying thud. He stood with irreverent casualness, confident that his audience would hang on every word. Everyone loves a secret, and the bigger the secret, the more focus it generated.

"First of all, this talk about UFO's, it's all true. There are UFO's, one crashed in Area 51, we recovered bodies of aliens in the wreckage, and we have been using that technology to fly top-secret flying machines for the past fifty years while denying that they are among us. That's always the first question everyone asks me. We're thick with them. We should stop being so arrogant as to think that they wouldn't exist. I've told that story so many times, it's a relief to get it out of the way. Now for the important stuff." Max looked at him with amazement, while Scarlett stared at him without betraying her thoughts.

"You think that our country is run by people who have been elected by voters, who have the omniscience to pick the right one every time. The truth is, the average voter doesn't know shit about who to vote for. They don't even remember who they voted for in the last election. The government is run by a group of powerful people whom politicians answer to. Your election took them by surprise, and you make them very, very nervous. They don't like a politician whose strings they can't pull anytime they want. Hell, Max, you're not even a politician. You're the X factor. They don't know how to deal with you."

"There are several sacred cows in politics. One is the energy industry. If they can't make money off of it, they will fight it, even if that one change means that humankind will be better for it.

Remember a guy named Tesla, back in the early part of the twentieth century? He created a generator that runs off of the earth's magnetic field. Free energy. When he died, after they had driven him to bankruptcy and spread the word that he was a fraud, all of his notes on his invention disappeared. He had applied for a patent, and there is no record of its existence. Gone. Wiped from history so that they can keep making a profit."

Max finally found his voice. "Who is behind all of this?"

"The same people who are behind everything that happens behind the scenes in this town. They have been manipulating politicians to do their dirty work for generations. They don't have a name. I don't even know how many of them claim to be members of a particular organization. They're more like a group with a continuity of interest. They took lessons from the Illuminati, the Mafia, and the Nazis. If they acquire a name, they can be identified. If they can be identified, they can be eliminated. Congress has been infiltrated, so is the Supreme Court. It's how they get things done."

"You know that new oil derrick blowout out in the gulf? That was no accident." Sinclair paused to pour himself a drink. "Those mercenaries hired by foreign oil blew it so they can jack up the prices and get our politicians all riled up. Then the prices go up at the pump, the voters go wild, and your ratings go into the toilet. And they won't stop there. These guys want to sink you and take over. A coup."

"By the time you get back to Washington, there will be the biggest shit-storm in history. You have got to be careful. I don't think that they will try to assassinate you, not yet, anyway. They didn't go after Kennedy until they realized that they couldn't count on him to continue the arms race. When they feel they are losing control of you and your agenda, that's when they begin to fight dirty." He took a long sip and went on.

"You think Oswald killed an American president all by his

lonesome? Give me a break. They not only do the deed, they set somebody up for the fall. The Warren Commission? They were afraid that if they announced that Kennedy's assassins were walking the streets, America would fall into anarchy, and the world as we knew it would enter the last war. Back then, people thought that when the bomb fell, all you had to do to survive was to take the door off the hinges, pile some dirt on top, and crawl underneath. Fools. Don't get me started about the idiotic ideas floating out there. There is no reality, as you like to say. There is only your perception of reality, and how you act on it.

"Clinton didn't get attacked in his first term," Sinclair went on. "He presided over a good economy and peacetime, and they reined him in with distractions at home. Subpoenas and depositions and rumors were enough to bring him back in the fold. See, if they want, they can have you dead tomorrow, but my bet is that they are going to try to make you look impotent and inept to bring down your popularity. That's the word I'm hearing from my sources. They will give you just enough rope to hang yourself, and they won't be sending any flowers to your funeral."

Max stood and faced Sinclair with a determined glare.

"I didn't get elected to hide out and do nothing for four years, and I don't intend to back off just so the status quo can pad their trust funds. If it's better for the country, I'm going to push for it, and I won't live one minute in fear that someone is going to snuff me. Do I make that crystal clear?" Max was pacing in the aisle. Sinclair gleamed with delight.

"I like that in my president," he exclaimed.

CHAPTER 10

Roger suddenly became stoic. "One more thing before you get off this jet. It's been haunting me for more than twenty years. The dangerous faction is a group controlled by your Dad's old enemy, Pryor. He's the one behind Adrianna's death, the Patriot Group bombing, and the attempt on your life last month before the election. He controlled the Secret Service from his position as Director of Homeland Security. He wanted Blythe to win; the presidency was in their pocket, and you were too much of a loose cannon to them. They hate change. Pryor put in his own people to substitute for your regular detail, and I'm the one who got that information to you in time. I am telling you this so you can have your revenge."

"I'm supposed to be telling you about foreign threats to the United States," Roger continued, "and they want me to keep you in the dark about the way things really work around here. But I saw how you ran your campaign, and I was a friend of your father back in the day, when he took on the same people who tried to stop him from protecting Americans from their own government. I was heartbroken when they killed Adrianna, and it almost killed him."

Max stopped him there, raising his hands for pause. He didn't speak, feeling the volcano of emotion boiling inside of his mind.

His hands became fists, and Sinclair watched as the redness spread on his face. The rage consumed him, and he spent several minutes trying to contain the overwhelming thoughts of revenge.

❖ ❖ ❖

"I thought you knew about Pryor. That son of a bitch has so much power, Max! He was behind the bombing, but he wanted *your father* eliminated, not Adrianna. She was just collateral damage. He didn't care if he killed everyone in that room, if he could get to your dad. They were longtime enemies, starting back in the days of the Senate hearings. Your father humiliated Pryor in front of the world, and he swore his revenge.

The only thing that saved your father's life was that Pryor's people planted the bomb in a flower pot that was strong enough to contain some of the blast and direct it upward, and your dad was standing behind a pillar at the time. As you remember, he almost died, but he lived to put you in a position to do something about it."

Max closed his eyes and watched the scene play out in his head. He was sixteen, and his father came into his bedroom before leaving for a social event with Adrianna. The senator was smiling, dressed in a black tux and looking dapper in a way that would put his image in all of the society pages. After thirty years in Washington politics and a highly publicized resignation, every appearance in public was met with a flurry of press attention. John Masterson and his stunning love, Adrianna, could go nowhere without their pictures appearing within minutes on all of the major internet news. He sat on his son's bed and spoke.

"Max, I'm finally going to do it. I'm going to ask her to marry me." Max had always thought of Adrianna as his mother, and she had home-schooled him from the age of three. He couldn't imagine life without her. She had lived at Fairlane for as long as he could remember. He looked at his father with a puzzled look.

"Dad, does this mean that she won't be my tutor anymore?"

"No, son, your life won't change a bit."

"Then go ahead and do it. I don't see what the big deal is."

"Someday, it will be a milestone in your life."

His son's response was unexpected, but Max had been taught to express his feelings honestly, and doing something for the sake of tradition had always taken a back seat to the pursuit of clearly defined goals.

"I take that as a sign of approval."

"Can I be your best man?"

"I was hoping you would say that, son. I wouldn't have anyone else, and Adrianna feels the same way." His father nodded and and walked out the door. The next time he saw his father was in a hospital bed, bandages covering his cuts and burns. His father was crying. It was the first time Max had seen tears in his father's eyes. The sorrow on John Masterson's face was intense.

"She's gone," he said in a quiet voice. Then he looked away. Max had grieved, and so had his father, and that memory was indelibly etched in his mind.

CHAPTER 11

The sound of the landing gear brought him back to the present, and Max assumed a seriousness that had been lacking moments before. Sinclair leaned back in his chair and exhaled a sigh of relief. He had fretted for days about how this would play out, and now that he had supplied Max with the information he was duty-bound to reveal, he had rolled the invisible boulder into Max's lap. It would be up to Max to deal with it from that point forward, and he had faith that justice would be done, in the right time, and in the right place.

"I'm briefing you about what I know so that you can do something about it. If word gets out that you know these things, I'm a dead man. I accept that. I have lived a good life, and I have always done what was, in my mind, in the best interests of our country. But now, they are planning something that I can't abide by. It's domestic terrorism on a huge scale, and this country will suffer for it. You need to stop him."

"Tell me their plans," said Max, trying to maintain his composure. So many irrational thoughts ran through his head at the moment, the anger keeping him from dealing rationally. Suddenly, he became very calm, and Sinclair watched him transform into a figure of serious determination. This was Max's time to think and his time to act, and

Sinclair resolved to support him in his own way. Scarlett knew, too. She would free Max from the duties of politics and let him resolve problems in a new way.

Sinclair was pleasantly surprised when he felt a glimmer of hope. He thought that his years in Washington had drummed that out of him, *This president has the ability to inspire and lead. I can see it in his eyes*

"I don't know much yet, but what I can tell you is that Pryor wants to destroy you in a very public way. He intends to make the American people turn on you, to humiliate you. He wants to sit back, turn on his TV, and watch them rip you to shreds. He's a sick bastard, and his position as Director of Homeland Security has given him access to all sorts of terrorist toys. Why do you think that he convinced Congress to shift control of the Secret Service to Homeland Security? He was behind the effort to kill you during your speech at the Kennedy Center. By the way, that hologram idea was pure genius. I never even thought of that one."

Max ignored the compliment, focused on the matters at hand. "Have his people infiltrated the Secret Service? I have to trust those guys," said Max, cloaking his concern. "No, he brought in a crew of imposters to do that job. He made a few phone calls to reassign the team that had been protecting you, and nobody questioned his authority. He was running things, remember?"

Max looked perplexed, wondering whether the talented and dedicated Secret Service had been ruined from within. "Who can I trust, other than you?"

"I'll give you a list." Sinclair wirelessly transferred the information, along with a number of classified documents that he had brought to the briefing. He would hold back nothing from this president. He trusted him, and he believed that Max would finally be the person that would pull the country out of the malaise that had engulfed it… If he could keep Max alive long enough to do his job.

CHAPTER 12

Max stepped directly from Air Force One into a waiting black SUV, one of many identical vehicles that held the Secret Service, the Press Corps, and essential staffers who accompany the President of the United States on any foray away from Washington. His face was furrowed with worry. Andrew Fox, his Chief of Staff, noticed immediately. The normally jovial Max Masterson was more serious than he had ever seen in public, and he was concerned that the private briefing on Air Force One had burdened him with more reality than even the strongest person could bear.

"Mr. President, are you okay?"

"Yeah. I just have a lot on my mind right now, and don't call me that. I'm not comfortable with it yet. Max will do when it's just you and me."

Andrew remained focused on the stern look that had appeared on Max's face during the flight to the Gulf. "Anything would like to share? Do I need to fire somebody? I need to start earning my keep as your Chief of Staff."

Andrew's attempt at humor made Max smile, but it was more of a forced grimace. He didn't dare disclose to Andrew the thoughts he had of revenge on the man who was responsible for the death of the first woman he had loved, who was a mother to him and had loved his father with unselfish devotion. It was a seething hatred that boiled inside his mind at the moment, and when the time was right, he would strike back with all of the combined might of his armed forces. At the moment, Pryor had been able to evade detection, but nobody hides for long in a world without privacy.

After I'm officially sworn in, and not before. I need to do this for the United States as Commander in Chief, Max thought as the caravan drove through the bayous and marshes near the coast. The details of Adrianna's death and the devastating effect it had on his father weighed on him more than he could put into words. He composed himself as the entourage sped toward the Gulf Coast location, chosen by his advance team to provide visual effect for the American people on the news channels.

He knew he could do nothing to undo the damage that had wreaked havoc on the economy and ecology of the region, but he had to do something, and he had needed to get out of Washington before he went crazy. During the ride, he reviewed the documents uploaded to his iPad, and by mental dictation, he detailed an outline of his plan to eliminate Pryor and those like him before they could ruin everything he stood for. As he dictated, he realized the power he held in his exclusive control: he was the Commander in Chief, and he could direct the United States of America against its enemies, wherever and whenever they were found. The idea that the enemy was inside the United States—and that it was composed of U.S. citizens—was his most consuming challenge.

CHAPTER 13

Max stood on the beach and directed his gaze intently at the old man in the rowboat. He entered the scene as a black speck on the horizon. As the weather-beaten, flat-bottomed skiff approached, the details gained a color of their own, and he could see the man's brown-streaked T-shirt. It displayed the two-tone green symbol of BP, the oil giant that had once again turned his bayou into a sludge-infested cesspool the color of coffee. He rowed because he had to. A motor would have fouled and stalled the second the sludge entered the intake port, and the grizzled fisherman trusted his wiry muscles over a mechanical contraption anyhow.

As the boat came closer, Max could make out the inscription on the shirt. WE ARE BRINGING OIL TO YOUR SHORES it proudly proclaimed, obviously written to introduce BP to the U.S. market many years before, and eerily prophetic of the many spills that found their way to the shores of the Gulf Coast over the years. Max thought about how utterly worthless this trip would be, but it would get good press, and his advisors had wanted a soundbyte. It was a part of the job that he was rapidly learning to detest.

From the lines on his face, Max could see that the fisherman was a beaten man. He had endured more than a soul should. His hard life had given him no respite from the realities of survival in a world where he eked out barely enough on a good day. He had started his life as a fisherman and later became a shrimper, spending his life dragging the gulf at night for weeks at a time, and being paid at the dock by the pound before heading out again. All to make a living. When the fertile shrimping grounds of the Gulf were smothered in oil from the Deepwater Horizon disaster, he had changed professions again.

Now he was an oysterman, working the shallow waters of the coast in clear violation of the government's ban on harvesting seafood in the areas fouled by the latest oil well explosion. Today, he returned empty-handed, and for the old man, he would have spent another day broke and tired if he had chosen another location to pull his boat ashore. Today was his lucky day, and the media opportunity was not staged. He just happened to be there when the hoopla converged on his solitary life.

Max kicked off his shoes and peeled off his socks. If he had been alone, his actions would have attracted no more notice than a passing glance, but he was the President-elect of the United States, and the mere act of picking his nose would have warranted at least a sniping comment from the New York Times. As he rolled up his expensive trousers, a murmur arose from behind him. Looking toward the marina parking lot, he quickly counted more than a dozen black SUVs that had transported his entourage from New Orleans Louis Armstrong International Airport to the bayou.

"Keep them back," Max ordered to Andrew Fox and his Secret Service escort, who were busily erecting an enclosure with rebar and yellow crime scene tape. "And take off those damned black suits. You are going to fry your brains in this sun." Andrew immediately complied, relieved that the sea breeze could be felt through his dress shirt. The Secret Service ignored him, assigned to wear their electronically sophisticated sport coats in every condition. The coats also concealed the arsenal each man carried to protect the president.

"The least you can do is take off those ties," piped in Andrew. "This is supposed to be a casual photo opportunity."

"Sorry, sir, but we can't do that," said one agent closest to Andrew. "We have our orders."

The press was herded into the makeshift press box, where they stood in the bright winter sun while Max did his thing in front of the cameras. In contrast to the Secret Service, they had no qualms about stripping down to allow their skin to catch a bit of the constant sea breeze, and soon they stood in dress shirts and undershirts.

If the camera crews had their way, they would have gone the next step, and stripped down to their underwear, but there is something about covering the president that commands a form of silent decorum. Still, the thought ran through their minds, and they made mental notes to pack a bathing suit and tropical clothes on their next foray into the American South. Even in winter, the temperature could nudge eighty degrees Fahrenheit. They quickly realized that this president was going to be more of an outdoorsman than the last guy.

Max trailed his Secret Service escort on his impromptu walk up the beach toward the point. He had to get away from the crowd and find clear water. It was an urge he had to follow, but he knew with overwhelming certainty that he wouldn't find solitude or clear water here. As far as he could see in either direction, lines of turd-like blobs bobbed in the incoming tide.

He bent over and picked up the child's flip flop that lay abandoned on the beach. It was a miniature version of an adult sandal, black, with the inscription CHAMPION on the strap. He could imagine the small child, bundled against the sun, writhing to spend one more minute playing in the sand and the clear water, before it was time to leave. It brought it all into perspective somehow, at least for him. They had ruined it for everyone. He absent-mindedly slid the sandal into his suit pocket, and walked toward the old man.

As the boat bumped up against the chocolate shore, Max walked forward and extended his hand. The recipient of his handshake was not much for social decorum, and he had lived his life without concern that what he did or what he said would be misconstrued as politically correct. The words that came out of his mouth were inspired by his heart.

"I'm tired of the guvmint tellin' me what to do or keepin' me from doin' stuff that don't hurt nobody." The old man thought he was in trouble. Most of his life was spent in trouble, and he took the well-dressed mass of humanity as his lynching mob.

"I'm not here to hurt you. I'm here to help you," replied Max.

"Bullshit." He reached back into his boat, pulled out a bottle of amber liquid, and took a draw. He didn't offer it to Max, cradling the bottle in his arms, wondering what would come next.

"Do you know who I am?"

He stared at Max with yellowed eyes. He focused for a few moments and said, "Are you the lottery guy? Did I win?" Max smiled and extended his hand again. "No, I'm not the lottery guy. I'm the President."

This time, the old man shook his hand. "If you's the president, how you gonna fix dis mess?" He took a long swig, and extended the bottle to Max. Max took a sip, and he realized that the old guy had a hankering for good quality tequila. He looked for the worm, took another swig, and gave it back. The bottle went back into the boat as quickly as it had come out.

"I don't see how I can," Max responded. "I have an idea about who did this one and the last, but I can't fix the damage they did. All I can give you is my promise. We're gonna find the bastards and kill 'em, and then we're gonna come down here and have the biggest beach party you ever saw." It was all impromptu bullshit, and he cringed at the thought of lying about it, but he felt helpless to do anything at all. *This is a feeling that the most powerful person in America should never have*, he thought. *I haven't been president for more than a few days, and I have already violated one of my own Maxims. It is better to say nothing about an issue than to lie about it. This will not happen again.*

"That's good for me," he replied. "You hafta to earn my respect, and the first thing you need to do to earn it is don't bullshit me." He rubbed his shirt with both hands in a futile effort to wipe off the brown goo that covered everything, and pulled the lanyard rope from inside the boat. "You work for me. I don't serve you."

Max thought about those words. They came from the heart, of that he was certain. He reached for the loop of the rope, intending to make the job of pulling the boat ashore easier. The man brushed his hand away.

"My father was a religious man, and he prayed in private. His favorite passage in the Bible was in the Book of Matthew: Ask and it will be given to you; seek and you will find; knock and the door will be opened to you. For everyone who asks receives; he who seeks finds; and to him who knocks, the door will be opened. He practiced it in his life, and I have been entrusted to carry it forward now that he has passed. I'll be damned if you are going to stand in front of me and turn down my help."

Max gently pushed the man aside and grabbed the brown rope with both hands. He pulled, and the slimy lubricant worked. It slid between his hands with a slithery sound, and Max fell into the brown goo, covering his skin and clothes from the neck down.

The press, which had been restrained 50 feet away, broke into unrestrained laughter at the scene of the unplanned mayhem, still recording the events that were unfolding. By the time Max managed to stand, after two unsuccessful attempts at it that put him back on his butt in the brown sludge, he was laughing hysterically. He couldn't see what he looked like, but he could easily imagine, and the reaction of the press corps intensified with each movement. Any effort at maintaining dignity had gone by the wayside. Max's young Chief of Staff and Press Secretary Bill Staffman stood silently snickering, but even the members of the newly formed cabinet had no immunity from the infectious laughter. Soon, they succumbed, and each movement reignited uncontrolled giddiness from everyone who watched the scene unfold.

In his best Creature from the Black Lagoon imitation, Max lumbered toward the waiting press corps. He waved his goo-covered arms wildly and walked stiff-legged toward them. In child-like response, several members began screaming for effect, which only heightened the laughter. Soon, he stood several feet away.

"I know you expected to see me swim here today," exclaimed Max in his most ironic presidential tone, "but instead, I think I'll introduce you to the dirty world of international politics." He smoothed his hands on his oil-covered arms, and began gesticulating wildly, splattering the oil on the clean shirts and blouses of everyone within twenty feet from where he stood.

"I need to take this attention-getting opportunity to inform you of the cause of this latest oil spill. I was briefed in Washington before flying down here today. International espionage has taken place here in the Gulf of Mexico, *for the second time.*" Murmurs began as the press reacted to the idea that the Deepwater Horizon explosion years before was also the result of industrial espionage.

"We have been attacked by terrorists who want to harm our economy and our American way of life. But we won't let them hold us down for long. We can clean this up. We now have the technology to plug the well quickly and to remove much of the oil from the water before it does widespread harm. And we will track down the cowardly bastards who did this and put them away. The United States of America will not be a target for our enemies, and they will soon know our wrath."

CHAPTER 14

Max accepted a fluffy white towel and began wiping the sticky brown sludge from his exposed skin as the Secret Service ushered him toward his waiting helicopter, Marine One, the president's Helo. He was in dire need of a bath and fresh clothes, but the tiny sink and toilet would suffice until he returned to civilization. Clothes were hanging from a hook on the back of the door to the head. They were the right size, but they weren't his clothes. They were golf clothes, and Max had never played the game.

"What the hell are these golf clothes doing in here?" Max yelled to nobody in particular, but expecting an immediate response. As he emerged from the cramped bathroom, a female voice came from the co-pilot's seat. "Because your handlers are taking you on a golf outing, and I must say you look very pretty dressed in bright yellow, Mister President." The sound of Rachel's voice was melodious, and brought back his smile. She couldn't resist the opportunity to tease him mercilessly. "Do you need me to carry your golf bag, Sir? I'm a good caddy, and I'll wash and polish your balls after each shot."

Max laughed. "I'm sure they got that covered, all except the ball polishing part…Come to think of it, the president's girlfriend will henceforth be his designated ball polisher from this point on. Attend to it immediately, my able assistant!"

"Yes, Mr. President, should I alert the press?" Andrew was relieved to see Max back to normal, and wondered how long it would last. Rachel had that effect on him, and he played along.

"And may I suggest, Mr. President, that we also appoint this capable woman to act as your co-pilot in all future trips outside of Washington, as she is attracting a large contingent of voters who are keenly interested in your love life, sir?"

"You may have our legal staff prepare a presidential proclamation to that extent, Mr. Fox, while I spend a little alone time with our co-pilot...We need to do an in-flight check...or something..." He pulled her back into the tiny makeshift changing room and closed the door. Immediately she was in his arms, kissing him passionately and fumbling at his belt. "I'm going to initiate you into the mile-high club on every flight," she whispered breathily in his ear. She pulled his golf shirt over his head. Max found a front zipper and pulled, pleasantly surprised that her flight suit concealed nothing more than his favorite Victoria's Secret bra and panties.

The day had not gone anywhere close to plan, but Rachel's presence had brought Max back from the serious thoughts that occupied him at the oil spill. He needed her desperately, and their passion could not wait. He couldn't remember the last time they had been alone—if traveling with a full flight crew, security detail, and political aides could be considered alone. He groaned, not only from the intense pleasure of the moment, but also from the realization that the President of the United States can never be alone.

"We have got to keep meeting like this," Max said as Rachel's flight suit slid off her shoulders and slowly crumpled to the floor.

CHAPTER 15

ndrew Fox was to accompany Max on each of his forays away from the White House. He had assumed the essential role of keeping Max on task as he had attempted to do during the campaign. Minutes into the job, he realized that his duties would be unlike any job he had held in the past. Max Masterson's life was an eclectic combination of passion, exercise, and deep focus that allowed him to work and play with equal intensity.

As Max and Rachel were wrapped in passion in the makeshift changing room/bathroom, Andrew sat on the mall jump seat staring forward through the cockpit at the green rolling hills that stretched into infinity below. He tried to focus on the detailed notes on his iPad, and he tried to update the log of activities that had taken place, checking off each event and reviewing the details of the next one, ensuring that every detail was arranged. But he couldn't get the thought out of his mind that the President of the United States was having sex no more than fifteen feet away. He shifted to the personal calendar, writing FIND A GIRLFRIEND...QUICK!

He looked across the cabin at the two Secret Service agents assigned to the President. They seemed oblivious to the President's activities. They sat stoically in the other jump seats, gazing out the windows at the view on the ground, occasionally scanning the horizon. *If I don't get the hang of living in DC, it's going to be a long time between dates,* he thought as the drone of the helicopter mercifully took the edge off his state of arousal. Andrew tried to focus on the day's agenda, but his imagination was getting the best of him. *I've got to get a life, and soon.*

Somewhere over South Alabama, Max strapped himself into his seat, and Rachel took the co-pilot's seat once again.. He focused on his surroundings, and was astounded at the amount of gear that had been packed inside, still leaving room for four comfortable passenger seats and two drop seats for his Secret Service contingent. It reminded him of how close to death he had come before he became president. Their seaplane, piloted by Rachel, had almost been knocked from the sky by an assassin's mortar round. The dum dum bullet had missed the control cables by inches. He wondered if another attack would just bounce off the armored shell, or whether there was some kind of technical gadgetry that would save them.

He looked at the golf clothes with disdain, and pondered what other surprises the day held in store for him.

The next stop for Max was nine holes of golf with the Governor of Alabama, and then back to the White House for briefings that would go into the night. The other members of the transition team were busy vetting candidates for key governmental positions, and the incoming president was required to make final approval of his cabinet and agency heads. None would be retained from the Blythe administration. Least of all, the Director of Homeland Security.

◆ ◆ ◆

The press contingent in Alabama was not the same as the one at the oil spill. They were more of a skeleton crew assigned to get video clips of Max and the Governor, a photo opportunity that politicians crave to show their constituents that they are important. With this president came the unprecedented chance for members of any political party to boost their popularity and poll ratings. He had run as an Independent, and they could gain votes by being seen with the winner.

Andrew was convinced that the golf idea was a bad one. It had not occurred to him that the president of the United States was not an avid golfer. He had just assumed that every president played golf. He heard Max's dismay when he changed into the golf clothes that had been arranged for the scheduled appearance, and he took careful mental note that Max would not be doing this again. *He's not your typical politician*, he reminded himself.

CHAPTER 16

From the start, the golf appearance took on the characteristics of the typical train wreck. Max exited Marine One in his brand new golf clothes: bright yellow, his least-favorite color. He looked clearly uncomfortable, and upon shaking the governor's outstretched hand, he was turned toward the cameras to stand next to the large, red-faced man. The governor beamed, his white teeth making quite a contrast to his shiny face. It appeared to Max that the man had been waiting in the bright sun all day to get that sunburn, and he took an immediate dislike to this loud stranger who was ostentatiously feeding off of his popularity.

"I don't do golf," Max announced, the first words spoken after the cameramen had paused in their efforts to preserve the moment for posterity. The governor, taking his comment as a joke, laughed heartily.

"Don't worry, Mr. President, I brought along a good friend of mine, golf legend Henry "Shank" Mulligan, to be here today, and he can teach you a few tips before we tee off. Come on up here Shank, Ol' Buddy, and meet our new president." Mulligan, fresh off a full security scan from the advance team of Secret Service agents that preceded the arrival of Marine One, was allowed to approach. He was trim and tanned and looked like the prototypical pro golfer: dressed in clothes that bore his label, with his logo emblazoned on his hat and both sleeves. Max briefly imagined that he was probably wearing underwear that bore his logo, too.

"Mr. President, it's a pleasure to meet you. I would have voted for you, but I was in Australia for the Open."

"I don't do golf," Max repeated.

Andrew cringed, and stepped into the awkward moment. "Shank, I'm Andrew Fox, the president's Chief of Staff. I didn't realize this," he said in a low voice, "but Max doesn't play the game, and I was wondering if you could take him around behind the clubhouse somewhere and maybe show him a few things before we tee off. I know you probably get paid thousands of dollars to do this, but believe me, if you make Max look good in front of the cameras, you will receive a letter of gratitude signed by the President of the United States worthy of hanging on your wall and an accompanying digital image that you can use in all of your marketing efforts. Come on, Shank, do it for America."

"I'd be proud to," said Shank. He sized up his high profile student, standing awkwardly in his fresh-out-of-the-box golf clothes. It was evident that he had no interest in the game. Max saw the media event as an opportunity to appear like an ass for the second time of his first day in front of the cameras.

Looking at Andrew with scorn, he leaned in his direction and whispered, "From now on, you will let me know when you plan to have me do something that makes me want to waterboard you. Do you have any more surprises for me today?"

"No sir, just a speech in front of—"

"No speeches. Make a plausible excuse, like the President had to take his Chief of Staff to the emergency room with internal injuries sustained in a golfing accident," Max said in a hiss.

Andrew took a few steps backward, and held his computer bag

in front of his face. "If you spent a few seconds with me each day, this wouldn't happen."

Max sprung forward and grabbed the iPad with both hands. He lowered it slowly, bringing his face within inches of his young advisor.

"You didn't know I hate golf? You picked out this polyester clown outfit? When have you EVER seen me in the presence of balls of any kind? I can forgive you for thinking that I might want to, say, kick a soccer ball, or even shoot a hockey puck or spike a volleyball, but *GOLF*? I don't do golf…" He let go of the computer bag and walked over to his golf instructor, who was busily texting to two unsuspecting women at the same time.

"Come on, let's get this over with. But before we do, I think it would be better if I picked out some of your signature clothes from the pro shop…You know, for marketing and branding, that sort of thing," Max schmoozed.

They began walking toward the clubhouse. "You know, Mr. President, I was thinking the same thing," replied Mulligan. "By the way, who picked out that outfit?"

While Max was changing into more tasteful golf attire, Andrew scrambled to rearrange the day's itinerary. The logistics of moving from one public appearance to another had become monumental, and the security team had already been deployed at the next stop, Montgomery, Alabama, where Andrew had arranged for Max to speak to the NAACP at a monument for Dr. Martin Luther King. *I even wrote the speech myself,"* he thought with regret.

When Max emerged with Mulligan at his side, he was wearing more subtle and tasteful golf clothes, adorned on both sleeves with the Shank logo, a snowy Egret in flight with a golf ball on its back. The logo also appeared on his golf hat and his newly acquired golf sunglasses, in addition to his golf underwear, which Shank threw in for good measure.

"Now the key to golfing for pleasure," Shank began, "is not your score, or how many strokes you take, it's how you look in front of the cameras." They practiced looking good for the next twenty minutes while the press was sequestered out of sight, preparing for the photo opportunity that would be broadcast worldwide by dinnertime.

Max's first two shots hooked into the woods that lined the first tee. Making a slight adjustment, the ball shanked right over a manicured mound that concealed the eighth hole. Within seconds, two Secret Service agents came running, stopping at the top of the mound to determine the source of the shot.

"He sunk it. He got a hole in one," they radioed.

"You're shittin' me," Max and Mulligan said in unison.

That evening, as the broadcast of Max's golf outing ran non-stop with a voice-over of the day's events, Shank Mulligan was interviewed.

"No, he really is a terrible golfer," he explained.

"But he really looks good in my golf clothes."

CHAPTER 17

Two helicopters left Alabama in a rush. One held the President of the United States and half of his Secret Service contingent, while Rachel co-piloted the remainder to Tallahassee Airport, where Air Force One sat waiting to transport Max back to Washington. Max gave his pilot special orders to head to a favorite location in Florida as soon as he took off his golf shoes. He pitched them out the window somewhere over Pensacola Bay. It would be the last time he wore golf attire.

"Andrew, radio ahead and have them supply me with a surf ski and snorkeling gear, and I want you to find something for Secret Service to paddle, too. I don't want any power boats on the river. They make too much noise."

"What's our itinerary, Mr. President? I'll alert the press," Andrew replied, still shaken from the oil spill fiasco and the golf fiasco. He didn't want to make any more mistakes on his first official day on the job.

"I have had about as much press as I can stand for one day. This is for me, not that enormous entourage. You are not to broadcast my whereabouts to the press, or anyone else, do you understand? Make them think that I'm in Tallahassee. Tell you what…have someone dress up in those awful golf clothes and rush him aboard the plane. At a distance, they'll think he's me," he chuckled. "A part of each of my days as President will be spent out of the public eye, and it is your job to help me accomplish that goal. Pulling a Max is as important to me as anything you can do for me. Oh, and by the way, I'm not doing this in my underwear. Get me a bathing suit." Andrew made a mental note to have snorkeling gear and swim trunks stowed on any trips abroad.

Marine One landed at the park at the headwaters of the Wacissa River in a remote part of the Panhandle of Florida. The river is spring-fed, and the clear water and white sandy bottom were unique to Florida. The water quality at the springs far exceeded that of drinking water that had been purified through man-made processes, and the Floridan aquifer that flowed beneath the limestone bedrock was a national treasure.

On their excursions throughout Northern Florida as a child, Senator Masterson had made a point to stop at as many springs as possible so that his son would gain an appreciation of nature. The values that the senator instilled in his son evolved into a need to protect that treasure. Max had quickly developed a love for that time together, and he sought out the solitude and natural beauty of those remote places.

After a quick change into swim trunks, Max took an obligatory jump off the diving platform. Swimming with powerful strokes, he let the current propel him toward the waiting surf ski, which waited at the point where the spring flowed into the river. Donning a dry T-shirt, hat, and flip flops, he inspected his watercraft. It was a Kevlar composite racing surf ski, nineteen feet long, with a rudder operated by pedals in the footwells. It weighed less than thirty pounds from stem to stern, designed for long-distance offshore races. He was familiar with similar human-powered craft, and he estimated that there was nothing on the water that could move faster. He had a familiar surge of adrenalin as he inspected the carbon fiber paddle that accompanied it, anxious to test his limits.

He looked over at the two canoes that had been supplied to his Secret Service contingent. Livery canoes are average in every respect, accommodating beginner canoeists on weekend day trips, and capable of carrying two passengers, a large cooler, and the family dog. They are not as tippy as the surf ski, and due to their width, Max could predict that they would be slow. At least he wouldn't have to rescue the black-suits from the bottom when they tipped. He quickly became resigned to a leisurely float, and he amused himself by poking fun at his security detail as he strapped his snorkeling gear to the hatch with bungee cords.

"You are required to wear the orange life vests that you see there, and I'll wait right here while you guys put them on. We will not leave without proper safety precautions," Max prodded, fully aware that two of his protectors were seasoned Navy SEALs who had probably faced death in treacherous waters many times.

"Mr. President, why aren't you wearing one?" questioned the man with the broadest shoulders. He looked ridiculous in a canoe, but with his broad chest covered in a bright orange life vest, he resembled a bad Halloween costume.

"Dang, the whole river can't be more than fifteen feet deep at the deep end, and I can probably walk across most of it without getting my head wet," complained another.

"Quit complaining, or I'll just go by myself," Max teased.

"Alright, we're ready," proclaimed the third as he awkwardly took a seat at the stern.

They launched and paddled quickly away from the headwaters. "Follow me, I have something ahead I know you will enjoy," said Max with the enthusiasm that freedom provides.

CHAPTER 18

After a few minutes, it was apparent that the surf ski powered by the President was about three times as fast as the two canoes powered by four exasperated Secret Service agents in constricting orange vests.

"Fuck this," said the first one, shedding the vest in one contorted move. At his example, all of the paddlers shed their floatation devices, piling them on the floor of the canoes in contempt. Max amused himself by continuously circling back and prodding them.

"Can't you go any faster?"

"No, Mr. President," they proclaimed in unison.

"We're almost there."

They were perspiring and cussing under their breath.

"Where?"

"Here," said Max, steering toward a small, clear creek on the left. He disappeared behind a curtain of wild rice that lined the river canal, prompting the paddlers to increase their pace. They steered into the current at the place where they had last seen him, and caught a glimpse ahead just as Max and his superior watercraft negotiated another turn in the high reeds.

"Damn, I thought White House detail was going to be a cake job," puffed one.

"You got that right. He's making us work for a living," complained the paddler at the bow.

"Just shut up and paddle," muttered the one in command.

When they caught up with Max, he had already donned snorkeling gear and had free-dived to the bottom of Big Blue Spring, a hole in the earth which discharges millions of gallons of pure water each day. The view that they saw, however, was the unoccupied surf ski bobbing in the middle of a remote area, and the President was nowhere to be seen. They panicked and radioed Marine One in unison. Their voices came through as a unified message, undecipherable to the pilot and other members of the security detail. "Please repeat," asked a member stationed back at the communication hub.

"We've lost the president."

Max, having stayed down at the bottom of the 45-foot-deep spring for as long as he could in one breath, popped to the surface in a burst of water and expelled air.

"Never mind, we found him."

"If it wasn't my job to keep him alive, I'd be tempted to kill him myself," proclaimed the agent in the stern .

CHAPTER 19

Max was reliving his youth, and although he was years ahead of his protectors, he had found a way to rekindle the joys of his childhood from time to time. "You guys should really try this. It's a rush like you wouldn't believe." He ran his wet hair through his hands and put his still-dry T-shirt back on. Straddling the surf ski with both legs, he unlashed the kayak paddle, put his feet in both footwells, and took off again, steering around both canoes and shooting downstream, back to the main channel of the river with powerful strokes.

His security escorts struggled to turn their canoes, and they nearly succeeded in dumping themselves in the water before pointing in the direction of the current. By the time that they recovered, Max was out of sight, and the anxiety of their failures was compounded. As they emerged from the high grass and entered the main channel of the river, they were relieved to see Max coming their way, paddling toward them against the current.

"I think I'll just float for a while," he said. "After we go downstream awhile, we need to turn around and paddle against the current to get back, and I don't want to have to tow your sorry asses back to the helo." He settled in behind the canoes and stopped paddling, allowing the strong current to carry them downstream.

"Mr. President, you say you have been here a few times?"

"Oh yeah, when I was a kid, I used to paddle down the slave canal to where it meets the Aucilla River, go down to Nutall Rise, and then turn around and paddle back. It's pretty remote, with gators and wild boar. One time, I even saw a manatee give birth. Not a place you expect to see in Florida."

"Slave canal? Why do they call it the slave canal," questioned one agent, who bristled at the idea. His ancestors had been slaves, and he had never been able to reconcile the idea that one man could own another and treat him like a commodity that was bought and sold.

Max wanted to cherish the silence and enjoy the abundant wildlife, his way of decompressing from the stresses of the day. But he owed his companions an explanation. After all, he started it, and he wasn't through testing their ability to protect him from the unknown.

"Back before the civil war, the plantation owners needed a way to float their cotton on barges from the headwaters to the Gulf of Mexico, and this river ends up in a swamp. They had slaves that they used to construct a canal between this river, the Wacissa, and the Aucilla, which is a direct route to the Gulf and deeper water. Then it was easy to load their valuable cargo onto ships." Max slowed the surf ski by silently back-paddling while the current pulled the canoes farther downstream.

"The interesting part of the story is that the canal was never used. The Civil War intervened, and the South declined. The Union blockade ended the cotton industry, and after the war, trains did the work that the slaves used to do," Max explained. They had reached the slave canal, hidden to the right behind willow trees. If you didn't know it was there, there was no way to find it without a detailed map. Miss the concealed cutoff, and you ended up in the swamp.

Max took the cutoff.

Two more seconds, and Max was concealed by trees and high grass. To his protectors, it was if he had disappeared without a sound.

CHAPTER 20

He paddled at full pull, using the foot-controlled rudder to maintain maximum speed around the turn. As the bow of the surf ski rounded the narrow bend of the river, he passed into full view of the mama gator sunning on the sandy right bank. The squeaks of her newly-hatched babies greeted him from the opposite shore. No sane person would intentionally come between a mother alligator and her babies, but his intrusion was purely accidental.

Max immediately realized his predicament.

He was about to get chomped.

The eleven-foot-long alligator slashed her tail once and lunged into the water. He paddled on pure adrenalin now, not bothering to turn his head to respond to the source of the splash.

He knew that she was inches behind his rudder.

If he wanted to live, he had to paddle.

The surf ski was nineteen feet long, but it only extended three inches on either side of his hips. At twenty-nine pounds, it would be no obstacle to the five thousand pounds per square inch produced by the jaws of the ancient reptile. If he brought the man-powered racing kayak to a full stop, it would tip him into the water. Besides, and at this point stopping was definitely not an option. He saw the eyes and snout of the gator pop to the surface to his left ahead of him, and he looked on as the leathery mouth began to open, revealing jagged rows of teeth.

She was looking at him.

Max kept paddling. When he came abreast of the gator, he placed the blade of the paddle directly between her eyes and hoped that the depth of the water would keep her from planting her powerful legs in the sandy bottom. If she was floating, he could sink her long enough to propel his watercraft beyond her jaws.

If she was planted on the bottom, she could have him for lunch.

Without breaking form, he aimed his paddle directly between her eyes, and he was relieved when the massive head submerged for the moment he needed to get by. Propelling the surf ski as fast as his aching shoulders could go, he sought his escape. A wake extended behind him, creating small waves that hit the sandy banks on either side. He imagined the eyes of the gator glowing yellow as she watched his retreat. Fifty more strokes, and he came to a tree that extended its full length across the Slave Canal. A lush bush of poison oak covered the center section of the narrow passage. On the right, he saw light beyond the obstacle and steered the rudder toward the hole in the foliage. *Great,* he thought, *I get past being served for lunch, and now I have to worry about catching a nasty rash...* Once beyond the downed tree, he turned and looked behind him. There was no sign of the gator, but he was not in a trusting mood.

He paddled for as long as his tired muscles would thrust him downstream, and then he allowed the sleek craft to tip him into the water. It was cool and clear, and the invigorating wetness brought him back from exhaustion. Its spring-fed waters maintained a temperature of seventy-two degrees year-round, and he floated until his body temperature and breathing returned to normal.

I wonder how frantic my Secret Service agents would be if they knew that the President of the United States was almost devoured by a huge reptile on their watch? he asked himself. *I can only imagine the predators lurking in the Oval Office. And there are no corners to hide.*

CHAPTER 21

He could hear it before he could see it: the sound of a helicopter's rotor pushing the humid air aside as the aircraft approached the secluded spring. Then the massive rotors appeared above the cypress trees with a loud *thrup-thrup-thrup*, followed by the dark blue body of the craft, the presidential seal prominently displayed on the fuselage in gold. The turbulence tore the Spanish moss from the branches, and it floated slowly toward the water in elongated tufts of grayish green. The helicopter maneuvered above the circular opening in the trees—not much wider than the reach of the powerful blades—and hovered thirty feet above him.

From doors on either side of the helicopter, two dark figures emerged and dropped from the sky, landing twenty feet away. Max treaded water as two Navy SEALs in wetsuits and full scuba gear swam furiously in his direction. The SEALs approached with strong strokes, their faces covered by masks. Max was amazed at the speed at which they converged on him, and he wondered whether they would crush him between them. When they were at arm's length, they pulled off their masks and pulled the regulators out of their mouths in unison.

"Just relax, Mr. President, we're here to save you," exclaimed one, while the other attempted to roll Max onto his back with arms that resembled tree trunks.

"But I don't want to be saved," sputtered Max as he slipped beneath the hold and pointed his finger in the face of the SEAL in front of him. "I was enjoying a restful dip in my favorite spring until you guys came along."

"Sir, it is my duty to protect you from danger, and I would give my life to defend you from harm—"

"Did it ever occur to you…what is your name?"

"Shields, sir."

"No, your first name! There will be no formality, as long as you maintain respect."

"Benjamin, sir. Well…Ben,"

"And you?" Max shouted.

The other Navy SEAL treaded water silently, witnessing the exasperation of Max, and wondering whether he and his companion were about to get re-assigned to somewhere cold and lonely on the first day of their privileged duty.

"Mr. President, sir, my name is Jonathan Schlitz, but my friends call me Schlitz. I prefer it. I'm duty bound to protect you," he said over the roar of the helicopter.

Max contemplated his next move, knowing that if he attempted to exercise independence that violated their stringent training, he would likely be trussed up, stuffed in a metal basket, and hauled by cable into the helicopter, which continued to hover overhead.

I have been coming to this spot since I was a young kid, and one of my favorite things to do is see how long I can hold my breath at the bottom of this spring, Max thought. While I'm here, I'll be damned if I am going to let them spoil my fun in the name of security! What I'm gonna do is take three deep breaths and free dive down to the bottom, thirty-five feet down below, and I'm going to hang upside down from that piece of limestone down there until I can't do it anymore. Then I'm going to float to the top all by myself. "After I'm done having my fun, you can take me home." He didn't waste his breath with a lengthy explanation. The sound of his voice was nearly drowned out by the rotor wash. Max could see black SUVs pulling into the clearing near the boat launch on shore. One of them was already stuck in the white sugar sand, wheels spinning and throwing dust into the air.

"Yes, sir, Mr. President!" They replied in a unified baritone. Max took three deep breaths and flipped under the surface, pulling his way toward the bottom of the spring.

From shore and from above, the scene of the President of the United States disappearing beneath the surface, followed quickly by the SEALs, was enough to cause unrestrained panic.

"The president is down. I repeat, the president is down!" they yelled into their communicators.

They watched helplessly as the water whipped in circular waves from the hovering blades. The effect was to obscure what was happening beneath the surface of the clear water, and the anguish of those on land became horror as each second ticked away.

After two minutes and fourteen seconds, Max popped to the surface with Ben and Jonathan within arm's length, regulators still in their mouths. Max was ecstatic.

"A new record," he managed to say between deep breaths of fresh air.

Immediately, the Navy SEALs communicated with the hovering helicopter.

"Drop a basket, and get Wizard out of here. The other helo can pick us up."

The abrupt intrusion into his placid respite was startling, but he was coming to understand that his ability to be alone had gone away on election day. He had become the property of the United

States of America. With that position came the sacrifice of trips like this—it was deluded to assume that the president had a reasonable expectation of privacy.

And his inauguration was still over a month away.

CHAPTER 22

Air Force One was to be flown to Tallahassee, where it would remain on the tarmac until Marine One returned from the Gulf. With it was Rachel, who had been eagerly training to fly the presidential jet and helicopters since days after the election. That was one of the perks of being the president's girlfriend. If she wanted something, she asked for it, and they gave it to her. She had no intention of being an ornamental woman, quietly spending her lengthy time apart, waiting for her man. *While Max is away having his idea of fun, I'm going to have a little fun of my own.*

It was her time to take the controls under the watchful eye of Commander Mark Tillman. In his career as Chief Pilot of Air Force One, he thought he had seen it all, from piloting George W. Bush on 9/11, to avoiding certain death as they evaded a SAM attack over the skies of Saudi Arabia on a clandestine peace mission. But he never thought he would be giving flying lessons to a beautiful woman young enough to be his daughter and using the most sophisticated and protected flying machine in history as a trainer. It went against all of his instincts, but in the twilight of his long and impeccable career, he intended to do whatever the new president wanted him to do. He would do it with gusto, no questions asked.

"How am I doing?" Rachel asked.

"Well, I'd say you're doing fine, considering that we are presently on autopilot," Tillman replied smiling. He couldn't resist the opportunity to tease his young protégé, who he was rapidly coming to like. He could easily see why the president had taken a shine to her. She was worlds apart from the political wives and girlfriends he had met, and he had met more than his share.

"By the way, you are presently the most protected woman in history."

"I am?"

"I need for you to understand something," he replied. "Any time this big bird flies, all of the power and might of the United States of America flies with it. You don't realize this, I'm sure, but the president is a target whenever he goes out in public. Air Force One is the most visible symbol of that might. We have the most sophisticated anti-missile technology ever invented, and we have a continuous escort from the most tricked-out fighter jets that our defense contractors can put in the air."

"I'm amazed at how easy it is to fly. I don't suppose Max would like it much if I tried any stunt flying."

"Young lady, if you try anything at all, I'll see that your license is suspended until President Masterson is in the history books." She smiled at the thought. *Max as an old man, having the distinction of being a former president, still guarded by Secret Service. I wonder how he will take to that. I wonder if I'll still be around to see the day.*

She considered the sobering reality of loving a person who symbolized ideas so vivid that he was a constant moving target, and her smile transformed into a look of determination. She focused on the task at hand. "I think I'll leave the flying to you, and I'll be satisfied to sit as your co-pilot for now, sir. And believe me, I won't do anything to get my wings taken away."

Rachel pursued her passions without restraint, whether they involved Max or not, and flying gave her the satisfaction she needed to feel fulfilled. Max was so preoccupied during the transition that she needed to be away from the constant buzz of preparation that surrounded them. The press of people soon became overwhelming. She was amazed at his ability to mentally insulate himself from the activity that surrounded him, but she needed frequent escapes from that reality. Flying supplied that extra thrill that gave value to her life, and she had accumulated enough flight time to rival Amelia Earhart, her childhood idol. On this training flight, she could focus on flying. *I think I'll leave the protecting to the people trained to do that sort of thing.*

CHAPTER 23

On the flight back to Washington, Rachel surrendered the flying to Commander Tillman. Whenever Max was aboard, she could sit in the co-pilot's seat while the enormous jet was on the ground, but standard operating procedure put her in the main cabin during the in-flight transporting of the president. She waited in the private cabin in the rear and watched through the open door as he emerged from the conference room. His solemn face alerted Rachel that something was seriously wrong. Max made his way in her direction, his head held high. He shut the door and turned to face her. His remote gaze made her briefly wonder if he had noticed she was there. He sighed wearily, and held her in his arms. Max hugged her tightly. It was not a hug of passion this time. "Did you have a bad golf game?" she asked. "What's got you so glum, Darlin'? I know how much you like to get away and go paddling. I—"

He reached up and placed a finger against her lips.

"I need to tell you about my day."

Rachel felt a pang of trepidation from his tone of voice.

He was bone tired, not just from the physical activity, but from the burden of knowledge that he had acquired. He realized that he was surrounded by enemies he never knew existed, not just those who he could readily identify. There were bad guys lurking in the shadows, and the knowledge that his father's life-long enemy was responsible for the Patriot bombing that killed Adrianna had become a larger boulder in his lap as the day wore on. He continued to hold her tightly, and he whispered to her quietly.

"Pryor was behind the death of Adrianna," he said.

"No!"

"And there is nothing I can do about it until we locate him, and I need to get his people out of the picture before that will happen," he responded. They laid together on the bed, fully-clothed. For the remainder of the flight, Max recounted his experiences and shared his thoughts.

She's my most-trusted confidant. I depend on her more now than ever. She gives me her opinions, but above that, she gives me the unselfish support I need to survive the day. Right now, I don't know who else I can fully trust.

◆ ◆ ◆

When Air Force One landed, Max was whisked without delay to Fairlane. He hadn't officially taken residence at the White House, so his home was his resting place until Inauguration Day. As soon as Max emerged from the limo, surrounded by security, he walked purposely toward the private entrance that only he could enter. It was nondescript side door, with an arch of limestone that concealed it from a front approach. The security system recognized him and him alone, and when the Secret Service contingent attempted to follow too closely, Max interceded. Turning quickly, he made them stop short.

"I am the only one who can enter through this door. I had it installed years ago, and the security system only recognizes me. If you enter through this door, you'll be stuck in a sealed room until I let you out. Go through the front door, and I'll meet you near the den." As the agents made their way around the front, Max quickly entered the house and sealed the door from the inside. He didn't wait for them to catch up, and he strode purposefully into the den, unannounced.

"Max, Max!" they all spoke at once. Scarlett was in the middle of the room, surrounded by the transition team. iPads and papers were strewn on every flat surface, and the buzz of activity was a palpable reminder of the tasks they had been assigned before his trip.

"Have you fired and removed every one of Blythe's people yet?" he whispered to Scarlett, dispensing with formalities.

"No, we thought we would vet the ones who deserve our attention," said Scarlett.

"I want them gone. *All of them.*" He stood directly in front of the table where Scarlett sat, his scowl revealing his thoughts.

Something must have happened since this morning, she thought, oblivious to the events that had transformed him. She had no fear of him, but Max had never displayed anger in her presence, or seemed to be the kind of person who would. This side of the president was new. His jaw was set, and his eyes took on a piercing countenance. "We usually keep some of them to tell us how things are done," she said.

"All of them gone. *Now.*" He was no longer whispering. He turned to the transition team, which huddled behind the stretch of tables that occupied the middle of the room. "Tell me," he said, scanning their faces, "Which of you worked for Blythe or worked for Homeland Security before you came here?" There was a prolonged silence, and three people, a man and two women, timidly raised their hands.

Max turned toward Scarlett. "I want the Secret Service to gingerly escort them out of the building, now. And I want a complete background check on everyone that remains." He turned back toward his staff. "If I find out that any of you are lying, you will never work in government again."

A fourth person, a dark-haired middle-aged man, stood and silently left the room.

Satisfied, Max concluded the meeting. "It's been a long day," he said. "I want the rest of you to go home. Tomorrow, each of you should bring a comprehensive list of potential cabinet appointees and staffers. I don't want you to collaborate on the list until we reconvene in my kitchen at 8:00 A.M."

CHAPTER 24

Max's father, retired Senator John Masterson, never cared for the nicknames he acquired during his many terms in public service. Not that his disdain changed anything. His Senate colleagues had given him the name "Minuteman," and it stuck. It described Senator Masterson's impatience for long-winded speeches—he had habit of walking out of marathon hearings before the speaker had finished. This trademark characteristic described the senator's life until his death when Max was twenty-six years old.

Max was instilled with a similar impatience for meaningless detail and tradition. He dreaded the idea of being in endless meetings and enduring shallow talk. He believed to the core of his being that his role as president was to manage the big ideas, leaving his subordinates, including the United States Congress, to work out the details. By starting with large concepts, Max was able to stay on task and pursue the path that his father had laid out for him prior to his death. Senator Masterson had the plan inscribed on gold plate and mounted on the wall of his den at Fairlane, and Max had gazed at the words nearly every day since he was a young boy. He had long-since memorized the list, but he still stopped to read it each time he walked into the room:

ALWAYS SPEND LESS THAN YOU HAVE.
SPEAK IN POSITIVE AFFIRMATIONS.
KEEP YOUR MESSAGE SHORT AND TO THE POINT.
RESPECT THE OPINIONS OF OTHERS.
EDUCATE THE PEOPLE BEFORE ASKING THEM TO DECIDE AN ISSUE.
THE INFORMED WILL OF THE PEOPLE DICTATES WHAT IS RIGHT.
MAINTAIN WHAT IS RIGHT, AND RIGHT WHAT IS WRONG.
AMERICAN INTERESTS MUST PREVAIL OVER FOREIGN INTERESTS.
MEASURE EACH DECISION BY WHAT IS BEST FOR AMERICA.
MAKE AMERICANS AWARE THAT THEY ARE A PART OF THE WORLD.
IT IS BETTER TO CONFESS THAT YOU DON'T KNOW THAN TO LIE.
DON'T QUOTE A STATISTIC UNLESS YOU CAN BACK IT UP WITH FACTS.
PERSUADE, DON'T DECEIVE.
COMBINE STRENGTH WITH COMPASSION.
ABOVE ALL ELSE, BE A PATRIOT.

Max followed the maxims. He had been taught by his father and his mentor, Luke Postlewaite, that if a president can rise above the incessant tug of politics, the greater good can be achieved through his efforts. Much of what he had been taught by them was character-building more than rote memorization. They had the mutual goal of teaching Max the selfless above the selfish, and they made sure that he understood the meaning of the word *patriot*.

His lessons were presented in the Socratic method. The teacher asked the question and the student analyzed all sides of an issue. A quick answer was met with a rebuke. He was expected to reason out of dilemmas, and to make the hard decisions that had to be made at the end. Sometimes, there was no right or wrong, only the *better* decision. He had to be *the problem solver* to confront the challenges of his presidency, and beyond that, he needed *the power to persuade.*

Classroom teaching was balanced by exercise. Max was trained in the martial arts from the time he was old enough to talk, and he had become an expert in efficiently dispatching his opposition with an economy of movement. Most times, a match was over soon after it started. Still, Max never ascended from green belt status when he was training. "That's the student's color, and you're the student," his father would say.

The lessons were private, as were the competitions. He competed only against young men and women who were just a little better than him. He became gracious in defeat, but he always looked forward to the rematch. And most times, he prevailed the second time around. Both of his mentors, Postlewaite in particular, became keenly interested in Max's responses to defeat, and his response to victory, too.

They paid particular attention to the matches involving female opponents. The macho-misogynist male attitude of certain politicians had frequently led to their defeat, both politically and personally, and that way of thinking had the potential to cause Max to fail in his life's mission. Women in politics did not seem to suffer defeat as a result of the misconduct that brought down their male counterparts, and he was presented with examples of defeat that involved sex or greed. If he was to serve with honor, he would need to avoid those character traps.

The lessons would start with the allegations against the politician, his defense, and the physical evidence. It was an informal prosecution, and the wisdom was in the answer to the eternal question: "Why?" Max would sometimes shrug it off and respond, "Women need a reason: love, security, or companionship. Men just need a place." Sometimes, that was an appropriate fallback answer, and it became the standard response when the idiotic behavior of a politician ruined a lifetime of career-building. Other, times, greed, power, or testosterone-driven thrill- seeking were more appropriate answers, and he learned of potential landmines to avoid.

"You will never be able to escape the urges that go along with being male, but there are non-verbal ways of setting yourself apart from the herd," Postlewaite counseled. "When you meet a woman, make a point of shaking her hand and looking straight into her eyes. Resist the urge to look at her breasts. When she breaks eye contact, look at her breasts and take a mental picture. Then resume eye contact, and don't break that connection. It's a powerful habit. Practice it and master it, but never reveal it."

Max's lessons on enemies were taught by his father. In Senator Masterson's long career in Congress, he had confronted and defeated most of his political opponents, but it wasn't his opponents that were the subject of his forceful diatribes. Enemies were his scourge, to be conquered and destroyed. All enemies were opponents, but not all opponents descended to the level of enemy. Enemies lacked the ability to negotiate or compromise. They were singularly obsessed with the attainment of their cause.

"Son, if you don't defeat your enemy, they will defeat you," taught his father. "Choose your enemies carefully, but when you do, you must devise and execute a plan to defeat them before they realize that you are on to them. Most attacks begin with deceit, and they will use false efforts at compromise to buy time. Before the battle begins, you must prepare for it wisely."

CHAPTER 25

Willie B. Somovich combed his thick, black hair over his forehead, obscuring his uni-brow. When he had styled it into his trademark look, he sprayed it with copious amounts of hairspray in a sticky cloud. It was predicted to be windy in Chicago, and he wanted to make sure that the paparazzi wouldn't get an image of his hair being out of place. He had little cause for worry. At this stage of petrification, his recognizable look was more like a helmet.

Willie had spent the previous ten years of his career as host of the conservative talk show "Willie B Right." The format for the show was predictable and repetitive, weighing in heavily on conspiracy theories that were so ludicrous and unprovable that they gained a life of their own.

"I create the truth, my flock!" he would pronounce. "You must believe to achieve," he would respond to skeptical callers. His messages had no more substance than hot air, but to the faithful listeners who provided revenue to him and his advertisers, every word that he spoke was money in the bank. They bought his books and came to his seminars, which took on the tone of an Elmer Gantry-style revival meeting. Most of all, they bought the products he hawked at every "station break".

The conspiracies were created in the studio during planning sessions between Somovich and his producers. They judged the value of each one by the amount of listeners who believed his nonsense enough to call in and fill up airtime. Some of the regular callers and guests would go on to commercial success by writing books about Willie's theories, and some would ghost-write books that would be published as Willie's profound beliefs. Each one had become a best-seller, and Willie B. Somovich had become a very rich man.

The show ran each weekday afternoon from 1:30 to 3:00 PM. His commentary occupied the first segment, followed by an hour of call-in guests, who he interrupted at every opportunity. Most of the sentiments that Willie expressed were nonsense, but his listeners and viewers didn't mind. His approach to the world was unique. He would start each show with a quote that described his character with micro-precision: "Life doesn't make sense, so why should I?" Once reason was dismissed, all of the messages were cloaked in a conservative mantra. Anyone who questioned the basis for the theories was immediately criticized for their lack of adherence to conservative ideals. If they refused to back down, Willie would question their patriotism, and they never called back.

"Good afternoon, Conservative Americans!" The background jingle had been created exclusively for Willie, sung by a country singer who had once been at the top of the charts, but his only gig nowadays was to sing *The Willie Song* at every event at which his meal ticket appeared.

"Today," Willie began, "we will be talking about the ideals that made this country great. My topic of the day is: We must buy up all of the Middle East oil we can, so the Chinese can't get their hands on it, and we need to borrow their money to do it. My argument is this: They need oil to run their factories over there, and if we have all of the oil, they can't out-produce us. They produce almost everything we use here in this country, so we need to beat them to the oil wells." Willie seldom made sense, but lately, his thought-processes were more jumbled than usual due to a hidden addiction to painkillers. His growing habit was unknown to everyone except the doctor who made a good living writing prescriptions for Willie, whether he needed pain-killers or not.

His first caller was a long-distance trucker from the Deep South, who was calling from the highway while driving a load of used tires cross-country. "Let's take our first call from Trey from Tuscaloosa. Welcome to "Willie B Right!"

"Willie, Trey here. Long-time listener. First-time caller. Here's a BooYah to Ya, or as we say in Tuscaloosa, Boo Y'all to Y'all."

"Good one, Trey. And BooYah back to Ya. What is it you wanted to talk about?

"I wanted ta talk to ya 'bout that there idea ya'll had 'bout buyin' up all the oal."

Trey's image on split screen, broadcast from a Skype phone built into the steering wheel of his semi, was quite a contrast from the carefully coifed Somovich in the broadcast studio.

"That's one heckuvah accent you have going there, Trey," Willie replied.

"I ain't got no accent, ya mangy dawg...Y'all got the accent, if ya ask me. I—"

"Now, now, Trey." Willie interrupted Trey in mid-sentence. It was a standard part of the program. If he allowed the caller to get out a complete sentence, they would be having a conversation, and Willie delighted in cutting Trey off before he could get there. "I like accents. They remind me of the fact that we are not all alike, and some of us are less alike than others. Now, what was the matter in which we are about to engage?"

"Engage! I ain't gonna engage to no fella. I gotta a girl back home—"

"Next caller," said Willie.

The next caller was a university professor from Berkley, California, named William. No last names were permitted. William had the temerity to attempt to challenge the premise upon which the day's topic was based, and in doing so, he challenged the extent of Willie's knowledge on the subject. He was not a frequent viewer, or he would have realized that having an intellectual conversation requires *two* intellectuals in the conversation, and Willie was going to have none of that on his show.

"Hi, Willie," said Willie.

"My name is William, and I'm calling about—"

"No. You're a Willie, I'm a Willie, we're both Willies. Equals, if I may." Willie always said "if I may" at the end of a sentence when he was on the air with someone he presumed had greater knowledge than he did on a topic, which happened a lot. He was at his best when he could make an intelligent caller sound stupid. The goateed man in split-screen shifted in his chair. He appeared uncomfortable.

"I prefer to be called William, if you don't mind."

"Well I do mind, Willie," said Willie. "I prefer to be called Willie, and I think that's a perfectly nice name, don't you think?

Smelling the bait, William ignored the question. "I would like to challenge the presumptions used in forming your hypothesis about buying foreign oil to stimulate the U.S. economy, and thereby defeating China's—"

"Well, well, Willie. You misunderstood. I'm surprised that a man with your credentials wouldn't understand that I was talking about jobs for Americans and taking back the rights of every American to keep those jobs at home!"

A gong sounded, and a pre-recorded cheer resounded through the studio.

"But I thought—"

"Next caller!" said Willie. The sound of the connection being severed was amplified for effect. "Schmuck."

And so it went. Another typical day on the Willie B Right show.

CHAPTER 26

Glen Aspect was the polar opposite of Willie. He fervently believed that all who disagreed with him were Neanderthals, and he told them so. He contended that government should take care of all of our needs, but he bristled at the label of Socialist.

"Why can't we all get along?" Glen was starting his morning talk show in the usual way. It followed a set format, and for his most faithful listeners, it struck a chord. They couldn't get enough. Aspect would start with his message of the day, addressing recent national and world events that were violent enough or so potentially catastrophic as to evoke worry. Then he would shift to a discussion of how the government should help, followed by clips of somewhere in the world where innocents were being slaughtered. In the end, he would do a sixty-second editorial about altruism, and how if we all just did the right thing, the world would be a better place. He didn't take calls from listeners. He didn't care what they had to say. His concern was with ratings, and they told him all he needed to know.

"The last thing I need to hear is some yahoo from Topeka calling in and questioning my flawless judgment," he told his producers during the daily staff meeting. They had been reviewing the format for the show, and Glen was adamant that he remain isolated from public opinion. "It just doesn't fit my program. I will not be flailed by call-ins who I can't control. I don't work like Somovich, and if his viewers start in on me, I'm going to have a bad day. I don't like bad days," he explained.

The next day, the show would start the same. Nothing changed, and Glen had another segment that essentially presented the same material with different players, all bent on changing the world with peace, love, and getting along. The fallacy of his argument, that lasting change must address the core of the problems, was never mentioned. Glen Aspect's view of life was simple: As long as the world continued on the same path toward perceived annihilation, his talk show would never be cancelled, and his personal prosperity was guaranteed.

"The ultimate obscenity is nuclear energy. It doesn't choose its victims. Everyone becomes its victim," he started in his daily editorial. The opening statement had to be what he called a "headline grabber," and each one was carefully crafted for maximum controversy by his staff of seven writers.

The mornings were devoted to his show so that he could book the afternoons for guest appearances on other talk shows to discuss his views. The irony of the situation was that Glen didn't have many views of his own, and his appearances were written and rehearsed for maximum play on all of the major networks. He was a regular contributor by virtue of his ability to talk in the time allocated for his segment, and his staff wrote the questions for the interviews. All the networks had to do was park Aspect in a chair and let him read from the script.

"Remember Three Mile Island? Chernobyl? How about Fukushima? Hiroshima? Nagasaki? Well, I'm here to tell you that we have our own nuclear disaster waiting to happen again right here in the good ol' United States, and all it will take is one big earthquake in California. That's right, folks. The Diablo Canyon nuclear plant is built on one of the biggest earthquake faults in the U.S., and it's a disaster waiting to happen. And mark my words, it will happen."

Aspect didn't waste any time seeking comment. He was the Chicken Little of the talk show world, and people loved it. There was no need to explain his views. His genre was sensational fright inducement, and he knew it. Glen Aspect was a real-life horror ghoul dressed in an immaculate pin-stripe suit.

CHAPTER 27

Bob, Phil, and Jerry sat in their usual Thursday night "meeting." At least that's what they called it, but it was more of a structured excuse to get away from the wife and kids for awhile, drink beer, and eat chicken wings. They had been doing the same thing for so long that it had become a habit. Jerry never let a Thursday pass without reminding his fellow members that he held the record for consecutive meetings, which made Bob and Phil eternally regret that they chose the birth of their children over the meeting. Most of all, they regretted that Jerry would do anything to maintain his string of attendance, and they would never be able to steal that badge of pride, no matter what. Jerry could be on life support, and he would still find a way to be there.

Jerry took the opportunity to start the meeting by waving a drumstick covered with Blazing Volcano sauce so hot that it had been rumored to eat the flesh off of unsuspecting hot sauce rookies. He announced, "Let the meeting begin!" and they turned toward the big screen situated at the end of the bar. Their focus was the political news of the day, and they had long since programmed themselves to filter out the information they deemed not worthy of discussion.

This Thursday, they chose to focus on reports of the new president, Max Masterson, and his vice-president, Scarlett, who they had privately confessed to each other that they would screw in a heartbeat if their wives wouldn't find out. They then took a male oath of secrecy by saying in unison, "If you tell anyone I said that, I'll personally kick your ass." They each took a prolonged gulp of beer and bit into a wing before reviewing the clips of the day.

"They all make shit up, and they put their slant on whatever you say. The more words you speak, the more they have to twist and misconstrue, and in the end, they can have you spouting nonsense," announced Jerry as they watched a report from the Bull Network's Glenda Reasoner that dealt with the new administration's lack of party loyalty.

"You can say that again," Bill replied as the televised commentary shifted to talk show hosts Willie Somovich and Glen Aspect, two hosts they loved to hate. "Did you see what they said about our boy Max the other night? That shit about him just sitting up in the Oval Office and not caring about us common folk? If you ask me—"

Jerry cut off Bill before he launched into one of his weekly diatribes.

"He isn't even in the White House yet. Glenda says that he's down at the oil spill getting his hands dirty—"

"Would you guys shut the fuck up? I want to see the Special Report."

Phil resented the fact that he was always the last to speak. By the time they got around to him, he usually had nothing to say, but on this occasion, he was ready. The three turned from their bickering and watched as the president-elect of the United States fell into what looked like floating turds, not once but twice, and came up covered in brown gook. As they watched in rapt amazement, Max approached the camera and flung the slimy mess at the laughing press corps.

"Oh Lord, we're in for an interesting four years," said Phil.

"What do you mean? I'm going for eight," replied Jerry.

"Well, if you guys want him in for eight, then I'll go for twelve," announced Bob.

Jerry and Phil just shook their heads as Bob, convinced that he had finally one-upped his old buddies, drained the last of his draft with a satisfied gulp.

CHAPTER 28

The Trump Plaza in Jersey City is the jewel of high rise residences in the greater New York metropolitan area. At 55 stories tall, it is the tallest residential building in New Jersey, commanding an unrestricted view of the Statue of Liberty, the Hudson River, and all of Manhattan. The penthouse condo of the building had been sold back in Trump's heyday to meet his financial obligations on other projects, purchased by a corporation named PGM, Inc., which existed only to purchase properties in tall buildings in major cities along the eastern seaboard and west coast of the United States. Nobody knew what the initials stood for, and they didn't care. All transactions, for all ten of the luxurious penthouse residences that PGM had purchased to date, were made by remote wire transfer, and all ten sales were closed without the presence of a single human being. None of the residences were occupied, and their opulent furnishings were only for show.

In the weeks leading up to the inauguration, there was a flurry of activity in each of the units, as men disguised as movers brought large, innocuous looking boxes into the buildings. They had the proper credentials to present upon request, and their activities were never questioned by the management. The movers had the keycards necessary to enter the building, and another key card gave them access to the penthouse floors, which were inaccessible by anyone not possessing the electronic key. The total time that the units were occupied was approximately two hours, during which the workers installed ice-making machines and carefully connected them to the power supply. Inside each icemaker was a carefully engineered device of mass destruction: a tritium-enhanced, super EMP bomb.

It wasn't a bomb in the conventional way. An Electromagnetic Pulse device did not produce a structure and people-destroying explosion. The EMP bomb was designed to emit gamma rays in a concentrated discharge. The effect of it's detonation was to save those people and buildings, but take away all of the pillars of living in a technological society. Gamma rays emitted from the sun have disrupted electronics and communications on earth. The EMP produced gamma rays in a much shorter burst. At levels much higher than the indiscriminate gamma radiation produced by solar flares, the device was capable of crashing the grid and plunging a city into darkness in less than a minute, and paralyzing all modern transportation. If used in the intended way, the bomb could be pointed in the direction of a target city, sparing civilization outside of the target area.

In his briefing with Adam Pryor weeks prior to the incident, Darkhorse was given the details of his mission. "You know why we own those high-rises?" Pryor now inquired.

"No sir, I don't care. After this is over, I'll disappear like I always do, and you can do whatever you do, and we can all part ways. I just do my job. You pay me. It's as simple as that."

Darkhorse had spent a lifetime guarding his identity from everyone. He had never maintained a lasting relationship, not even a casual friendship. He liked it that way. *If they don't know you, they can't get to you*, he thought, and that more than anything guaranteed his continued existence.

He didn't trust Pryor to leave him alone and alive after it was over, and he had carefully devised his exit strategy. He would be gone before the bombs were detonated, and he would be in a place where nobody would look, even if they knew he was involved. His only contact was Pryor himself, and this power whore would never give him up.

Pryor was proud of his plan, and despite his assassin's aloof response, he outlined the details. "I am going to run Masterson out of office and regain control. I don't want to kill a lot of people to do it, but there will be collateral damage. Survival of the fittest. You understand that, don't you?" He turned his back to pour himself a drink but continued to watch Darkhorse in the mirror above the bar. Pryor continued to speak as he watched his hired gun shift uneasily and scan the room for available exits. There was something about this conversation that was becoming very creepy, and he wasn't about to remain any longer than necessary.

"You do understand," Pryor continued. "I know you do. The people who maintain my lifestyle are counting on you to understand. I managed to get my hands on eleven weapons that this country has never seen before. Homeland Security intercepted them a few years ago in a container load down at the docks of the international seaport at Port Everglades. They were shipped from the Ukraine by way of Germany. Terrorists bought them up when the Soviet Union collapsed. I hear they paid for them with crappy cars and kitchen appliances." He laughed as Darkhorse stared.

"It turns out that the Soviets had improvised an EMP bomb that doesn't nuke a city like conventional nukes. They modified them to take out all of the electronics and shut down the grid. They have some kind of cone inside that lets us direct gamma radiation in any way we want, and I'm about to take out all of the electronics and shut down the power anywhere inside the blast area. Hell, if I could find out how to get one of these babies up six miles, I could take out the whole country. But I don't want to do that."

Darkhorse stood up to leave.

"No, don't go. I haven't got to the good part yet." Pryor moved toward Darkhorse, intending to grab his arm. When he saw the menacing look that his advance had provoked, he backed off and continued talking. "Do you know what will happen when these things go off? I'm not talking big mushroom clouds and destruction here. I am just going to take all of society away for awhile."

Darkhorse became curious long enough to delay his departure. "What do you mean by that?"

Pryor giggled with glee, and Darkhorse realized that this megalomaniac's sole purpose in life was mayhem of unprecedented proportions. He hadn't signed on to become one of the world's most reviled mass exterminators, but it was too late to back away from the plan.

"I am going to shut down the grid. I am going to fry all of their electronics. Everything they take for granted will cease to exist. No cell phones. No satellites in geostationary orbit to transmit signals of any kind. No TV. No heat. No refrigeration except Mother Nature. No transportation. You won't be able to take a cab or ride the subway. A city of twenty-five million people all hoofing it around, looking for a bicycle or a horse. After they eat up all of the food, they will be looking for their next meal. They don't store more than a few days of food in Manhattan, and the hoarders and panicky city-dwellers will panic *en masse*." *Pryor took a long sip of scotch, cleared his throat, and glared at his newly attentive audience.*

"All of them. There will be chaos."

Darkhorse was silent, running the resulting chain reaction of events through his head. *New York would die in the darkness, and the mass exodus would begin.*

"To test my little project, I have a little surprise in store for our new president," Pryor concluded.

"Can I go now?" Darkhorse was raring to get out of the room.

"Yes. I'm sending you to Washington to deliver a package for me, and I don't want you to be late," he replied.

"Listen, Pryor, as long as you pay me in full and on time, I don't care about your mystery and your grand plans. Personally, I don't understand why you don't just take him out." Darkhorse brought his grimacing face within inches of Pryor. The intrusion into his space was enough to cause the madman to take two steps backward before responding.

"That didn't work very well for you during the campaign, and now you expect to assassinate the most protected person in the world. Were you planning on using a slingshot this time? Maybe you'll hide up on some grassy knoll and shoot at him this time? Pryor was becoming more abusive as he drank, but he was far from losing control. Now that he's in office, surely you realize that I don't want to make a martyr out of Max Masterson…" He spat the name in disgust. "He is the symbol of the future that those idiots, the voters, attached their dreams to. If I eliminate Masterson, his legacy will live on. Can't have that…not that…"

Darkhorse wanted to respond, but chose to bite his tongue and wait out the tirade as he had done in the past. It was a survival technique.

"Just watch what happens when I detonate this package on Inauguration Day, and our new president gets whisked away for his own protection. Just see the American people turn on him. You'll see. You'll…see." He drew out the words for emphasis.

Pryor's blood pressure was rising, his face flushed and perspiration formed on his forehead and cheeks. He had no intention of revealing all of the details of the plan to anyone, especially the one person who could implicate him in years of mayhem directed at his enemies. He would have his revenge, and it would be in a humiliation more public than a mere assassination. He sought to extinguish the hope for the future that Max had created, and in doing so, he would preserve the status quo.

◆

CHAPTER 29

M y boy," began Luke Postlewaite, Max's long-time mentor, "I used to be a hippie back in the '60's, and I had long hair for awhile until I tried to find a job. Then I realized that all of those firebrand radicals were mostly unemployed, and I had to cut it. Now, I don't have anything to prove to anybody, so I try to grow it long. All I can grow now is a silver ponytail that looks like it came off roadkill."

Luke had come to Fairlane to congratulate Max on his spectacular win, but he had a more important purpose for his visit. The Masterson estate had been built to the exacting specifications of Max's father, and there was a long-hidden secret in the basement that Max would find extremely valuable in his new job. But for now, Luke chose to warm his stockinged feet on the hearth of the massive stone fireplace and tell stories while sipping his favorite brandy. The senator had wisely stocked the wine cellar with kegs of Napoleon brandy, thinking wisely that supplying his old friend with his favorite vice would bring him to visit more often. It was more than Postlewaite could consume in a lifetime.

Postlewaite was rapidly becoming inebriated. His tolerance for alcohol had declined with age, and what used to happen only after three snifters could now be accomplished with one. He swirled the amber liquid and downed the last of it, then he brought his story to a close. "Max, back in those days, we didn't drink much. Smoked a lot of pot back in those days. The trouble with that was that it made me horny." He smiled at the memories that came back to him after more than half a century, dredged from a place in his mind that was timeless. He was twenty again, if only for a moment, reminiscing about the freedom of youth in the late 1960's. "Come to think of it, everything made me horny."

They both laughed heartily.

"I went through that rebel stage," Luke continued, "fighting with Nixon supporters, and believing that love could conquer all. But while my friends were getting messed over in Viet Nam, I was student-deferred, and that's when I met your Dad. We were friends from then until the day he died. He had greatness in him from the start."

Max sat patiently, waiting for Postlewaite to finish supplying him with the wisdom that had been dispensed to him thousands of times over the course of his instruction from the age of sixteen. It didn't matter that Max was now the President-Elect of the United States or that the world now clamored for his time incessantly. There was always time for Luke's wisdom.

"But enough of that. I'm here for an important piece of unfinished business," he concluded, shoving his memories back where they had been stored. "Your father, God rest his soul, made me swear that I would never tell you about this until you became president, and it has been my temptation to reveal it to you every time I came to visit. It just wasn't the time for it."

Max's intrigue was sharpening with every word. Still, he waited. He knew from experience that he would bear the wrath of Luke Postlewaite for interrupting before the old man finished his thoughts, and he still had the mental scars of past tongue-lashings.

Abruptly, Luke lifted his feet from the hearth and plopped them into his shoes in one motion. Without bothering to tie the laces, he turned to Max and exclaimed, "Come on!" His enthusiasm was contagious, and Max jumped to his feet as Postlewaite shuffled toward the door.

CHAPTER 30

The entry to the basement of the Masterson estate was inconspicuously placed in the center of the house, adjacent to Senator John Masterson's ornate den, where he spent most of the last days of his life. To occasional visitors, the door looked like it might be a broom closet, and Max had rarely been allowed to enter as a child. He hadn't opened the door for years. An old key was needed to enter, and Max had never been told where it was hidden.

Postlewaite reached behind a landscape of Monticello that had been commissioned by Thomas Jefferson in his early White House days, and he removed the key that hung from a nail on the back of the frame. The painting had previously hung in the White House adjacent to Jefferson's bedroom, but it mysteriously disappeared after Clinton left office. Historians assumed that Bill Clinton had removed it along with the other items when his administration vacated the presidential residence, but this time their suspicions were unfounded.

Still, the explanation of how the painting had come to Fairlane had never been made, and Max had lacked the interest or desire to research its origins. He just assumed it had always been there, along with the other artifacts that his home contained since his childhood.

Postlewaite turned the key and descended quickly down the oak stairs. Max was close behind, pausing only to flip the light switch, which bathed the stone walls of the basement with a yellow glow.

"This place was built on the foundation of a plantation house," Postlewaite explained. "They used to hide runaway slaves down here before the Civil War, but Union troops burned it to the ground as they retreated to Washington after the Battle of Bull Run. Your dad bought the land after it laid vacant for a hundred and twenty years, and he rebuilt the house on the same foundation. The stones must have come from brooks that flowed out of the mountains, and they mortared these walls sometime in the early 1700's."

Max looked at the old walls with a new fascination.

"Here's what I brought you down here to see…" Luke raised his hand to the stone wall and pushed. Balanced on a central fulcrum, it spun open with minimal effort, a credit to the craftsmanship of Freemasons who had constructed it in secret, centuries before he was born. There was a room, more like a primitive apartment, with bunks that lined the walls on three sides. It was uncomfortable quarters for slaves waiting to escape by train to the Northeast states, but it had served its purpose at the time. Senator Masterson had left it in the same condition he had found it, and other than an occasional cleaning, the room was intact.

On the far side was a large, brass embossed door that was adorned with reliefs of African-Americans working in the fields, with a large house in the background. The green tarnish concealed the details, but Max could make out figures in the foreground that appeared to be running. It was a visual picture of their lives, pounded into the metal by the people who had been given refuge there.

Postlewaite strode to the door and used the same key to unlock the latch. Max pulled on an enormous metal ring, and it opened with a loud creak. When it had opened fully, the lights came on automatically, and Max could see that it extended in the distance for hundreds of yards before it curved to the right. "Max, this is your private entrance to the White House," proclaimed Luke.

"How? Why? My father never told me…" Max was astounded by the sight, and excited by the possibilities that could come from it. "All my life, from the time I was a little boy until now, there was a massive secret beneath my feet…" He choked up, unable to express his feelings or to fully comprehend what this discovery could mean.

He did know that he was free of the geographical constraints of the presidency, and this was his escape. He could come home whenever he wanted, and nobody would know. If this was an underground passage from his home to the White House, he was free to sleep in his own bed, in familiar surroundings, and he had a buffer between his identity as president and the private person that treasured time alone.

"Back long before the civil war," Luke explained, "when Thomas Jefferson took office in 1800, he commissioned the tunnel to shelter members of Congress, the president and his family, and occupants of the White House in the event of an attack from the British. He was worried that the Brits would retaliate for our support of the French in their long-standing war in Europe. He was right, but Britain didn't retaliate until after he left office. They were rightfully pissed for our burning of York, which the Canadians renamed Toronto."

Max was preoccupied with the sight of an electric vehicle, not much larger than a golf cart, and two well-preserved mountain bikes that were parked at a rack near the tunnel entrance. They were all covered with a patina of dust, but they all appeared to be in operable condition. The vehicle was hooked up to a charger, which he assumed was connected elsewhere to a power source of some kind.

"Is this how we get around? Where does it go from here," he inquired.

"Until right after the British burned the White House in the War of 1812, the Masons continued construction of a tunnel as an escape from the Capitol. From the time of the burning in 1814 until its completion in 1834, a crew of stone masons worked on Washington's buildings by day, and at night they dug deep below ground with hand tools, lining the passageway with limestone diverted from the surface. When they began the stage that passed below the Potomac River, they added an aqueduct that diverted water from the river to the tidal basin. It all looked like part of a big reconstruction project for the Capitol, and the tunnel's existence was kept secret from all but a select few."

Max sat in the electric vehicle and realized that it was a golf cart, customized to resemble a convertible presidential limousine from the early 1960s, but on a smaller scale. He turned the key and noticed that the mechanical gauge indicated that it was fully charged. He noticed an electrical cord that ran from a wall socket and a plug that attached to the vehicle, and he disconnected it. He wondered whether his father had sneaked down to do the maintenance work himself or if he trusted someone else with his closely-guarded secret. Luke joined him in the passenger seat and continued his lecture. He wasn't to the point of slurring his words yet, but they had taken on a more rounded tone.

"Andrew Jackson was an insomniac, and stumbled upon the secret entrance in the basement of the White House late one night while investigating noises. He thought he was hearing ghosts, but it was really just the sound of small charges the tunnel builders had placed to progress through granite that was blocking their forward progress. Realizing the importance of the tunnel, he pushed for completion at an accelerated rate. He traveled by horse through the tunnel and dined here without anyone knowing the wiser. He had more than a few meals in the old house's kitchen in those days, I have heard. He was rumored to have been so pleased by this secret escape that he would travel without an escort, something that presidents throughout history have only dreamed about doing." Luke puffed with exertion.

His age and sedentary lifestyle had made even the most minimal activity an effort.

Max took the pause to speak. He knew that his elderly muse detested interruptions, and after more than a few episodes of being chastised for speaking when he should have been listening, he learned to time his words. "The White House is across the Potomac, ten miles away. Do you mean to tell me that this tunnel is ten miles long, and goes beneath the river?" He was incredulous at the size of the project that had taken the Capitol's stone masons twenty years to complete. He wanted to hop on a bike and pedal as far as he could see in the distance where the tunnel curved ahead, but out of respect for Luke, he waited in the electric vehicle.

Luke caught his breath, and with a gleam in his eye, he continued. "Your dad and I used to get liquored up late at night, back in the days when he was a senator." His breathing was labored, and his sentences became abbreviated, allowing Max to get a word in edgewise during the longer pauses. Luke laughed at the memory. "One night, we were feeling our oats, right after Clinton left office, in that gap between the election and before he moved out of the White House—"

"You mean, like I'm waiting in right now? How long does it take Blythe's people to move out? I heard that he's still in rehab, and that nobody has laid eyes on him since the election."

"Nevermind old Blythe. You kicked his ass pretty good, and he won't be showing his face in public anytime soon. He managed to get his slush money hidden in a few banks in the Caymans, and…"

Luke paused to inhale, but Max knew from the look on his grizzled face that he would not be allowed to change the subject of the conversation—more of a lecture—until the old man had finished his story.

"So," Luke continued, "we got in the car and drove under the river to the White House in the middle of the night. The Clintons were off in New York for some damn fool reason, and the White House had a lot of security to keep people from coming in everywhere except from our little Hidey Hole in the basement. There was nobody around, so we snuck in…"

Max shook his head and smiled. He remembered his father's legendary reputation for adventure, irreverence, and his impish affection for practical jokes. He could imagine it all; the drunken underground drive to the White House, the laughing and whispering, and the nighttime burglary. He admired their brash disregard for the consequences of breaking into the most secure residence in the world.

"When we got there, we had to use this key to unlock the door. It opens into a closet near the kitchen…" Luke gasped for air and continued. "John, your dad, tripped over the hose of some floor-cleaning machine, and he fell face first on the floor of the kitchen. We spent about ten minutes laughing hysterically, and going, shhh… shhhhh….The thing is, we had both been to the White House for dinner and had taken the tour, and we knew the layout of the place.

When we got up to the first floor, a lot of the furniture and paintings were packed up to be moved. I guess the Clintons were in the middle of taking their share of the antiques before they left town. Your Dad saw a painting of Monticello he loved. Jefferson had it commissioned while he was president, and it used to hang in the hallway outside of his bedroom. It looked like it was headed out the door, so we snatched it on our way out."

"You're kidding me."

"No. We took it."

"The one that hangs in my hallway? You stole it from the White House?"

"No, we took it back…It's all perspective, Mr. President." Luke chuckled.

"Well, let's go."

"Really? You want to sneak into the White House? In the middle of the night? Cool," said Luke, his gray ponytail poking out of his collar. He was way beyond caring about his public persona, and the thought of reliving an excitement of his younger days had him raring to go.

Max put his foot on the accelerator and pushed lightly. The vehicle moved forward silently. The speed startled him, and he backed off the accelerator. It stopped so abruptly that they nearly tumbled over the hood. With no windshield and no seat belts, the possibility of tumbling out was a good one.

"Get this thing going, my boy, we have an unannounced White House visit to make!"

This time, he eased into the driving, and soon they were traveling southeast at the peak speed of 25 miles an hour. In the confines of the tunnel, it seemed like they were flying.

CHAPTER 31

The quiet electric motor allowed for talking, but the wonder of the moment kept both passengers silent as they made their way toward the White House. The tunnel curved at times, and Max could only see ahead for a few hundred yards. At regular intervals they encountered large spider webs in the darkness that spanned the width of the passage, and after having to wipe the sticky silk off of their faces a few times, they learned to duck.

The nearly 30 minute trip landed them at another metal door, and Luke jumped out with key in hand. "Come on," he whispered, excited at the idea that they were reprising one of his life's biggest adventures. It was not lost on him that this time, he was helping the president-elect break into his own house. The irony of it all was that Max would have been arrested the moment his presence was detected, *and now what could they do, charge the president with trespassing?* He smiled at the thought.

They encountered a large floor-polishing machine in the closet that effectively blocked their way. They pulled the polisher into the tunnel and stepped inside the closet. The door to the tunnel closed automatically, and they stood in the darkness. Luke slowly turned the doorknob and whispered, "Don't want to scare the shit out of the kitchen help." He chuckled.

Opening the door, he signaled that they were alone and stepped into the kitchen. Max followed, fascinated that two intruders, never mind that one of them had legitimate reasons for being there, had been able to sneak into the most guarded house on the planet.

"Where are we going?"

"You'll see."

"No, really, Luke, I want to know."

"The Oval Office. The rest of this place is pretty boring."

Max pushed Luke gingerly aside and looked him straight in the eyes.

"Listen to me, old muse. I'm not going to have you get shot by whoever is walking the night shift. I'll lead." Max quietly padded up the stairs to the main floor. They opened the door from the kitchen, triggering a silent alarm. Nobody went anywhere inside the White House at night without the Secret Service knowing, and according to the motion detectors that monitored their movements, they were unauthorized to be there. There were no residents or guests during the weeks before the incoming president took office.

"Raise your hands above your heads and turn around."

Max and Luke did as they were told. They faced three black-suited Secret Service agents, all holding guns directed at their hearts, the laser red of their sights were an indication of their imminent deaths if the triggers were pulled.

"Max?"

"Mr. President?"

"Stand down!" The guns were lowered in unison, and they stood in disbelief at the next President of the United States and an old guy who looked harmless, although he did look a bit looped.

"I'm glad you recognized me before you shot me. A lot of people would be very disappointed if I left office before I actually took office," Max said, pre-empting anything they could conjure up that resembled a question.

"I came in unannounced to test security, and you are to be commended for your excellent training and dedication. I would like you to meet my presidential advisor, Luke Postlewaite. He and I are to have unlimited access to this building, and no, I will not inform you of how we entered ."

Still in shock and wondering how they pierced perimeter security without a peep from anyone, the agent in charge announced, "Computer! Recognize President Max Masterson and presidential advisor Luke Postlewaite. Scan for future recognition, and clear them for free access."

A voice came from nowhere they could discern. "Acknowledged. Welcome, Mister President."

"Now, please direct us to the Oval Office and give us some time alone." Max was enjoying his unlimited status, and he punched Luke in the arm when he began giggling. *They were pulling this off.*

Once in the Oval Office, Luke began his search for the liquor cabinet, and Max took his seat, for the first time, in the comfortable chair behind the Kennedy desk. He stared out at his surroundings, and spun around to revel in the view. He had arrived.

CHAPTER 32

Max opened the center drawer of the desk. It was deep and bare, save for one item: a large, gilded, leather book. It bore the Seal of the President of the United State of America, but there were no words on the cover. He knew what it was, and his heart rate rose. *The Diary of the Presidents.*

Many people had speculated about its existence, but few had seen the legendary book with their own eyes. Fewer still knew what it contained. But Max knew, and of all the books that had ever been written, he longed to study this one the most. The book contained the road map of his predecessors, the presidents who came before him, and their intimate thoughts, unvarnished by political rhetoric. He wanted to know their mistakes and fears, their thoughts about how the office should be, but most of all, he wanted to understand the mistakes they had made and their suggestions to their successors about how to avoid similar mistakes in the future.

Max held the gold-trimmed journal in his hands, marveling at the heft of the leather-bound book, perfectly preserved after nearly 300 years. He turned the pages with care. The early ones were parchment and brittle to the touch, and he tenderly gave this irreplaceable piece of history the reverence it deserved. Here was the handwritten wisdom of the ages, an instruction manual to guide incoming presidents away from the mistakes of the past.

More words were written by Jefferson and Lincoln than all of the others combined, owing to their genius and their prolific writings throughout their lives. Others were much more concise, some just a few paragraphs. All of the entries were heart-felt and non-political, intended to rise above the tawdry world of politics. He read further, smiling at one particular entry halfway through the book.

"I didn't think I was better than anyone else. I just knew I had a higher destiny than selling men's clothing," wrote Harry Truman.

He thumbed through the pages, from back to front as left-handers are known to do, pausing randomly to read the words.

Abraham Lincoln: *"America will never be destroyed from the outside. If we falter and lose our freedoms, it will be because we destroyed ourselves."*

Calvin Coolidge: *"Nothing in this world can take the place of persistence. Talent will not; nothing is more common than unsuccessful people with talent. Genius will not; unrewarded genius is almost a proverb. Education will not; the world is full of educated derelicts. Persistence and determination alone are omnipotent. The slogan "press on" has solved and always will solve the problems of the human race."*

Theodore Roosevelt: *"It is not the critic who counts: not the man who points out how the strong man stumbles or where the doer of deeds could have done better. The credit belongs to the man who is actually in the arena, whose face is marred by dust and sweat and blood, who strives valiantly, who errs and comes up short again and again, because there is no effort without error or shortcoming, but who knows the great enthusiasms, the great devotions, who spends himself for a worthy cause; who, at the best, knows, in the end, the triumph of high achievement, and who, at the worst, if he fails, at least he fails while daring greatly, so that his place shall never be with those cold and timid souls who knew neither victory nor defeat."*

Max recognized the words. They came from a speech Roosevelt made in Paris in 1910.

Thomas Jefferson: *"The same prudence which in private life would forbid our paying our own money for unexplained projects, forbids it in the dispensation of the public moneys."*

It appeared that Jefferson, a hero to Max for his genius and ideas that had shaped the early days of the United States, and Lincoln, who had endured the impending breakup of his country, were by far the most prolific of the contributors to the diary, and he looked forward to being able to sit quietly and absorb their wisdom. He was certain that he would benefit from a cover-to-cover reading. To think he was holding in his hands the collected wisdom of the presidents, written in their own hand, was beyond inspiring.

"Luke, I had heard rumors about this. This is what you brought me here to see."

"I thought I would never see the day," Luke answered.

He was sitting in a comfortable chair, cradling a snifter of brandy that he had pilfered from the liquor cabinet. He had been watching Max's total absorption into reading the diary, and he was beaming with pride. This man, who he had treated like a son after the death of his friend, John Masterson, was the President of the United States of America, and he was sitting, for the first time, at the desk where he belonged.

"You know," Luke continued, "I have sat in this room on several occasions, and years ago, I had the experience of spending the night in this haunted place. Saw a ghost, too…at least I think it was a ghost…" Luke paused, waiting for Max to absorb the meaning of his words. "But right now, I think I'll try to find the president's bathroom," he said, standing on unsteady feet.

Max didn't respond, absorbed in the pages of the journal he held in his hands.

"Max, we need to have an exact copy made, and convert it to digital, too. I want you to be able to access it any time you need guidance, except… I don't know if I want you to dwell on the collected wisdom of guys like Grover Cleveland or William Henry Harrison." Luke cackled in his own amusement, and Max realized that their adventure was coming to an end. Luke was crocked.

"Come on, let's get you home. This time, let's take the presidential limo."

During the hastily-assembled motorcade ride back to Fairlane, Max realized that Rachel didn't know he was gone. He had left her sleeping soundly in their bed before Luke had arrived for his typical late evening visit. It was after 2:00 AM when they returned. After he was certain that Luke had made his way to a guest bedroom at the far side of the house, Max crept quietly into the bedroom.

"Where have you been?" exclaimed Rachel, eyes wide open and sitting erect in the expansive bed, her shapely legs bare. It was obvious that she had been waiting for him to come back for hours, and judging from the half-empty champagne bottle in a bucket of melted ice and her state of relative undress, she had made plans for romance. He had unknowingly stood her up, and she was not pleased.

"Don't get in a swivet, my sweet. I just rode over to the White House with Luke, and we took an unannounced tour," he said in a level tone.

"Then come to bed, My Darling President," she said with a smile.

CHAPTER 33

The next morning, Max took a run on the trails along the Potomac. The river was waking to the sun as the mist of morning swirled above the water in wispy clouds. It was his time to think and to work out the cobwebs in his mind caused by the previous night's drinking with Luke. If he had been sipping brandy instead of beer, he would still be lying in bed feeling very creaky at this time of day. Max knew that he would be exercised, showered, changed, and done with breakfast before Luke would show his face in the kitchen, looking like he had slept in a tent next to the highway.

What normally would have been a solitary ten-mile, out-and-back loop through the woods was now a group activity, the cost of being protected. Four Secret service agents had been assigned to accompany him, and they were in better shape than Max from years of training on a daily basis. They had to be, to maintain a steady seven minute mile pace while carrying water bottles, Power Bars, sidearms, and communicators. They could call in support at any point, and it would arrive in seconds. A Blackhawk helicopter maintained a constant visual on Max from above, its stealth rotors barely audible above the sounds of morning.

Max insisted on taking the lead so that he could come upon the familiar sights of wildlife that he loved to encounter along the trail. The animals were used to his occasional runs, but the sight of his heavily armed security team would have startled them into hiding, and he would have been deprived of this simple pleasure.

At mile five, the trail wound around a granite knob and began a meandering course back to Fairlane. Max gestured for a break, and asked for water and a Power Bar. The mylar wrapper proved to be impossible to open, a fault of modern packaging that seals and vacuum packs food from the outside world. He struggled to open it for more than a minute, embarrassed by his inability to perform this simple task.

"I'll get it," said one of his companions. Before Max could react, the Power Bar was snatched from his hands, tossed in the air, and shot. It fluttered into the hands of another agent, the top of the mylar sheath neatly sheared from its berry-flavored contents.

"You guys are good," said Max, trying to contain his shocked amusement. "I suppose next you'll try swatting mosquitoes with a hand grenade."

They all laughed at the mental picture, and Max scanned each of his four fellow runners. They hadn't broken a sweat.

I could still do that, if I had more time to workout, thought Max, wiping the sweat from his forehead with his sleeve. *Maybe I'll make them run twice as far next time.*

CHAPTER 34

When Max had returned from his most interesting run in memory, he showered and changed into casual clothes. He entered the kitchen, ravenously anticipating a hearty breakfast. Rachel sat at the table, still in her bathing suit, fresh from a morning swim. She sipped green tea from a large, flowered mug that she had claimed as hers.

"You missed a good swim," she exclaimed, smiling.

She looked stunning, her tanned skin complementing her yellow bikini. She felt comfortable there, not choosing to cover up her trim figure from admiring eyes, especially Max's unapologetic gaze. She stood to give him a kiss, and returned to the news report she was viewing from Glenda Reasoner, who had made her career by tracking Max's every move. The report of the day dealt with his early years after the senator's death, and the seemingly endless stream of women that accompanied him at social events. A different woman for each event, it seemed, and Glenda took particular delight at pointing that out at every opportunity.

Max ignored the report of his escapades, deep in thought about the previous night. He had failed to inform Rachel of his newfound ability to go to work underground. He kept that secret to himself. He felt guilty about his nondisclosure. *She will learn in good time. I know she'll be delighted. I need to remind myself that she will need to be cleared with security. She wouldn't be able to enter unannounced without the Secret Service knowing that she holds the special status as the president's girlfriend. They are funny about those sorts of things. In the meantime, Fairlane is my base of operations. I prefer it that way.*

◆ ◆ ◆

Rachel had moved from Glenda Reasoner's report, but the subject was fresh in her mind. *Why does he keep me? Where does his devotion start and end? I see how women react to him. They all want him, and he could have his pick any time he wanted.* She stared at a photo of Max that accompanied a feature article posted by all of the major news agencies, which had become gossip and rumor agencies, too. She was learning to filter out speculation from fact. To do otherwise would have plunged her into self-doubt and insecurity, and she knew that the press created most of the reports about Max's love life from thin air. Slow news days were the worst.

She ran thoughts through her head in the early morning as she had done all of her life. She greeted each day with optimism and joy, a quality they shared. But while Max rose at 5:00 AM each day, exercised before breakfast, and followed these with coffee and planning, she relished her sleep. He was usually long gone by the time she got up. There was never time to procrastinate, and less time to doubt or worry.

She recalled what he had told her about the reports of his dalliances with other women, and it gave her comfort. They had been at a beach late in the day, watching the dolphins play as the sun set in a spectacular display of purple and orange. The water was smooth as glass and took on a green sheen that made it look like it was suspended in time. She couldn't imagine a more romantic moment. He had held her hands in front of him and looked into her eyes with a gaze so intense that she felt that he had gained access to her soul. Her excitement rose, her heartbeat made her breasts heave with anticipation. He had stared for the longest time, but she didn't dare interrupt the moment for fear of breaking the spell. In his low, calm voice, he had explained his state of mind clearly and concisely.

"When you truly love someone, there is no room in your heart for anyone else."

She loved him desperately. He was the ruggedly handsome object of feminine desire, who epitomized success in every way. Max had been at the top of everything he had attempted, and that aspect of her man was incredibly sexy and intimidating at the same time. She was not so naive to think that she was more special than any other woman who sought his love, but still, she realized that he had neither the time nor the inclination to do any of the things that the press had tried to pass off as fact. If she believed a fraction of the gossip and innuendo, she was doomed to a life of self-doubt, and she wasn't made that way.

Max didn't pay any attention to the press, seemingly insulated from the constant focus. He was driven to accomplish much and worry little, and she could see the genuine affection he had for her. He was open in his displays of affection for her, and that gave her a bubble of confidence that no other woman could pierce. She took consolation in the stories that were impossible to be true; when they reported that he was out with the starlet of the week, he was with her. All of it was created by publicists who had been hired to boost the career of beautiful women by linking them to Max. It worked, too, but Rachel had to consider the source. It was all fluff.

Through with reflection, she retreated to the bedroom to shower as Max made his typical breakfast of fruit and poached eggs on toast. She dried her hair and quickly pulled on her flight uniform, not bothering to apply makeup. She was in a hurry. It was Wednesday, time for her to head over to Andrews Air Force Base for another lesson in flying Air Force One.

CHAPTER 35

R*edundancy,* he thought. *If the president won't let me do my job in the way I have been trained, I will find a way to do it his way. He's going to make me gray in no time if I keep reacting instead of strategizing.*

The challenge for Justin Armstrong was in thinking like Max, anticipating his every move. The Secret Service head had had free reign since the fall of the previous administration, and he was amazed at the sudden gap in security when they departed. Protecting the president had become his sole purpose in life, but he had forsaken everything to rise to the top.

He had never been much of a husband to his first wife or his second, and his daughter from his first marriage had to beg for him to take time off from his obsession to be a part of her life. At sixteen, Jessica spent more time with her boyfriend than either of her parents, but once these years had passed, he could never get them back. All he had from her first years of life were pictures of birthday parties he had missed, the empty chair at the table with a cardboard sign labeled in a child's hand in magic marker: DADDY.

Armstrong rationalized that his wife and daughter had accepted his role as a highly-decorated Navy SEAL, and later, as an upwardly mobile member of the Secret Service. His constant absence from the family for months at a time had taken its toll in loneliness and longing, and he couldn't blame his wife for taking up with a horny insurance agent while he was off doing black ops in the mountains of Pakistan. He couldn't share his triumphs with family; SEALs took a solemn, life-long oath to remain loyal to all of their members, and family fell outside of that circle. There would never be a tell-all book from a SEAL, or a reality show. He was, and would always be, a SEAL first and a spouse and parent second. It had to be that way.

Armstrong could have been the nation's darling hero if he had disclosed that he was a part of the team that had killed Osama Bin Laden. But that would have ended his career as a SEAL, and that thought, to him, was unthinkable. After all, what would he do in the civilian world? He was SEAL trained and duty-bound. He was where he wanted to be, despite the regret. There would be days tied to a desk. The mere thought of doing busywork made him nauseous, but it had to be done.

He busied himself with the duties of the job, creating codenames for the president and those in his inner circle for use by his Secret Service detail. It was tradition, and he took delight in the choosing. He wanted the words to have a connection to their personality. He knew with silent pride that his choices would become a part of history. The codename he chose for Max was Wizard, for his habit of disappearing and evading security.

Before becoming the most guarded person in the country, Max had mastered the cheap thrill of keeping the press guessing, emerging from places they never suspected. When it came time to leave, which seemed to happen less than a minute after the press had found him, he would disappear without warning. While other candidates would spend hours quoting statistics and droning on and on about the issue of the day, Max had made his comments short and to the point, and then he was gone. Rachel's codename was Flygirl, and aviation was so much a part of her that no other words would suffice. He knew that his subordinates would refer to her by other names in private, as men do, but if he heard any of them using those words in his presence, it would be misconduct that would get them reassigned. They knew it, and in their daily briefings, he reinforced his rule.

When it came to Vice President Conroy, Armstrong became more judicious in his choice of words. Previous codenames had little connection to the person, and in his research of the history on the subject, he was disappointed that his predecessors were so lacking in imagination. Obama was Renegade. Clinton was Eagle. Poor Gerald Ford was Passkey. Scarlett Conroy's code name would be Hairbrush, he decided, for her penchant for combing her hair before every speech. *History will support my decisions*, he reflected.

CHAPTER 36

T here are two ways to take back our country. One is by over-whelming force, and that would involve a coup. We would need to convince the American people that Masterson is intent on ruining our country, and we would need to take control of the combined force of our military." Adam Pryor sat passively on the deck of his mansion in the Hamptons, casually discussing the overthrow of the United States government and the demise of his nemesis, Max Masterson.

The longtime Director of Homeland Security had officially retired on election day, announcing to the public that he was returning home to take a position with a think tank named the National Security Foundation. In his reality, Pryor was leaving before he was forcibly removed. For more than thirty years, he controlled the security of the United States, or perpetuated the illusion that the country was secure from terrorism. He used this position to ensure his personal wealth and the wealth of those who placed him in that position of power and control.

Pryor owed no allegiance to his country, and he had no stake in the prosperity of the nation. He recited this chant on a daily basis, and perverted the meaning to suit his selfish agenda: "To thine own self be true." To his way of thinking, that meant he would sacrifice the lives of other Americans to accomplish his personal goals, and over the years, his mania made the needless sacrifice of lives a goal rather than a consequence.

Adam Pryor was warped by hate. In his mind, discrediting the new administration by launching a massive terrorist attack on the United States would vindicate him. During his time as the head of the Department of Homeland Security, Pryor had no supervision and no peer. He was free to do whatever he chose, while creating a branch of government that failed to exist before September 11, 2001. The first large-scale terrorist attack within the borders of the United States spawned Homeland Security, and for the following decade, Pryor had a free ride.

Along with the ephemeral duty of protecting America from the unknown came a great deal of power. Pryor used that power to control and eliminate his political enemies, and he was ruthless in creating the path to their devastation. The word in Congress was that if you messed with Homeland Security, your days in politics were numbered, and ignoring that adage had ended the promising career of a large number of politicians.

They had suddenly found themselves defending scandals that sprung up following their efforts to question the functions and funding of Pryor's department. It didn't matter that the allegations would prove to be false after the firestorm of titillating controversy died down. By that time, public interest was turned elsewhere, and the powerless politician was left floating in a sea of mistrust and hostility.

He had been publicly humiliated by Max's father, John Masterson, during Senate hearings long before Max was born, and that hate had never subsided. It was merely transferred from father to son. Max Masterson and his presidency had inherited an anger that could only be quenched by the humiliation of Max and everything he stood for, in the most public way possible.

His audience was composed of two members: a man known as "Darkhorse" and another known only as "Bob." This meeting was their first in person. All previous communications were made by secure wireless contacts at remote locations. Nobody would suspect that the Director of Homeland Security would be involved in a plot to destroy the presidency and install a dictatorship in its place, he was confident of that. Pryor had instituted the same policies that he was in the process of circumventing. If anyone was capable of using security to cause mayhem, Pryor was an expert.

"I need you to move fast. At precisely noon eastern standard time on Inauguration Day, January 18, we will detonate the first and smallest of those devices in Washington. It is designed to disrupt anything with electronics. All vehicles with electronics and all communication devices, we will make useless. We are going to spoil a celebration of patriotism." He smiled in a wicked leer.

"At a time I choose, the larger plan will begin. We will place EMP bombs in high-rise penthouse condos that we own in six major metropolitan areas. They are to be on the top floor of the tallest buildings we could find. They are designed to knock out all geostationary communication satellites and power stations in each city with one blast," declared Pryor.

"You are going to kill a lot of people," responded Darkhorse. "How will it feel for you to be hated worse than Hitler?"

Pryor ignored him. "I don't intend for you, or I, or anyone who is involved in this mission to be revealed to the public. We are going to shift the blame to Masterson and gain the support of the U.S. military in ensuring the continued existence of our way of life. You, Darkhorse, will be my minister of mayhem, and I expect you to maximize that mayhem at every opportunity." Pryor's voice took a sinister tone, and privately, the two mercenaries harbored doubts as to his mental stability. "These bombs are not designed to kill people. The electromagnetic pulse emitted from these explosions will be focused on eliminating satellite communications, the grid, and all electronics within the blast area. We will knock out all electronics in large metropolitan areas and bring down the power grid that supplies all of the comforts of society. They won't be able to talk on the phone, watch TV, cook their food, or even keep warm."

"But why?" said Bob.

"Survival of the fittest, that's why." Pryor was beginning to show outrage at the insolence, his face reddening with anger. He would not tolerate the questioning of his commands from a subordinate, and he considered everyone a subordinate.

"You are being paid an outrageous amount of money to carry out my commands without question," he rose from his Adirondack chair and pointed his index finger inches from Bob's face. The swift motion was unexpected, and Bob backed off.

"The city dwellers are weak. They are like sheep being led to slaughter. I don't need to kill them. When I turn off technology and they lose the comforts to which they have become so dependent, they will die from the struggle or kill themselves to end their discomfort. America will become a nation where only the strong will persevere, and we will become stronger than any time in our history as a nation," Pryor proclaimed in his most self-righteous voice.

"The American people are like sheep. As long as they have full bellies and a shelter over their heads, I can make these wage slaves do anything I want. You think Lincoln freed the slaves? I'll tell you this. The only difference between this country in 1855 and today is it is no longer a matter of race.. They're all slaves, and they're still living hand to mouth. If I can control the money and the basic necessities of their lives, I can control whether they live or die," proclaimed Pryor.

He's truly deranged, thought Darkhorse. *Once this job is over, I'm going to disappear for good. That crazy son of a bitch has used and abused me for the last time.*

Bob was oblivious to the implications of Pryor's plan. He was good at taking orders from people with the money to hire him, and in his tiny niche of technology, he was an expert. The years he spent in Pakistan defusing nuclear devices had prepared him to do the work that the former Director of Homeland Security required, but this time, he was arming nuclear devices, not disarming them. He heard the discussion, but his involvement in decision-making ended with which route to take to get to the destination and the proper wrenches needed to install the devices at the locations he was given.

His crew would accompany him on his three-week trip by truck to assist with the installation, but for all they knew, they were installing expensive icemakers in rich people's penthouse condos. They would be spared the true intent of his mission. It was an easy diversion; move the devices into place and send the crew to the nearest bar to wait while he armed the devices and programmed them for detonation by cell phone.

Once installed, Pryor could carry out his plan by speed dialing three preset numbers for each location. Each device had its own numbers, and Bob's employer had memorized the codes. Once installed, he destroyed those codes, so that total control over detonation resided within the mind of Pryor.

The only exception was the device entrusted to Darkhorse, and he had installed and programmed that one minutes before their meeting. In three weeks, he would be paid enough money to live for a year. It was more money than he had ever seen at one time, and it was more than he could make in two tours of duty in the Middle East. He felt lucky to have been chosen for this special assignment.

CHAPTER 37

Once Bob and Darkhorse had been given their orders and had been dispatched to perform their tasks, Pryor reminisced about his singular victory over the Masterson family, and the many defeats that had forged his hatred for them and everything they held sacred. It was a coup of his design; after the House of Representatives had voted unanimously in favor of funding to harden the nation's infrastructure against solar storms and man-made gamma radiation from EMP bombs, the Senate almost unanimously voted the measure down. It was unprecedented, and it was solely of his making. Pryor had secretly labored, through the use of threats and the calling in of favors, to convince and coerce the United States Senate that the bill was too expensive, and that the security of America was secure on his capable watch.

Max's father, John Masterson, had attempted to appeal to the reason of his fellow senators during a speech before the Senate Standing Committee on National Security. "The Carrington event is the only example we have of the effects of gamma radiation on our ability to communicate. It had nothing to do with man or the ability of mankind to wreak havoc," he said in his commanding voice. "It was a solar superstorm that happened in 1859, before electronics, before electricity. The only electrical disturbance it could have caused back in that time in our history was to the telegraph system that was still in its infancy. It shut down the telegraph everywhere and caused sparks to ignite paper that burned down more than a few telegraph houses. It essentially shut down modern communication," he had explained. "Today I stand before you with a problem that is a billion times more dire than the solar storm that shut down the primitive communications of 1859. If we don't harden our electronics against the very same gamma rays that the sun emits, all of our electronics are vulnerable to attack. Not from nature alone, but from a device that is man-made, the EMP bomb. The irony of this story is that the same event could shut down our communication infrastructure today, and we have done nothing to protect ourselves from that eventuality. Senators, the House has unanimously approved this bill to protect our communications infrastructure from solar storms and EMP attacks, and we must do this to protect our way of life."

Senator Masterson's reputation as the protector of American privacy and dignity would have no influence on his peers. The day before, the House of Representatives had unanimously passed a bill authorizing funding to harden the sensitive electronic infrastructure against an EMP attack, but the Senate voted the matter down in a nearly unamimous vote against. His message had fallen on deaf ears.

Pryor relished his victory over Senator Masterson more than any other accomplishment in his long career as Director of Homeland Security. Contrary to his official duties as protector of the nation's security, he fought to preserve the one vulnerability that he could use to control the nation and nurture his megalomania.

The day following the Senate vote, the following article was posted in WorldNet Daily:

ACCORDING TO A RETIRED SENATOR WHO HAS RAISED ALARMS OVER EMP, THE U.S. SENATE HAS DROPPED A HOUSE-APPROVED PLAN THAT WOULD PREPARE THE UNITED STATES TO DEFEND ITSELF FROM AN ATTACK FROM ANY ELECTROMAGNETIC PULSE SOURCE—WHETHER IT WOULD BE FROM A NATURAL SOLAR FLARE OR THE DETONATION OF A SPACE-LOCATED NUCLEAR WEAPON BY ENEMIES INTENT ON DESTROYING AMERICA'S INFRASTRUCTURE.

A demonstration of Pryor's power was his ability to take a unanimous vote of the U.S. House and turn it into a defeat in the Senate, and the next day, the bill to protect Americans was scarcely noticed by the press.

"The news is what we say it is. Keep them dumbed down, and pacified, and in the dark, that's what I always say. You don't have an opinion until I say you do. I don't make sense because the world as I let you know it doesn't make sense," Pryor had pontificated. He had manipulated the world of politics for as long as he had directed Homeland Security, and he lacked remorse. Through fear and intimidation, he had created a dynasty of one. This time, he had the ability to carry out his grand plan. A decade after the defeat of the EMP bill, H.R. 5026, he had his plan in place.

CHAPTER 38

The terrorist didn't perceive himself to be anything more than a young man just trying to make a living. He was trained by his nameless superiors to follow orders without question and to execute those orders with exacting precision. He entered the Statue of Liberty by the service door, dressed in the same coveralls as the rest of the restoration crew. The statue had been closed late in 2011 for restoration of its ever-corroding metal sheath and to install a second stairway for public access to the top. In recent years, the existing stairwell had become unstable, and public safety inspectors had mandated the closure until safer access could be made. The last thing they wanted was the death of visitors to America's most visible symbol of freedom, a gift from the French to the United States in an era forgotten by time.

He passed the plaque on his way toward the stairs, and paused to read the inscription, resting the large backpack at his feet.

GIVE ME YOUR TIRED, YOUR POOR,
YOUR HUDDLED MASSES YEARNING TO BREATHE FREE,
THE WRETCHED REFUSE OF YOUR TEEMING SHORE;
SEND THESE, THE HOMELESS, TEMPEST-TOST TO ME,
I LIFT MY LAMP BESIDE THE GOLDEN DOOR!

"I'm just doing my job," he said aloud. He kept his voice low, but there was no audience for his words. The building was officially closed to the public until repairs had been completed, and security provided by the National Park Service was reduced to a skeleton crew while workers completed their repairs inside. He was more than an hour and a half early, plenty of time to unpack his payload and slip out of the building in the gray morning, as if he had never been inside.

He made his way slowly up the stairs toward Lady Liberty's arm and the torch, ever-mindful that it was too fragile to accommodate the constant wear and tear of public access. That route to the top had been closed to the public since 1916, and that insured he would have no visitors while he placed the small bomb at the peak. He was an expert locksmith, and any barriers between him and his goal were quickly dispensed with. All thoughts he had about his weight causing a catastrophic break in the famous statue were dispelled quickly, when he realized that the arm and torch had already been fully restored in recent years.

He was alone.

CHAPTER 39

Max held Rachel's hand as they walked through the colorful field of wildflowers that graced the Fairlane estate. There was no lawn, replaced by his father years before his birth in a fit of practicality. Senator Masterson had ordered the green expanse of nothingness plowed up and hauled off, and replaced by a hundred sacks worth of native wildflower seeds that gave birth to a garden that bloomed year-round. The senator had been practical that way.

The seeds had naturalized the landscape over the years, and the only landscaping was the addition of a flagstone walkway that wound through the grounds toward the Potomac and back, over small babbling brooks and through the forest that lined the river banks. It was an idyllic escape that Max and Rachel made a part of their daily routine whenever they were home, once in the early morning when the song of birds served as their alarm clock, and once before or after dinner, depending on when the golden glow of the setting sun was touching the tops of the trees.

"I don't feel like the White House is home to me, Max said. "It's more like a symbolic home built into a fortress. You can't be alone there, free to walk around naked if you want to." Rachel giggled.

She and Max had spent many an evening lounging nude or walking around the spacious estate without a stitch of clothing, but those evenings had gone the way of their privacy.

"I remember that game of strip hide-and-seek we had that night when the moon was full." She laughed as Max pulled her close, their bodies melting into one. He could feel her heart pounding in excitement, and she could feel his desire building. It happened every time he held her.

"So do I." He recalled their passionate lovemaking under the stars. "You and I really left our inhibitions with our clothes that night." He smiled, reminiscing of the days when nobody knew where they were or what they did, a carefree time.

Rachel was his, and he was her one and only. She had never told him that, but he had never asked. She knew the stories of his early years, throughout his twenties and early thirties. He had a reputation for being a suave and confident, dedicated to bedding beautiful women and getting constant exposure in the press. Max's image got more exposure than his words. He was known for one sentence interviews, but that suited glamour reporters well.

The press had no interest in depth or insight. They wanted a cutline beneath an image and something to run for fifteen seconds by deadline, showing Max in the company of yet another "female companion." If they dated more than once, the name of the woman would be found, and she would have her brief glimpse of fame as a possible romantic interest. Three dates would elevate her to relationship status, accompanied by an article detailing her background. If the young woman consented to an interview, Max invariably terminated their relationship. There were few who had lasted beyond the romantic interest stage.

When Rachel attracted Max's attention, all of the carousing with social-climbers had ended abruptly, and the press immediately went into withdrawal. They attempted to dig into Rachel's background, but the information they found was sketchy. No previous romantic relationships beyond the puppy love stage during high school. No arrest record or any indication that she had any vices at all.

Her father had been a highly decorated pilot who served in the first Gulf war, and he had gone on to start his own helicopter manufacturing firm, designing high-tech helicopters for military and business applications. Rachel's mother shared her striking dark hair and svelte figure, staying at home to rear Rachel and her younger brother, Tom, who had grown up to be a married CPA with a nice wife and three kids. It was all bland fare for the readers and viewers accustomed to the glamour and fabricated scandal of Max's past, and it was deemed not newsworthy.

The fascinating information about Rachel had to do with her interests. She shared her father's love for flying, and at 13 she had soloed her first single-engine plane. In the years between her first flight and her 26th birthday, she became licensed to fly nearly everything from her dad's helicopters to passenger jets. Flying was her passion, and she had accompanied Max on the campaign trail on most of his forays, acting as his pilot. That way, she could spend more time with him while remaining active doing the things that gave her the most satisfaction. While Max was off doing his own thing, she could usually be found at an airport.

Although the press could sometimes predict where she could be found, they were totally stymied in their ability to get a statement from her. Their frustration wore on for the first two years of the relationship between Rachel and Max, until the information became sensationalized gossip, rumor, and speculation.

Articles with the headlines MAX DATING MUTE BEAUTY and MASTERSON'S FEMALE COMPANION; TALK MUCH? were featured in one week, to Max's delight. He loved messing with the press. Rachel had the intuition and intelligence to know that any words that came out of her mouth would be sensationalized, chopped, and slanted to suit the particular audience that each segment of the press serviced, and she had steadfastly refused to fall into that slippery pit.

"The earth laughs in flowers," said Rachel, quoting Emerson. She paused to pick an Indian Paintbrush from a naturalized bed of identical flowers that covered a small hill that faced the sun. Its orange, red, and burgundy colors were visual therapy that helped them slow down from their hectic lives, if only for the duration of their visits to this special place.

They kissed and held each other for a long time, turning their heads to the west to gaze at the setting sun. From the private vantage point where they lay, they were invisible to the world, but to each other, a sexual intensity grew. Max ran his fingers through Rachel's long, brown hair. When he reached the back of her head, he pulled her even tighter, until they were fused in passion. They made love in the darkening shadows—the highlight of the day—and into the night.

CHAPTER 40

WASHINGTON DC

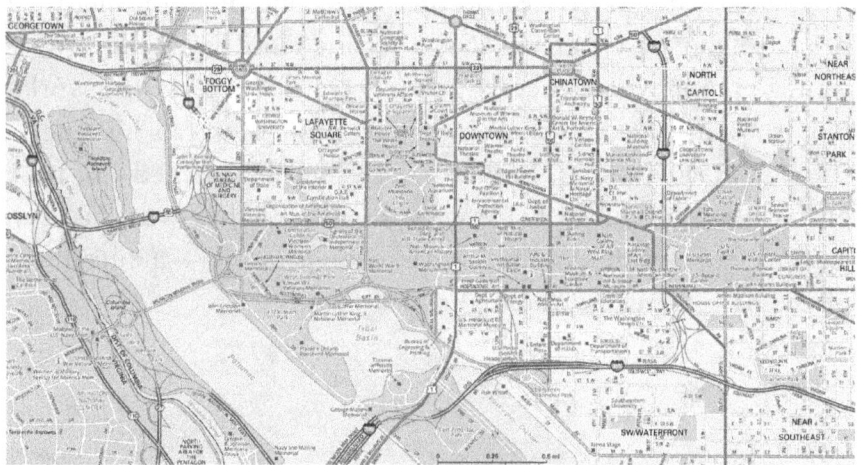

I naugeration Day is traditionally held on January twentieth of the year following the November election, and the significance of the date has been lost to history." Postlewaite paused for effect and took the occasion to take a long draw on his splendid cigar and survey the faces of 200 elected officials who had been invited to attend. "The reason for the delay between the vote and the swearing in is simple, I guess, but it is no longer logical," he continued. "It was to give our ancestors time after the election to make it to the occasion on horseback in the dead of winter. They then partied for five days prior to the ceremony and for five days after, before they got back on their horses and rode home with a glorious hangover." He was addressing his students, the politicians he had trained since childhood to excel in the business of politics. They were there to honor his two prize students, Max Masterson and Scarlett Conroy, who were about to become the President and Vice President of the United States of America. They had attained the pinnacle of all politics, and they were the culmination of his life's work.

In keeping with Max's disdain for mindless tradition, the site for the inaugural ceremony was moved from the Capitol Grounds to the Jefferson Memorial, where he had begun his campaign for the presidency by making his announcement at dawn. He also scheduled the nation's first annual Jefferson Memorial dance competition, in recognition of the National Park Service's well-known fetish for arresting people, all of them law-abiding citizens of the United States of America, for doing just that. Dancing. A meaningless regulation, and the law that made it more ridiculous, were obliterated from the mindless path that politics has been known to follow. Max had no intention of following traditions that had no meaning or to punish people trying to be Americans.

His audience that time was a hastily-assembled collection of the Washington press corps, who had been summoned before coffee to hear a speech from a political unknown. They were enraged when Max produced a one-minute soundbyte rather than the typical hour-long self-aggrandizement that politicians are known to produce on such occasions. They had nothing more to report on Max Masterson in the early morning hours of that day other than the words he spoke, and the words that resonated with the voters could be reduced to one message: Max Masterson was unique. That quality immediately set him apart from the usual suspects, the perennial candidates who spoke long about nothing other than the stale ideas that had been recycled from their previous failed attempts.

This time, they were all there, and they didn't know what to expect from this new president. The politicians and the press were there of course, but so were the glitter people, the ones who flew in from Hollywood to be seen. Max and Scarlett were ready, and the Chief Justice of the U.S. Supreme Court was there. The inaugural parade was ready, with the Marine Corps Marching Band and the high school bands, too. It began in the traditional way, with the flyovers of military jets and the huge mass of humanity who drove in for the occasion. It happened every four years, and the pomp and circumstance of the occasion was broadcast to the unlucky souls who couldn't make the trip.

This was the capitol at its best, the swearing-in of a new administration, with hope for the future and the discard of the old. In government, it was the most hopeful time. Most people attended the inauguration from the comfort of home. The audience for the event was expected to be over a billion viewers worldwide. Here was a man who was not a politician that was running for president, and America became curious about his reasons for doing such a damn fool thing. When he chose Scarlett Conroy to be his running mate, the viewership increased dramatically, and the special occasion took on an aura of royalty. Washington had not seen so much "new blood" since the Camelot days of the Kennedy administration.

The agenda for the day began with the swearing-in of the new president by the Chief Justice of the Supreme Court and the much-awaited inaugural address by Max. It was to be followed by the swearing-in of Vice President Scarlett Conroy. Her speech was allocated a larger segment on the program, which was provided to the attendees in paper form. There was no guest list. The inauguration is the welcoming celebration of the people, and anyone who chose to attend could do so if they could fly, drive, or get there somehow.

The sheer size of the audience was staggering, and they weren't just there for a parade. The inauguration of this president had a new life to it, a hopeful and visionary sense of purpose. Max sat in the black limousine, waiting for the motorcade to transport him the two blocks from the White House to the Jefferson Memorial directly across the Potomac Tidal Basin. Rachel was at his side, dressed in a coral white sequined dress with matching hat and gloves, looking very much like a young Jackie Kennedy. She had been swarmed upon by fashion designers and event planners for the previous three days, and she felt like the runner-up on a fashion makeover show, transformed into an image she hadn't chosen for herself and very uncomfortable with her new image.

Regardless of how she felt, her female admirers loved it. They gasped and clapped as she walked down the front steps of the White House, and she assumed that her life would never be the same again. Designer clothes were mandatory garb for times when she had to make a public appearance. Any other time, she could wear jeans and a T-shirt or her flight suit, which suited her just fine.

They sat silent for twenty minutes before Max had enough of the waiting. He was notoriously impatient when it came to down time, and when he reached that point, he had to move. "Why can't we just walk over there? I can see it from here," he exclaimed. Armstrong, who sat in the front seat, turned, his face ashen, and addressed his passengers. "Mr. President, we have our web of security deployed at the Jefferson Memorial and at all points in-between, but you would have to walk through the Ellipse, past the Washington Monument, and around the Tidal Basin to get there. My best guess is that there are close to a million people between here and there, and they are all going to want to touch you, shake your hand, and touch Rachel, too. It would be a breach of protocol for us to change plans at the last second, and I advise against it."

"Well, we're just going to have to breach protocol then, because I'm not going to sit in this limo one more second. Rachel, would you like to take a little walk with me? I have to make a speech over there on the far side of the cement pond."

Rachel giggled and held out her hand. "I'd be delighted to accompany you on your walk, kind sir," she replied. Max opened the door and stood. He smoothed his topcoat and extended his gloved hand to Rachel. She beamed at him and waved to the crowd, who stood en masse, hoping for a view. The weather was sunny and unseasonably warm for January, a perfect winter day. "I see that you have arranged a nice day for a tour of our national landmarks," she replied.

Max smiled. "I assure you, pretty lady, that this will be a day like no other."

They waited for a few seconds to allow the Secret Service to scurry to new positions along the way, and two Capitol Police motorcycles zoomed ahead to part the crowd. Capitol police on horseback were frantically summoned for crowd control. Then they walked, and the applause began.

The crowd did want to touch them, to the apoplectic consternation of their protectors. To avoid being pulled and detained, Max and Rachel extended their hands far enough to touch, but not close enough for a formal handshake, and that seemed to satisfy the surprised onlookers. With no way to cordon off the sidewalk, the motorcycles cleared the path while secret service ran slightly ahead and to the side of Max, and they were able to part the crowd with little difficulty. Most people were satisfied with a picture of the occasion, something to tell to their grand-children, taking a part in history. The entourage rounded the end of the tidal basin without incident, and they were able to maneuver inside of the cordoned area within two minutes, to the relief of the security team.

CHAPTER 41

The improvised EMP bombs were a new generation of terror device. They didn't kill people unless they were within a fifty yard radius of the blast. The gamma radiation that caused the damage could be focused by cone-shaped charges, and the tritium gas that enclosed the enriched plutonium core served as a magnifier, enhancing the explosion by a large factor. The net effect of this development allowed the bomb makers to be able to conceal the device inside a small container.

The disguise for the EMP bomb that was installed at Arlington House, the national landmark home of Robert E. Lee, was concealed inside of an air compressor tank. It had been placed under a tarp along with other construction equipment at the home, which was closed to the public during roof restorations. The antique furniture of the home, a legacy of Lee's family, had been wrapped with care in bubble wrap and trucked to a warehouse while repairs were made. On inauguration day, the tourist attraction would be closed, and no restoration would be done. All government workers have a day off when the next president comes into office.

Darkhorse had personally delivered the bomb two days before the event. It was as a matter of pride for him to do it right; there would be no second chance. He drove the pickup truck with the compressor towed behind on a small trailer that could be maneuvered by hand once it was removed from the hitch. He was dressed in coveralls festooned with the logo of the sub-contractor that had been the low bidder for the roof repairs. The truck and trailer drove slowly onto the grounds and approached the security station from the service entrance as he had observed the other workers do over the previous week, concealed from view by a stand of heavy woods along the river.

He presented a counterfeit work order to the uniformed security guard, who examined it with the nonchalance he expected.

"I thought you weren't going to start until next week on account of the inauguration and all," the young guard said in a strong Virginia drawl.

"I'm just here to drop this here compressor off before the whole town turns into one big traffic jam. Ya'll know how it gets," said Darkhorse, mimicking the drawl perfectly. He was a human chameleon when it came to entering and leaving unobtrusively, and he had learned from experience that the more alike he could appear to the victim of his deception, the easier it would be. He had no intention of lingering longer than it would take to unhitch the trailer and situate the EMP bomb due east. When he was done cranking the hitch to a level position on top of a cinder block and using a level and compass to assure that the orientation was spot on, he stood and looked across the river toward the Capitol. The morning sun made the white of the monuments appear golden, and the panorama of sights was special. Satisfied, he turned and yanked the door of the pickup open with a creak. He waved to the security guard as he left the manicured grounds of Arlington House, slowing to marvel at the huge limestone columns of the portico. *They don't make them like that anymore*, he thought to himself.

The location was chosen for two important reasons. First and foremost, Arlington House was located high on a bluff on the Potomac River. It overlooked all of Washington D.C. and was in a direct line of sight to the National Mall, where the Lincoln Memorial, the Washington Monument, and the Jefferson Memorial gleamed bright in the morning sun across the river. The gamma radiation could be directed toward the east, its effects would be felt to the White House beyond the National Mall, and as far away as Union Station and the Capitol. From the blast site and as far east as the horizon beyond the Capitol, the bomb would have its intended effect: it would render all vehicles with electronic parts inoperable, and all electronic communications would be cut off, along with the power grid that supplied electricity to the area.

The second important factor was a failing of security. Inside Washington, within the beltway, the president was the most protected person on earth. From across the Potomac, high on a hill from Virginia, he and the giddy audience for the inauguration were more vulnerable to attack than their collective imaginations could anticipate. The shaped waves of the electromagnetic pulse would direct heat, light, and gamma radiation on over a million people in a microsecond, and their lives would be transformed into a new reality in less time than it would take to blink an eye.

Darkhorse had arranged it that way, meticulous in the planning of it. As he drove along the Beltway away from Washington, he ran through a mental checklist of his handiwork. The bomb was shielded from detection inside the lead-lined metal canister of its air compressor disguise, and it could be triggered by a cell phone call from any location. It would be the last unshielded cell phone call from the Washington area for weeks or months if the device served its purpose. This would be his biggest attempt at widespread mayhem, and he reveled in the adrenaline the thoughts produced. It was a sexual urge for him. He knew it well. It was what he lived for.

CHAPTER 42

Pryor stood on a podium in the spacious ballroom of his mansion in the Hamptons. He wore a tuxedo identical to the other forty men in the room. He held a remote which operated four monitors located on the massive walls which surrounded them. What appeared to be large oil paintings by Albert Bierstadt and other painters from the Hudson River Valley School of Art in the nineteenth century were actually holographic images of original landscapes that hung in the Metropolitan Museum of Art in New York City.

The canvases were distinctive due to their size: each one was six feet tall and eight feet wide, and all were indistinguishable from the paintings that had hung in the gallery at the Met for more than a century. When he tired of one image, he could replace it with more than a million others from a database designed for the super-rich; it was grand in taste and guaranteed to satisfy even the most fickle of buyers.

Each of the attendees was summoned to the Pryor estate for a purpose, and art appreciation had nothing to do with it. It was Inauguration Day, and their host had promised that it would be an event that they would remember.

"I called for you to witness Masterson's crowning from the comfort of my home," Pryor announced in a loud, grating voice. He had been a powerful voice in his years as Director of Homeland Security, but in his career, he had never made a speech. His power was wielded behind the scenes, out of sight from the world, and he demanded anonymity. From his position, he had controlled the nation's largely enigmatic security force without addressing the public. He loathed the common folk who comprised a majority of the country, choosing to control others through threats and intimidation. Anyone who stood in the way could be ruined with a call to the right people. For decades he had ruined lives in the interest of maintaining the status quo for himself and the members of the elite group assembled before him.

"We under-estimated Masterson's appeal to the voters, and today, we will have our revenge." He activated the remote and the oil paintings disappeared, replaced by live broadcasts of the inauguration from multiple angles. Overhead cams were stationed on tall poles throughout the Mall, and the effect was to provide a continuous view of the action from every angle. Max was seen walking through the massive crowd, Rachel on his arm, beaming with his now world-famous visage. His face had yet to show his age. His dimpled cheeks, strong jaw line and dark, wavy hair brought his admirers to draw comparisons of his look to John F. Kennedy, Jr. and Errol Flynn, but it was an image all of his own. Pryor detested it.

"During my years with Homeland Security," he continued, "We came upon a shipment of a new type of terrorist device that was brought into this country through Canada. These babies came from the Ukraine, and were invented before the Soviet Union collapsed. A soldier guarding a Soviet research facility stole them and sold the devices for kitchen appliances and food for his starving family... can you imagine that?"

They all laughed at the feeble attempt at humor. Each of the privileged in the room had no concept of starvation or deprivation, having never experienced the slightest delay in satisfying their needs. If they wanted it, it was provided to them by the many that served them.

"We intercepted the shipment at a dock on the U.S. side of the St. Lawrence Seaway. Until then, we had never seen anything like it. Our tests showed that each one was capable of emitting electro-magnetic radiation, identical to the gamma radiation emitted by the Sun during solar flares, but it could be focused on targets and detonated without destroying people or buildings. It simply makes all of the electrical and electronic devices and all of the power grid go bye-bye." Pryor was beginning to show excitement as he explained his plot, his voice rising.

"It came in two sizes, a little one that you will see in action in a few minutes, and a big one that can take out an entire city," he explained, being careful to keep his explanations simple. His audi-ence was mega-rich, but few of them had pursued higher education to get to their station in life. They had inherited their wealth, not earned it, and an appreciation for noetic science was notably lacking from their educations.

Their time was spent in the appreciation of the finer things in life. Their most pervasive interest was preservation of the status quo: the maintenance of their wealth from the oil oligarchy and the banking, insurance, shipping, and fueling infrastructure that went with it. This secretive group of mega-wealthy were not entre-preneurs in any respect; their wealth had been accumulated by long-dead ancestors, and through the use of family trusts, offshore investments, and numbered bank accounts in foreign countries, they passed their bounty within their respective families from one generation to the next.

They were the idle product of a system which thrived on resisting change, and with the defeat of the Blythe administration, they had lost the control of government that they and their families had maintained for centuries. It was that perceived lack of control of that caused them to assemble at the time and place, and they placed their trust in Blythe to rid them of the renegade who would soon occupy the White House.

They stared at the monitors in silence as Max and Scarlett ascended the stage to take the oath of office.

"Repeat after me," said Chief Justice Robertson. "I , Maximum Masterson, do solemnly swear that I will faithfully execute the office of President of the United States, and will to the best of my ability, preserve, protect and defend the Constitution of the United States." Max repeated it, his right hand steadfastly placed on the Masterson family bible. When he had finished taking the oath of office, he took two steps backward. The Chief Justice turned to Rachel and ceremoniously delivered the bible and a copy of the oath to her. She pressed the bible to her chest tightly. Even though she was delighted to be next to Max on this occasion, her grim expression betrayed her feelings. She was overwhelmed by the enormity of it.

Max caught her eye, and leaned toward her as Scarlett took the oath of office. "Holding up OK?" He whispered the words so only she could hear.

"I'd rather be flying over this crowd than be stuck right in the middle of it. Please tell me we won't have to do this every day. I'm afraid to scratch my nose out of fear that my picture will end up on the front page of the Times," she responded. "I can see it now, banner headlines, *President's Girlfriend Picks Nose, Inauguration Ruined*."

"Not every day. Just most days, and I forbid you to pick your nose in public," he said with a smile.

She looked startled, realized he was joking, and grabbed his arm for reassurance. "What comes next," she whispered.

"You get to walk with me in a big parade, and then I get to make a speech over there on the front steps," said Max, gesturing toward the Capitol. "Then we have to hang out for about an hour while Scarlett makes a speech, and then everyone can go back to partying for a few days, while we entertain. It's going to be fun."

Rachel was itching to get out of the pressures of the huge crowd and wished she could go for a flight in the old Beech seaplane that had been restored and sat inside a hangar on the Potomac near Alexandria, Virginia, a short drive from Fairlane. The freedom she felt while flying was her favorite pleasure that Max couldn't provide. But in a way, he had. The seaplane was Max's inherited aircraft, even though he had never flown it. He claimed that his mind couldn't absorb too many stimuli at once or he would short-circuit his brain, a thought that she considered hilarious.

Contained in his casual statement was the universal truth that she felt made women superior to men: while men are stronger and linearly driven to accomplish great things, women can attend to details that get things done. One without the other accomplished nothing.

She smiled, and the cameras clicked. Her smiling face was the image that would survive the day. The inaugural parade proceeded past the Roosevelt Memorial, led by the Marine Corps marching Band. When they reached the Lincoln Memorial, they halted for a precision drill, leaving Max and Rachel surrounded by security. Both of them took the pause to change into walking shoes designed for the parade, which looked identical to the uncomfortable patent leather formal shoes worn for the swearing-in.

"I wish I could slip on my running shoes to do this, but red and white Nikes don't go with a tux. I suppose they'll want to dress me every day I'm in office," Max mused. The lack of privacy and independence that went with his position was a major sacrifice he had come to accept, but he didn't have to like it, and he resolved to resist every effort of his protectors and advisors to keep him cocooned.

"You're looking very pretty in your Jackie Kennedy outfit today, Ms. Rachel," he teased. She laughed, and the sound of her laughter gave him a butterfly feeling inside. For all of the pomp and circumstance of the occasion, she was unpretentious, a quality he valued in a woman. He doubted whether he would find anyone better, and he treasured every moment they could spend together. For the first time in his eclectic relationships with women, he felt he had found a soul-mate.

"Mr. President, I am charmed to make your acquaintance, and you just wait until I get you home," she flirted in her best effort at mimicking a Southern aristocrat.

The procession resumed, winding its way around the Lincoln Memorial and onto Constitution Avenue. Both sides of the wide promenade were a wall of people, all shouting and moving flags in a semi-synchronous wave. It was a patriotic gesture by the American people, a welcome entrance into the most responsible job of Max's lifetime. He stifled an urge to burst forward in a sprint to the Capitol, recalling earlier days when he ran the same route in the Marine Corps Marathon. This time, instead of trudging along in running clothes in a loose pack of anonymous athletes, he settled for being the center of attention.

CHAPTER 43

Are you going to let us down like the last guy?" a loud baritone voice bellowed. The crowd turned to the source of the sound, and Max could see a large man in a hooded sweatshirt, hands in his pockets. Sensing danger, the Secret Service converged on the man from multiple directions, and hustled him to the back of the crowd. The man fought back, swinging wildly. "I didn't do nothing wrong," he bellowed. "I just asked him a question is all," he yelled as he was brought to the ground.

Max wondered how many members of the crowd were there to protect him and how many were there to wish him well. "I don't want him arrested or hurt, and if you don't find any weapons on him, let him go and apologize for the inconvenience," he stated with conviction.

"Yes sir, Mr. President, we're checking him for weapons now," responded the closest agent. Although scanners and security checkpoints were placed at access points to the parade route, the size of the crowd had made any security measures inadequate, and Max was perceived to be in greater danger whenever he ventured outside.

Satisfied that the man was harmless, they released him, but twenty minutes had elapsed. By the time he made his way back to the front, the parade was blocks ahead. He stood dejected and resentful as the Florida A&M Rattlers performed at the back of the procession, and then he drifted with the crowd toward the Capitol. There the parade would pass by the grandstand, followed by long-awaited speeches by Max and Scarlett. He was in a dark mood, after being tackled and detained for asking a simple question, one that burned in his mind. He wasn't the only one to wonder, and he was far from the last. He approached a line of satellite trucks where the press sat, observing activity on monitors, filtering the newsworthy from the mundane. The closest technician looked up from editing and casually observed the man in the hooded sweatshirt as he flowed past. He looked at the footage, looked up, looked back again, and hollered, "It's him! Willie! Today is your lucky day!"

Willie B. Somovich was preoccupied with combing his hair over his unibrow and shellacking it in place before the cameras went live. Without diverting his eyes from the mirror, he responded, "Vince, if you interrupt me one more time..."

"No, Willie...it's the dude the Secret Service tackled...He's right there! Get him before he gets away!"

Willie launched his rotund body from his stool in front of his lighted makeup table, and slammed the aluminum door of the trailer open with a metallic crash. He didn't wait to descend the steps, launching himself into space as the broken door tumbled to the ground in splinters of glass. If he hadn't stubbed his toe on the threshold, he would have landed on his feet, but the stubbing changed his trajectory from a leap to a face-first lunge, and he skidded to a stop at the feet of the startled man.

"Sir, sir, may I have a moment of your time?" Willie was face-down, his face inches from the man's Converse Chuck Taylor All Stars. His white dress shirt was covered in grass stains and dirt, but his famous coif was immaculate. His investment in lacquered hairspray was his salvation.

"Are you that fella who is on the TV, who insults everybody all the time, that Willie B. Right ?" In the man's world, he was in the presence of royalty. He extended a meaty hand to Willie, and he pulled Willie to his feet in one powerful yank.

"Well, yes, yes I am, and I would like to interview you for my program. You are about to become famous, my friend," Willie responded, sensing that he was about to scoop his competitors with the first exclusive interview of the man who had the guts to confront the president with the question that would define the Masterson legacy.

"Me? Why me?" Today, he was newsworthy for the first time in his average life.

CHAPTER 44

Max's encounter with the man and the response by the Secret Service was viewed at every angle by an estimated one billion people. By the time he reached the podium on the Capitol Grounds where the inaugural speeches were to be made, he had a half hour to run the man's words through his mind a dozen times. Could he satisfy the nation? Would he let them down? How could one person make a difference? He realized that the same questions were being asked of him, and he needed to address them immediately.

The press had been diligent in researching the man's background, and the monitor showed his driver's license picture, a mug shot from a 2012 arrest for disorderly conduct where he pleaded no contest, and a continuous loop of commentary wrapped around the man's words, "Are you going to let us down like the last guy?" followed by more commentary. By day's end, he would be interviewed in special reports and featured on popular talk shows. With one fortuitous question, he had become an instant celebrity.

Pryor watched the events with particular delight. If his plot went as planned, Max would stand helpless as the cameras went black, before he could assure anyone that he could lead the nation. "I plan to make Masterson look like an incompetent fool in front of a billion people," he announced to his tuxedoed audience. As Max approached the podium, Pryor held the digital communicator over his head in a grandiose gesture of defiance. The entry of three digits would auto-dial the number that would detonate the bomb concealed in front of Robert E. Lee's mansion across the Potomac.

Max took the stage and began his inaugural address.

"America, thank you for being here, and for those of you who are watching from home, welcome." The applause caused a prolonged pause, and Max waited patiently for the opportunity to speak again. Finally, he continued. "I had some words written here that I thought you needed to hear." He pulled a paper pad from his coat pocket, and laid it on the podium. "But as I walked here in my first duty as president, I felt the love, and the hope, and the joy, and the expectations that you have for me. Especially, the expectations." Max paused again, and let the sound settle. "I sought, and was elected to, the most difficult and unforgiving job in the world, one for which I have been trained all of my life. My father gave me the training, and my mentor prepared me for this role, and the experiences of my life brought me here. But I was unprepared for the question one man, no different from any of us, asked me on my way to this podium. He said, 'Are you going to let us down like the last guy?'"

Pryor pressed the button. There was a brilliant flash, and the power went out from the border of the Potomac to the horizon.

CHAPTER 45

The first realization of the crisis was the immediate loss of power to the microphones and cameras. Max continued talking, but his voice didn't carry beyond the first few rows of the reserved section, where well-dressed dignitaries sat on padded folding chairs for which they had paid thousands of dollars to sit. The lights that provided the perfect ambiance for a presidential speech went out, too, along with every signal carried by a phone, TV camera, or wireless device.

Immediately, Max, Scarlett, and Rachel were hustled into the waiting limousine. Armstrong barked orders to the driver as the security detail formed a protective cordon, guns drawn against an invisible enemy. "Get us out of here, now! Clear the road!"

The turn of the key in the ignition was met only with a dull click. The driver muttered "Damn" and tried again. One more time. Another "Damn." He turned to Armstrong and said, "Electronic ignition. It's fried." He paused as they stared at each other, incredulous.

"Wish I was driving my old '66 Mustang right now, that baby wouldn't let me down," Max said.

"No electronics. You might have to put in new points, but I guarantee you that baby would run," the driver replied wistfully.

"What about Corvettes?" Max asked. "Would a Corvette run?"

"You might need to change the points, but that's no big deal. Anything with wheels that was built before 1968, but there aren't many of those old classics around these days. Mostly hybrids and electrics, but no gas-guzzlin' muscle cars like I grew up on," the driver replied.

Max leaped from the limo and began issuing orders.

"The only transportation that works right now is that horse over there, those bikes over there, and the pads on the balls of our feet. Bring the bikes here," he announced. Scarlett emerged from one door and Rachel from the other. "Rachel, you're coming with me. Scarlett, you will ride on that horse with that Capitol policeman to the White House. You are in charge of this emergency, and your first duty is to get someone to put the power back on. I want you, Andrew, and you, Bill, to pass the word that this inauguration will continue in one hour, and that drinks are on me."

Scarlett was not adapting well. Her agenda of the day was planned, and this crisis had disrupted that plan. "But my speech! I was going to make my speech!" Max grabbed her hands firmly, comforted in a miniscule way that his every action was not being monitored or recorded by the disabled electronics, but still, when he touched, she pulled back. The physical contact was unexpected and unwanted, and he sensed that he had crossed a barrier that he should not have been crossed.

He released her and studied her face. She was bewildered, and he needed her to snap back to the present. Catching her in his intent gaze, he spoke in a stern but comforting voice. "You need to take command. You will make your speech, but until we get the power back, nobody will hear you. I'm headed to my house, and in one hour, I will be riding back here in the damndest parade you ever saw. In the meantime, you're in charge of panic patrol, and you have a million people to entertain. Right now, I suggest you pass the word that all is well, and you get those park service people over there to start gathering firewood for a bonfire that rivals a University of Texas homecoming. We need to make the best of this. In a few minutes, my guess is that you will be surrounded by the best military force that this world has ever seen, and they won't know what to do, so I want you to make sure everyone is warm, fed, and in a good mood by the time I get back."

"This will not do. It will just not do. Our plans—"

"I'll show you plans. I have been planning to do this all day." Max turned to Rachel and pulled Rachel to him, kissing her deeply. The holders of the expensive seats looked on, stubbornly refusing to budge from the spot they had attained to watch the Superbowl of politics and wondering what was next on the list of activities. Collectively, they looked like a flock of birds, all turning their heads in unison at each movement. At the moment, they were fixated on the president kissing his girlfriend in front of a million onlookers, an event to which another billion people had been deprived.

"Max, they're looking..." Rachel had suddenly become conscious that they were in the least private setting for a passionate kiss, and pulled away, looking Max in the eyes. He was amused, and his impish grin foretold his secret motivation.

"All of you, listen to me! Are there any of you who would turn down a kiss like that?" They cheered. "Now, what are we going to do about this? You can't call anybody, and you aren't on TV, so I'm going to make this into the world's largest public party. We may as well make the best of it, right? If you hang out here for awhile, I'll be back in awhile. Right now, I need to go be president, but I'll be back, and we can get through Inaugural Day in grand style." Max left the details to Scarlett, who was already busy gathering whoever she could find and giving them instructions.

"I need a pen and something to write on." She announced to the crowd. Instantly, she was handed notebooks from purses and pockets. "I am going to the White House, and with your permission, I will wait 'til later to give my speech..." She became aware of the insignificance of her words, and stopped in mid-sentence. "Never mind about that. I have to plan!" The crowd cheered again. She walked toward the large Park Service horse, unsure of what to do next.

From behind, a uniformed officer approached and said, "Pardon me for being so forward, ma'am, but I'll get you on that horse." He placed one hand under her right arm and the other on her backside and hauled her aboard in one motion. Scarlett sputtered for a moment, indignant that her personal barrier had been violated, and mortified by the fact that she sat astride the rump of a horse in her inaugural dress, which had pulled up to expose her legs.

"Your undies are showing," someone shouted, which prompted Scarlett to blush, humiliated at her predicament.

"Well, I never...Take me out of here!" She swatted the horse, which caused it to rear up. To avoid tumbling to the ground, Scarlett wrapped her arms around the waist of the cavalry officer and hung on tightly as they charged forward into the crowd.

Rachel stood with her arm tight to Max. "You know, I can fly that old Baby Belle that your dad had restored, and as I recall, it had some good landing lights installed on the struts. I have been taking it up on some days when you're out politicking, and I'm getting pretty good at it."

Max turned to her, oblivious to the chaos that was spinning around them. "First of all, my dear lady, I'm not a politician, and second, have I ever clipped your wings? Ever?" He pulled her close and kissed her passionately once more, to the raucous applause of the onlookers. "We're going to go to Fairlane, and you can lead the way back in the helicopter. We're going to show whoever did this that we may be inconvenienced, but we are far from defeated," he explained quietly.

Max thrived on the unpredictable, and a clandestine call from Roger Sinclair the evening before the inauguration had cemented his plans. Sinclair had received a tip from a confidential informant, a member of a clandestine society of wealthy silver spoons with a community of interests. He disclosed that the inauguration would be disrupted in a major way, with the intention of embarrassing Max in front of the world. The informant had laughed as he said it, implying that Masterson would not last the first months of his presidency, resigning in disgrace.

The words had enraged Sinclair, but he refused to reveal his true feelings to his informant. The man was a wealth of information, and his only pipeline to the perpetrators of the plot. Their visit was brief, as the man, known only as "Bob", had stopped for the night at a hotel on the interstate north of Philadelphia on his way west, where he had been hired to do a "three-week job". He was paid well for the tip, as he had been paid in the past. Sinclair knew he could rely on the information, but without specifics, he was powerless to prevent what was inevitable. His only consolation was the fact that their intentions were to embarrass and not to kill. He communicated that to the president.

"How, Max? How are we going to get to your house? It's ten miles away, across the river. The Capitol is shut down, darlin'." Rachel was the practical one, and when she had command of the situation, she was calm and powerful, belying her exotic image of dependency on Max's strength. This time, though, the overwhelming unexpectedness had left her drifting.

"Don't worry. I have a huge surprise waiting for you at the White House," Max replied mysteriously.

"What kind of a surprise?"

"You'll see. We need to get ourselves and those bikes down to the kitchen."

Justin Armstrong, barged forward, shaking his head. "Mr.

President, may I have a few words with you? In there?" He gestured toward the disabled limo, its doors open on both sides and guarded by the Cajun driver. Realizing that the opportunity for a private conversation would be impossible immersed in the well-dressed mass of humanity that surrounded them, Armstrong abandoned the idea and resorted to cupping his hands and whispering in Max's ear. "All of our electronics are fried, and we can't communicate. I have taken an oath to protect you with my life, and I insist that you let me do my job. We need to keep you out of harm's way until the helos get here and extract you from this mess."

Max turned to Armstrong with a bemused look. "I know you want to protect me, but whoever did this is trying to embarrass me and our new administration in a big way. If they wanted to kill me and about a million people along with me, you would be scraping my remains off the sidewalk right now. Today is not my last day, and the last thing I want to show to the American people is an impotent president who cowers and hides in the face of an emergency. You and my security escort will ride with me to the White House, and I will need ten riders."

"Mr. President, in about ten minutes, I expect that Marine One and a squadron of fighter jets will be here to protect you and get you out of here," Armstrong pleaded, realizing that he was arguing with the most powerful man in the world.

"Armstrong, where are they going to land? I expect your people to get busy while I'm gone, clearing a space for the helo. Everyone will think that the jets in the sky are part of the festivities, but you know that they are useless as tits on a bull in this situation. When the helo lands, I want someone with a soothing voice to use the loudspeakers to tell these people that everything will be OK and to try to maintain order. Do you think you can do that for me?"

"No, sir, Mr. President."

"What did you say?"

"I have been assigned to protect you, and that is what I'm going to do. I can't leave your side," the burly Secret Service agent responded in a strong voice, conveying the determination that had propelled him through the ranks as a Navy SEAL.

"Then delegate, dammit! I need to get to the White House, and the quickest way to get through this crowd is the old-fashioned way." Max didn't wait for a response, quickly realizing that his protector, and the hundreds of agents within several steps of him, were going to do as they were trained, and he wasn't about to change protocol with a few words.

He smiled briefly and turned to review the collection of mountain bikes that had been hastily assembled. Most were Park Service bikes, but some were state-of the art titanium and carbon fiber wonder bikes that had cost their owners a fortune. They were guarded by their owners, who were nervously standing next to their prize posses-sions. In the nation's capitol, losing sight of your ride meant the difference between riding and walking, and the brightly polished, urban transportation was the best available way to move quickly in a city with no power.

"I need your help," Max announced to the bike owners, who zealously gripped their handlebars in a protective death grip. "I need to get to the White House quickly, and I would like to borrow your bikes for a while. You can pick them up later. And to say thanks, you will get a free ticket to the inaugural ball. How does that sound?"

A young woman, approximately Rachel's size and build pushed forward. "Here, take mine." She graciously surrendered her bike to Rachel.

Rachel examined the bike, wondering how to mount it in her inaugural outfit. She resigned herself to show some leg on the ride. "I'll take care of it for you," she said.

An athletic-looking man in his 30's stepped forward. From the look of him, he was probably a local resident and most likely a government employee of some kind, his neat, yuppie appearance betraying his status. He moved his bike in Max's direction. "She's my baby," he exclaimed with pride. "You won't find one lighter and quicker, and I want the bragging rights."

"Thanks. You can pick it up at my place after the party," Max said.

Max was satisfied that everything was in good hands, and gestured to Rachel. "Come on!" he coaxed her toward the mountain bikes that had been commandeered in the name of national security. The security detail quickly commandeered the remaining bikes, and they moved forward at the front, making a path through the crowd. "We'll be right back," Max announced.

Those within earshot clapped loudly and the ripple effect was huge. As they moved forward, the words "Here comes the president. Let him through!" were followed by a wave of applause as they made their way toward the White House.

CHAPTER 46

O nce they had reached the security gate, there was a glitch. The gate was powered by an electronic mechanism which locked automatically in a power outage, and their means of access was sealed for the time-being. Without hesitation, Max and Rachel propped the bikes against the fence and Max turned to hoist her over the top.

"I can do it, oh gallant one," she said with exuberance. The exercise had buoyed her spirits, and she was feeling less like a fixture at his side, which had made her feel unnatural and plastic. "I have been hopping fences all my life."

"I'll bet you didn't try this in a designer dress, though" he replied. "Don't any of you even think of trying to help," he announced to the security detail. "Secure the perimeter and address the crowd," he ordered.

The Secret Service turned their backs to them as Rachel placed her hands on the top rail and did a neat pirouette over the top. The crowd burst in raucous applause as Max approached the fence. In similar fashion, he vaulted the fence, landing on his heels hard, followed by an unceremonious fall to the grass, creating a grass stain on his inaugural coat. He recovered quickly, bouncing to his feet and looping his arm in Rachel's. They bowed simultaneously and ran to the front door, where the Vice President and the White House staff awaited.

CHAPTER 47

S carlett looked rumpled, but she had been able to find a comb and makeup and was busy reassembling her image in a large, ornate mirror in the main hallway. She was simultaneously barking orders to the assemblage, who would periodically run in the direction of their assigned tasks. Max immediately realized that in a city that had been rendered powerless, the lights in the White House were still lit. Scarlett turned from her mirror, anticipating Max's question.

"I know, I was surprised too, but it seems that all of the essential government buildings have been hardened against this kind of attack, and it's only the civilian grid that went down. We won't have any way of restoring power to the full area for a few days, but we should have the Metro running by the time people decide to head home. If they drove here and parked their car inside the blast zone, they are going to be looking for a ride, though…what a mess!"

◆ ◆ ◆

Andrew Fox and Bill Staffman were breathless with excitement. They had been monitoring the festivities from the Situation Room when the flash occurred and the screens went dark. From the shelter beneath the White House, they had been unable to determine the source of the outage, and had been forced to return to the first floor by a seldom-used stairwell.

"The subway is still down. So are the elevators, but I'm told we should have them repaired within a few hours. We are maintaining a perimeter around the White House, and we will continue to do so," explained Staffman.

"Communicators are being re-issued to the agents in the field, and we should have full restoration of our electronics inside of fifteen minutes. Those unlucky souls outside won't be able to call home anytime soon, though, and all audio-visual equipment on scene has been rendered useless. The press is going to have a conniption, not being able to report the excitement," piped in Andrew, Max's young chief of staff. He knew his last comment would provoke a smile from Max, and he was not disappointed.

"I didn't really think about it, but for the next few hours, we control the media, don't we?"

If brain activity created smoke, the Diplomatic Reception Room where they stood would have activated the fire alarms.

"Yeah, sorta," replied Andrew. "The Press Room is sheltered from EMP radiation just like the rest of the building. They had a Faraday cage built into the walls many years ago."

"Faraday cage? What's that?"

"I thought you knew. There's one in your garage at Fairlane. I noticed it the moment I walked in the door," replied Andrew.

"I remember my dad talking about this possibility when I was just a kid," Max recalled. "He would go on these tirades against his enemies in government and tell me how Congress had compromised our security by failing to use foresight. I was immersed in it so much that I didn't think about how he had taken his own precautions. You would have liked him, Andrew. Dead ten years and he's still taking care of me."

Andrew stayed on task. "A Faraday cage or Faraday shield is an enclosure formed by a mesh of conducting material. It blocks out the external electric fields that took out our electronics when the EMP device was detonated. We tracked the source to the Arlington House over near Arlington National Cemetery. Our security measures weren't good enough, I guess. We scanned every object in the Capitol, but nothing on the other side of the Potomac. Robert E. Lee's house has been closed for repairs for the past month, and nobody thought to go over there," Andrew explained.

Max was becoming impatient with Andrew's pedantic focus. "Thanks for the science lesson, but I need answers. Are you saying that the cars in my garage at home, and all of the audio-visual equipment in the press room were not affected by the blast?"

"Yeah, why?"

"Do you know how to operate one of those cameras?"

"Yeah, sure. Any idiot can do it. I took a video class in college, and I—"

"Andrew, I want you to go to the Press Room, get all of the equipment you need, and start recording smiling faces and upbeat words," Max interjected. Get another camera set up at the far end of the mall, and put a third at the podium. No other cameras are to be made available, and all recordings are to be kept from the press until we edit the material and give it to them. They will have to use what we give them."

Max scanned the room, looking for his press secretary, Bill Staffman. He spotted him at the back of the room, looking rumpled and alienated. "Bill, I have ten Secret Service agents milling around on the lawn, and I need them to bring their bikes down to the kitchen immediately. If they ask why, tell them because I said so." Staffman looked puzzled and dejected, but turned to carry out orders. "And Bill, I need for you to do the narrative on the images we will release to the press, digitize the whole thing, and get copies to all major networks as soon as I am through with my speech." Staffman turned to Max and beamed. "That's what I'm talking about," he intoned. "I think I'm beginning to understand you, Mr. President. I can give them a clear message of vitality and optimism that they will never forget."

CHAPTER 48

As Max and Rachel made their way to the kitchen in the White House basement ahead of the entourage of security and staff, Rachel finally had the opportunity to ask questions. "Have you lost your mind? Why are we going down to the kitchen? What's so all-fired important that you are ordering everyone around? Talk to me!"

"If you let me get a word in edgewise, I'll tell you. Remember that surprise I promised? It's down here. Luke showed it to me last week. He has been keeping it a secret since Dad died, and you and he are the only living people in the world to know beside me, at least for the next minute or so."

Max opened the utility closet and stepped inside. He pulled out the floor buffer and moved it aside, leaving the small space unobstructed. Then he pulled Rachel inside and closed the door. He turned on the light switch and pushed hard on the hidden panel at the back of the closet, and it swung open with a hiss. Rachel gasped in wonderment as the lights illuminated the tunnel, extending into the darkness. The EMP pulse had not penetrated to damage the electronics, and the power source was provided by the White House's shielded emergency generator. They stood behind the electric car, plugged into its charger inside of a metal cage.

"Another Faraday cage," Max exclaimed. *I'm beginning to see them everywhere.* "This is our private passageway to Fairlane."

Max and Rachel scrambled into the electric car. Max turned the key, and the headlights shone brightly. He turned to his Secret Service contingent. They were busy mounting their bikes after a tight squeeze in the kitchen closet.

◆ ◆ ◆

"You know how I hate speeches, so I'll be brief. This is a secret, and I'll have your balls surgically removed if you breathe a word of this to anyone. Clear?"

"Yes, Mr. President!" They had been well-trained.

"You are about to embark on a high-speed bike ride beneath the Potomac to my house. This is a test of your fitness level and your devotion to your elite status as my protectors. I want five riders ahead, and five behind. Your assignment is to clear the way to Fairlane at the far end of this tunnel, and I have no idea what waits for us when we get there. You will establish communications with your team on site and with the White House, and you will equip every car in my garage with communicators that have a direct link to both locations. I have been advised that we can assume that there may be other EMP devices out there somewhere, so we will only be driving cars that were built before 1970," Max announced.

"Why?" Justin Armstrong was the first to speak. His puzzled look betrayed a lack of knowledge of nuclear weaponry, and he silently cursed his ignorance. It was a huge gap in his training, and he knew his lack of knowledge could place the president in danger. He vowed to become an expert before another device wreaked havoc.

"No electronics to fry," Max replied. "The same gamma radiation that comes from solar flares was emitted when that EMP device was detonated, and if you were lucky enough to get a newer car going again, another detonation would stop you dead in the middle of the road."

"Mr. President, we will have those cars delivered to your front door, gassed up and ready to go. Which one will you be riding in?"

"I'm partial to the red, '66 Vette, and I'll be doing my own driving," Max replied.

Max pressed the accelerator pedal and the electric car lurched silently forward. Around the first curve, the cyclists encountered a spider web that spanned the width of the tunnel, the large spider situated in the center of the passageway. The lead cyclist broke through ahead of the pack, parting the web with his head. A portion of the web, together with its builder, stuck to his black suit, and he sputtered, frantically trying to brush the arachnid away with his right hand.

"Max, this is creepy," whispered Rachel.

"Yeah, we'll have to do something about those things when I get half a chance," he replied, intent on the planning. "I encountered a big one last week when I was down here. I didn't know that they could spin a web that fast." Rachel moved closer to Max and held his arm tightly. Her fright was peaking. "You need to know that I was briefed on possible terrorist activity a few days ago, and again last night, and I ordered that they keep me in plain sight. The terrorists are homegrown, and I'm betting that they are staring at a black TV screen somewhere, just like the rest of the world. Any image they have is of me standing at the podium. Even if they have people on the ground communicating to them, the only idea they have of our whereabouts is that I holed up in the White House about ten minutes ago."

Under the well-established protocol of protecting the president, Max would have been whisked away to a secret command center under a mountain outside of Washington, along with a contingent of every available member of Congress, his cabinet, and military decision-makers. He had ordered that protocol be abandoned. He was safer being unpredictable, appearing in public at times and places that could not be anticipated. If he was correct in his assumptions, his enemy not only knew of the protocol for protecting the president, he had established it.

"Rachel will lead the way with the helicopter, and I want an agent to accompany her to communicate with our people on the ground and in the air. By the time we get back to the Capitol, I imagine our military will be everywhere, and I would appreciate it if you told them we are coming their way. I'd hate for some field commander with his finger on the button of a surface to air missile to see us as a threat, if you know what I mean."

Armstrong rode powerfully alongside the electric car, relaying commands to his subordinates in rapid succession. Max chuckled when he yelled, "Whatever you do, don't shoot at us, and don't shoot at Flygirl's helo. We'll be coming across the Theodore Roosevelt Bridge in fifteen clicks, and I want a path cleared direct to the steps of the Capitol."

Rachel remained nervous and unsure, her mind leaping forward in time. She had not received combat training, and evasive maneuvers would be a challenge if she encountered anything that remotely resembled ground fire. She shuffled in her seat and looked at Max with concern. "I'm not sure I'm ready for this," she whispered. He stared ahead, confident. "Don't worry, you're going to be fine. The last thing they will expect is to have us come back there from the opposite direction like some big magic trick," he replied.

Max knew that his ultimate goal would be to avoid mass panic, and to do that, he would need to be back at the Capitol quickly. Fear of the unknown was the immediate enemy. Without contact with the outside world, the public rumors would spread rapidly, and his ability to lead effectively would be lost. Above all, he had to be

detail to prepare Baby Belle for flight, do the pre-flight check, and call in my flight plan, but I suppose there's no time for that today. I assume there is nothing but military aircraft flying in my airspace right now." She paused at the sound of the Blue Angels flying over the Capitol far in the distance. It was accompanied by the unmistakable thrup-thrup of military helicopters beyond the horizon. The sounds underscored the need to get back in a hurry, and the revving of engines in Max's personal inaugural parade would soon be drowned out by the roar of her take-off.

She broke the embrace and looked into his eyes. "You had me from the first time you smiled in my direction, and I had you from the time you first saw me in a bikini, boytoy," she bantered. "Get back to work." Rachel turned to finish her pre-flight check, and Max's smile dissolved as his mind returned to the many tasks that lay before them. There would be time for passion once they had survived the day.

"Armstrong, notify the White House over our secure channel that I want every operable camera pointed in our direction when we come across the bridge, and tell Andrew Fox and Bill Staffman that I will need our footage edited, copies made, and distributed to the press. Then, I will need official copies delivered to all of the major networks by every means possible. Tell Andrew to splice me together a message of hope and leadership using my words, and I want it done by the time I finish speaking at the inauguration. Oh, and tell him this: No speeches. He'll know what that means."

By controlling the message and keeping it short, Max was assured that the press wouldn't have the opportunity to distort the meaning or put their editorial spin on it. He had to convey hope and leadership, or whoever had committed this despicable act of terrorism would have succeeded at severing him from the base of his power: the people.

CHAPTER 49

"Please, Mr. President, please."

Armstrong stood in Max's path, his six-foot-four height and broad shoulders providing a barrier between Max and the Corvette. He towered over Max, but his face showed a fear that made the muscular Secret Service agent seem vulnerable.

"What is it, Armstrong? You have your orders, and we need to get back," Max said.

"Sir, from the time I became a SEAL, I took an oath. I take it very seriously, and I have pledged my life on it."

"This had better be important."

"If you value your life, you will walk over to that bathroom, and you will put this fucking thing on, and you won't give me a hard time about it." He stood over Max and intruded into his personal space, square jaw set, and his attitude was necessary.

Max stood face to face with his protector, absorbed in thought and oblivious to the reason for the confrontation.

"Sir, I can't let you go out bare-naked." He held out a body protector, molded to fit Max, with a few enhancements to make him look more like a Spartan warrior than the President of the United States. It would stop a bullet. No politician would be protected from an attack to the head, but it was something.

"Armstrong, if they want to kill me, they'll just blow my head off."

"Humor me."

He stood immobile, and Max realized that if he was going to make any progress, this was a battle that he would never win. "OK, OK, I'll do it for you, Armstrong, but we will talk about this later."

"I want there to be a later, sir."

Max slipped the vest over his head and smoothed the Velcro straps around his torso. He changed back into his inaugural clothes inside the expansive garage as the security team scrambled to prepare for their departure. They brought a tool kit and extra points for each car, in the event that more EMP bombs were to follow. By their pre-electronic status, the only part of the cars that could disable their progress was the points, which transferred a spark between the distributor and the spark plugs. They would fuse together in the massive gamma radiation emitted by the nefarious devices, but it was a quick fix that any amateur mechanic could perform in a few minutes. It involved popping the distributor cap off, turning a screw, taking out the fused points, and installing the new points with a screwdriver.

Each was carefully wrapped in a metal screen and placed inside of a tool box lined with yet another Faraday cage.

He marveled at the metal mesh that covered the walls and windows of the huge garage, protecting the car collection from outside radiation. In the senator's estimation, it had been just a matter of time before a massive solar flare or EMP attack would occur, and in his certainty, preparation was the only remedy for his concerns. Before Max was born, at least before the senator had adopted him, Fairlane had been hardened from EMP radiation by the construction of Faraday shields around the sensitive electronics of the house and out-buildings. The senator had prepared his home for the almost certain eventuality of an attack on the nation's infra-structure, and Max saw his familiar surroundings with new eyes.

All power to the house was supplied by a photovoltaic array in the garden, together with a small hydroelectric dam in the stream that flowed through the woods on its way to the Potomac. He had never realized or appreciated the efforts of his father to make Fairlane independent from the utility company until that moment in time. All of the aspects of society that he took for granted were turned upside down, and without the senator's foresight, he would have been powerless to do anything about it. But not this day, and not this time.

"Let's roll!" announced Max as he slid behind the wheel of the Corvette.

Rachel put her flight helmet on her head and strapped in. Before she took flight, she tested the communication system. "Okay, boys! Let's make an entrance they'll never forget!" Her voice provoked smiles from even the most stoic of her protectors as the mini helicopter rose and propelled toward the nation's capitol.

CHAPTER 50

Scarlett and the White House staff assessed their situation from the oval office. They assumed that they wouldn't be there for long; security protocol is to get the president and his family to safety, and to maintain order, and the next step is to relocate the vice-president to a secure location. But this day, the security protocol was scrapped in favor of the president's unorthodox inaugural plans. All communications had been knocked out, and any unshielded electronics inside a 12 mile radius of the detonation were useless. The head had been figuratively severed from the body. Max was temporarily unable to communicate with the nation, and the vultures were undoubtedly circling.

"I am going to need a few minutes to freshen up before I go back out there," Scarlett announced. "I want the public address system back up and running before I take that podium, and someone will need to find a car that is still running, because I will not be getting on the back of a horse ever again... do you understand me?" She barked out the commands to the assemblage of staffers that clustered around her, waving off their futile efforts at returning her appearance to her high standards. "Somebody find me my shoes!" She looked at her tattered hosiery with dismay. "Never mind! I need an entire outfit, and it better be spotless," she exclaimed, as several young assistants scattered in opposite directions. "Don't just stand there, do something! Now!"

Roger Sinclair stood impassively, waiting for an opportunity to speak with the vice-president alone. As the last of the staffers vacated the room in a hurry, he stepped forward until he was in the mirror's reflection. He waited until Scarlett acknowledged his presence. She paused from applying her lipstick long enough to address him.

"Hello, Darlin', it is so gallant for you to assist a lady in her time of dire need," she chimed in her best Charleston accent, 'but I thought you were in Philadelphia".

"I was, but I rushed back late last night to attend to some unfinished business. Besides, I'm beginning to think that you are getting used to having me around," he replied.

"Right now, I need a handyman, and you're handy," she responded. "I don't know a thing about how to get the power back on, and there are just too many tasks to perform."

"We need to unpack the Tesla generators and get them out there to the Mall," said Sinclair, still smiling from the greeting from his clandestine lover.

"You are going to get us caught, and I don't trust the staff to keep a secret just for me. News of my assignation with a man of your character would surely bring enough money to one of my poor ladies to pay for a bodacious townhouse, walking distance from here," Scarlett responded, ignoring his words for the moment. He held her tenderly in his arms, the first brief opportunity for them to be together in weeks. She craved his touch, nestling deeper. Suddenly, she pushed him away with a start and the look of pleasure transformed to a serious scowl.

"I mean it, Roger. I'm vice-president of the United States, and I take my position with all of the solemnity that the oath inspires. Y'all will just have to wait until I am through with this glorious day and can get out of these clothes. Now, what was that yammering about a Texas generator?"

"Tesla, he replied. Tesla generator."

Scarlet gave him a blank look.

"Are you making that up just to impress me?"

"No, my love, it's one of those secret inventions that will change the world, that's all, and we are going to use one to put the power back on. You want your speech to be heard by all of those people out there, don't you?" Roger replied.

"You know I do, and I want the world to hear. But the president, Max, conveyed a message to me to wait until he gets back, and he is the president after all," she said while applying the last adjustments to her makeup. "Right now, I think I'll be leaving those details to you," she said, rising to allow Roger to help her with her coat. He paused, debating whether to tell her the bad news, and decided to wait until her speech had been delivered. There would be a live audience, but no live coverage. Washington had been shut off from the rest of the world until satellite broadcasts could be restored, a reality of their situation that would best be delivered later by someone who could take the brunt of her anger.

Sinclair had met her during her first term, at a soiree held for freshman members of Congress. He was younger than her by a few years, but his stories from behind the scenes in the political world held a fascination for Scarlett that surpassed age. He considered her intelligence and exuberance for life to be an aphrodisiac, and he pursued her for over a year before she looked at him in a romantic way.

Throughout Scarlett's career in Washington, her love life was unknown to the press and the public. Owing mainly to the total lack of public appearances by Scarlett with a man or woman on her arm, the rumors hounded her. She kept her private life concealed from the public by design: First, it got her the sizeable gay and lesbian vote, but also, it kept the press guessing, all to her delight. It was free publicity, the lifeblood of the politician, and a huge fund-raising asset. In her estimation of life as it should be, Roger was the perfect mate; anonymous, interesting, and available, but only when she wanted him around.

"I need to focus. You need to get out there and get things back to normal," she commanded. "You don't expect me to go out there and set up the equipment myself in front of a hundred thousand people, do you? There are people who do that sort of thing for a living, and besides, I have already taken care of it. By the time you get your dress back on and head back out the door, I'll have the lights back on and a helicopter waiting to lift you over the waiting multitude," he replied. Sinclair was painfully aware that things would not be back to normal, and it was not the time to instruct Scarlett on the effects of an EMP detonation and how gamma rays render unshielded electronics useless. For the time-being, she only needed to be reassured that the power was restored and she would be able to make her pre-empted speech. Changes in the program did not come easily to Scarlett, and he knew that she had memorized the order of events days before the inauguration. She would not tolerate further change without making everyone in shouting distance extremely uncomfortable.

The aide returned with Scarlett's blue backup dress, which she had passed up in favor of the red only two hours before. They were identical in every respect except for the color, and the appearance of the familiar took the edge off of her agitation. "Oh, thank you for small pleasures," she cooed. Suddenly, she scowled. "Where are my blue shoes? I can't wear a blue dress with red shoes! Find them!" The blushing aide, anticipating her wrath, scrambled out of the room without a reply.

The helipad on the White House grounds was occupied by Marine Two, the president's personal helicopter, summoned hastily from its shielded hangar at Andrews Air Force Base. Communications had been restored for most of the military and Secret Service, but the Park Service Police that were charged with crowd control had been rendered silent due to their lack of shielded communication devices. They steered the crowd from the back of horses and bicycles, reminiscent of cowboys in the old West. For the moment, they were the only visible means of transportation other than by foot. Sinclair watched from the Lincoln bedroom as Scarlett entered the craft, trailed by three aides who still clung to their wireless communicators, a useless appendage for the moment, but a habit not easily broken.

CHAPTER 51

Max and the parade of classic American cars returned to the Inaugural in unexpected style, with Rachel leading the way. Her co-pilot was a Navy Seal who was personally assigned to her protection due to his ability to fly anything that had been built for that purpose, with the exception of the Space Shuttle, which had been mothballed before he obtained his wings. If it had still been in service, Rick Vance would have been an astronaut, not assigned to the protection of the woman most important in the life of the president of the United States. When he first received his duty assignment, he assumed he was doomed to a life of public appearances and boredom, but his first month on the job was contrary to all of his expectations. Rachel was exotic, exciting, smart and beautiful, and he harbored a secret crush for the woman he was duty-bound to protect. If he hadn't married his high school girlfriend and had two young kids to whom he was devoted, he may have pursued his feelings, but the nagging thought of being re-assigned to a remote post in the Antarctic lingered in the back of his mind.

Vance would coordinate their re-entry to Washington by a communicator that was shielded and hardened from radiation. He and the security detail on the ground were uncertain whether there would be multiple EMP devices to contend with, and communication during their return was essential to their ability to stay in flight. He admired Rachel as she flew low and in front over the procession, competent and in control. He allowed himself the luxury of a brief fantasy that she might someday be attracted to him, but he was certain that he would never be the apple of her eye. Like all of the Secret Service assigned to protect her and the president, there was a line that could never be crossed by the most base of cads without dire consequences, and he had a keen sense of the obvious.

The procession emerged onto the Beltway and wound around immobilized cars that appeared in their path at sparse intervals. The occupants had moved on, and the vehicles that remained created an obstacle course that they maneuvered in a snake-like fashion. Twice on the way, Rachel and Vance radioed about obstacles ahead, and one time, the procession on the ground stopped to clear the path, heaving a Cadillac Escalade onto the passenger side. It lay in silent repose, its four wheels pointing toward the center lane. There was a death-like quality to it, and the thought was chilling.

They picked up speed as they approached the Roosevelt Bridge, but slowed to a crawl as they made the right turn that took them along the Potomac toward the National Mall. Rachel hovered above and shouted with excitement to those below, "It looks like they got the lights back on! The whole place is glowing! It looks like nobody left the party, but then again, how could they?" The crowd turned at the sound of the approaching helicopter. When they could make out the driver of the shiny Corvette, they gasped and cheered.

On either side of the bridge, the crowd stood shoulder to shoulder, packed close in anticipation. In front, the TV cameras were strategically placed to provide the maximum effect of their return. Max waved, and the cheering became louder. The Park Service was on horseback, shooing back any of the observers who stepped off the curve into the broad avenue.

Max drove slowly past the Lincoln Memorial, while Rachel found the only landing area ahead that was not occupied, the center of the reflecting pool. The illusion of depth provoked a few screams, but she settled slowly into the eighteen inch deep water with no difficulty. Her landing was immediately followed by the Park Service dry platform, which had been extended from the edge of the reflecting pool to the landing struts by the time she emerged. She waited as Max approached, waving to the crowd in her flight suit. The sound of the crowd's approval was loud and enthusiastic, causing her to blush at the attention. Max left the Corvette idling at the curb and rushed in her direction. By the time she stepped onto the platform, he was there with his arm outstretched.

They returned to the closely guarded Corvette with arms linked. Max gallantly opened the passenger door to more applause. The etiquette lessons he had been taught as a child were now natural behavior to him as an adult, and this display of civility toward Rachel was not lost on those who looked to him as an example. By doing what was second nature, he was showing a part of his upbringing that had been lost to society as America declined over the previous decades. He had to show how a man treats the woman he adores as much as he would show how the president would treat a foreign dignitary. The Maxims would be followed without question.

Max hopped into the Corvette and the colorful procession of classic American cars proceeded down Pennsylvania Avenue toward the Capitol. Their clear view of the monuments was obscured by the crush of humanity, but they towered in the background. This was the playground of Max's childhood. Even if his vision was obstructed, he knew they were there, and he could detail them in his memory. First was the Lincoln Memorial, then the Washington Monument and finally, the Jefferson Memorial. Behind them to the west was a grand sunset, with the orange and yellow succumbing to reds and purple as the setting sun sunk toward the horizon.

Max was aware of the danger that sitting in a convertible posed for him. It hadn't worked well for Kennedy, and since 1963, no president had traveled a public route in a convertible exposed to a sniper's bullet. But this was Max Masterson, who was so adept at appearing where he was least expected that his security advisors had named it "pulling a Max". Their code name for him was "Wizard", for his ability to vanish in one place and reappear where he was not expected. If he could keep them guessing, he could stay alive. At least, that was his untested theory. Too much of his time was spent keeping him safe, and not enough time was spent with those who adored him, he figured, and he made his bold presence felt in person and electronically whenever possible. This drove his protectors crazy. The unpredictable has that profound effect on people.

All of this was contrary to the established protocol for protecting the president, which caused the "assassination pot" to grow to an enormous amount. The pot was a secret betting pool available only to those cynics in government at CIA, FBI, and Homeland Security. Anyone who was entrusted with actually protecting Max was banned from betting for obvious reasons, but that didn't stop the rest of them from trying to predict the day that Max would prematurely leave office.

None of his disdain for convention was appreciated by those whose job it was to keep him alive, but they had been duly warned before he was voted into office. The newly-elected president was going to do it his way, and millions of people were watching him do it in the most exposed and defiant way possible. In the real world, it was the equivalent of watching a NASCAR race in the hopes of watching a fatal wreck. They didn't know the when, but they knew that it was likely to happen, and the longer he stayed alive, the bigger the pot grew.

To add spice to the mix, he was being led back to his inaugural by his girlfriend, flying a helicopter, and followed by a parade of classic

American cars. They drooled in anticipation, with the hardcore cynics putting the most of their money on Inauguration Day. The press would label the detonation the "Inaugural Event". It was intended to disrupt Max's swearing-in as president and send him into hiding as a part of Pryor's grand plan. It was not intended to kill.

The short procession drove slowly through the crowd toward the steps of the Jefferson Memorial, where Max was scheduled to make his inaugural speech. The excitement was palpable, larger in scale than event planners could create in their wildest imaginations. For the rest of the world, it would be a non-event until the broadcast disk found its way into the hands of the media capable of broadcasting the events of the day. Those in attendance would hear his words, followed by Scarlett's prepared speech. Then came the inaugural ball, which Max had turned into the world's largest lawn party.

As he drove the mile or so to the speech venue, he was impressed that the Mall was as lit and festive as planned before the terrorist attack. The Inaugural Event had been reduced to an annoyance, an interruption that would be talked about by conspiracy theorists for generations, but today, the nation's capitol had been returned to a place of celebration that had captured the attention of the world. Whoever was responsible for the attack had failed, and had only succeeded in boosting Max's attention factor. The words of Max Masterson would be heard, not silenced.

Scarlett stood at the podium, beaming. She had managed to control the crowd by taking the stage early and rousing her audience with bits and pieces of her stump speech, along with continuous updates of Max's location. She had disregarded Max's instructions in a dismissive way, informing Roger that, "How does he expect me to speak to the American people without speaking? I can't just get up there and show my pearly white teeth and smile them into the comfort zone, can I? I'll do nothing of the kind." She reverted into her Charleston accent in times of great stress, and diverting from her day's plan had ruined the sense of decorum that governed all of her actions. She had only partly recovered from her unladylike and unplanned horse ride to the White House, and to expect her to further deviate from the program. Scarlett's own sense of importance was only satisfied when she was the center of attention of large groups of people, the more the better.

When lulls occurred, chants of "Where's Max" would begin with a low rumble and spread from mouth to mouth until the volume nearly drowned out Scarlett's amplified voice. Finally, she asked for quiet. She didn't get it.

To the West, the sound of a helicopter could plainly be heard, and all heads turned in the direction of the sound. From the raised speaking platform, Scarlett could make out Rachel's helicopter, followed by a colorful assortment of cars extending to the limits of her vision. Then came the slow approach up the length of the National Mall, moving too slowly for her tastes. All attention was diverted in Max's direction until she could stand it no longer. Finally, she made the announcement they had been waiting for: "Ladies and gentlemen, the President of the United States!"

CHAPTER 52

Max ascended the stage in two- step bounds, not stopping to shake hands with the picket line of dignitaries who lined the sidewalk that led from his Corvette. There would be time for that later, and he was anxious to get his message out and be gone. Rachel was escorted behind him, still in her flight suit. In keeping with his purposeful lack of convention, this inaugural would be a visual message that would endure long after the words were forgotten. He had no place for meaningless tradition.

"America, thanks for electing me," he began. He paused and waited for the applause to die down, looking out at the faces pointed in his direction as far as he could see. It seemed that the crowd had swollen to double the previous size in the time that he was gone, and he realized that the Washington insiders who normally disdained political events in favor of the comfort of their living room had been forced to witness the event live. There was no power on the public grid, and they had nothing to do. Washington as usual had become a single-event city for the time being.

"It's been quite a day for all of us, hasn't it?" he continued.

"The difference is, when I woke up this morning, I knew it would be a big day. I didn't know that someone planned to mess it up for the rest of you and keep me from being your president in the first few seconds. I thought they would at least wait until after the party…" Laughter rolled through the attentive group like a wave.

"I ran for this office to help my country be great again. I stand here today to tell you that I will not, cannot, be kept from that goal." Those who were sitting stood. Those who were silent clapped and cheered.

"You're the one, Max!" The chant spread, and he waited. Pulling Rachel to his side, he gave her a tight hug as she looked in his eyes in adoration. They held each other, the image preserved by the few cameras spared from the gamma radiation of the EMP blast. He returned to the microphone and continued. "I was elected to be the president of everyone, not just a few. There are people who are intent on keeping me from doing the job you elected me to do, content with our present stagnation and malaise. I promise you; they failed today and they will fail tomorrow, and they will fail every day after that. We will return to greatness as a nation. The United States of America will not be defeated."

The applause was deafening. It continued for long after the thought of continuing had left Max. He had no teleprompter, and no notes. Just the heartfelt words he chose to speak. He had no intention of making a long-winded speech, and by the time Scarlett had completed hers, his words would be remembered, and her words would be largely forgotten. *Too much information turns off the mind to the core of the message, and I have said what I came here to say. I need for them to remember. Not just today. Every day.*

"There will be other days and other topics to speak about, and you know I'm not a politician." Scattered laughter came from his audience. He had used that phrase thoughout the campaign for the presidency, but he had never articulated the meaning. It was time. "The president of the United States should transcend politics. The one person you elect to serve you is the representative of our entire nation, every man, woman and child. I pledge to do just that. I will leave the politicking to the legislature. That's what you elected them to do, and frankly, they are better at it than I am. I am focused on making America great again, and to making your lives better than ever before." *I need to inspire, to give them hope.*

After the applause had subsided so he could be heard once more, Max concluded his brief statement. "I will not always follow the tradition of politics, but I will not shirk the responsibilities of my position. I chose Scarlett Conroy to serve as our vice-president for a very good reason. She is a politician, and she is the best there is. She will make the speeches and she will attend the hearings and she will be our link to Congress. She will communicate the thoughts and desires of our nation to your elected Senators and Representatives, and together, the United States of America will lead again." I present to you, Scarlett Conroy, our Vice-President."

As quickly as he had ascended the stage, he left it. Scarlett pulled a stack of cue cards from her pocket and approached the podium. Scarlett began her prepared speech, but paused when she realized that every member of the audience had turned their attention to watch Max take Rachel's arm and walk slowly toward the White House. Her distress at the lack of attention was revealed in her facial expression. Her moment in the center had been replaced with envy. The speech did not resume until they had disappeared in the crowd of admirers. Regaining her composure, Scarlett resumed the speech.

By the time she concluded, Max and Rachel had been at the White House for an hour, busily reviewing the digital record of the inauguration and directing the distribution to the press, who rushed it to the nearest operable computers that they could find. There was no time to edit. The broadcast was presented in a 24/7 continuous loop, with no voice-overs, no commentary, all as Max had intended.

CHAPTER 53

I have silenced Max Masterson with the push of a button," exclaimed Adam Pryor with delight. "His new ideas are threatening to our way of life. We must band together to rid ourselves of this menace once and for us all."

A silver-haired man stood in a corner, quietly assessing the situation. He and the privileged members of the group had pledged to never refer to the membership by name, but he was known by all as the Chairman of the Board of Universal Petrochemical, a conglomerate of oil and gas companies that had a virtual lock on the price of petroleum and the multitude of products produced by petroleum.

Three generations before Doyle Effingham IV was born, his great-grandfather had single-handedly began the first purchase of oil from the Saudi royal family, and the organization immediately amassed enormous wealth that rivaled that of the sheikhs themselves. As Pryor spoke in his high, annoying tone, Effingham quietly placed his martini on a (antique French) table and purposely spilled it, causing the attention of the membership to be momentarily turned in his direction. Without a word, he strode confidently to the front of the room and stood several feet in front of Pryor, well within his comfort zone. "I assure the membership that Masterson will be cast from office and we will regain…" Pryor stopped in mid-sentence.

"Why don't you just kill the Son of a Bitch? It's not entirely unprecedented, you know," said Effingham in measured tones that betrayed his Yale background.

"My esteemed colleague," began Pryor, his voice rising to match his exasperation, "…surely you recall that Masterson received over eighty percent of the popular vote in the general election, and I am certain you remember what happened when Kennedy was dispatched on your father's watch, and how his death elevated him to martyr status, and how…"

Effingham interrupted again, betraying his lack of respect for the former Director of Homeland Security. "You will not pawn your incompetence on me, my family, or the esteemed members of this assemblage." Effingham's cheeks reddened with anger. "We pay you an enormous amount to ensure that our interests are protected, and in my estimation, you are a blundering idiot. Did it occur to you to have someone on the ground to report to us what happened after you set off that device? Did you?" His anger had turned into fury, and murmurs spread throughout the room. The membership had begun voicing their concerns in hushed tones.

"That's the problem with disruption of cell transmissions," Pryor responded. They won't have any way of transmitting a signal until they repair the cell towers. That should take days, and if the Secret Service is following established protocol, Masterson, Conroy, and a good portion of Congress are in a hidey hole under a mountain somewhere, cut off from the inaugural for days. I set out to illegitimatize the Masterson presidency. It's Phase One."

The assembled elite stood silent for a moment, watching the darkened screens, oblivious to the flurry of activity at the inaugural. The detonation had deprived the world of the delight of being electronic witnesses to history, but all unshielded electronics had been fused by gamma radiation, and that included all broadcasts from the National Mall that had been terminated when the electronics were fried.

Effingham strode purposely to the table that held the remote and activated the screens. Glenda Reasoner was the first to appear, with the footage of Max waving to the crowd from a candy apple red vintage Corvette, with the Washington Monument looming above a mass of humanity who were smiling and clapping. Masterson's girlfriend was seated next to him in a flight suit. "Our new President, Max Masterson, makes a grand entrance to the inaugural celebration, not thwarted by..."

Effingham changed the channel, and Glen Aspect appeared, with footage of Max standing at the podium in front of the Jefferson Memorial, the Presidential Seal prominently displayed on the front. In a voiceover, Aspect commented on the "Inaugural Event". "It may be an apt description, America, but Inaugural Disruption may be more accurate. Within an hour of the detonation of a device that we are only beginning to understand, Masterson had power restored and made a glorious return to his place on the podium." The camera zoomed into Max's confident face. The screens went dark again. Effingham threw the remote to the marble floor, where it shattered with dramatic effect. "He doesn't look like he's in a hidey hole to me. Your perfidy will not be rewarded. Fix it." He turned briskly and walked out of the room.

CHAPTER 54

After the festivities subsided, Max retreated to the Oval Office as Rachel slept in president's quarters, exhausted. The Oval Office lacked Max's brand, so he installed a plaque on the credenza behind his desk. It was a gold list, the Maxims. Created by his father and followed to the letter, the rules by which he would govern were a reminder of how the office of the presidency would transcend politics:

THE INFORMED WILL OF THE PEOPLE DICTATES WHAT IS RIGHT.
MAINTAIN WHAT IS RIGHT AND RIGHT WHAT IS WRONG.
EDUCATE THE PEOPLE BEFORE ASKING THEM TO DECIDE AN ISSUE.
AMERICAN INTERESTS MUST PREVAIL OVER FOREIGN INTERESTS.
MAKE AMERICANS AWARE THAT THEY ARE A PART OF THE WORLD.
IT IS BETTER TO CONFESS THAT YOU DON'T KNOW THAN TO LIE.
DON'T QUOTE A STATISTIC UNLESS YOU CAN BACK IT UP WITH FACTS.
PERSUADE, DON'T DECEIVE.
COMBINE STRENGTH WITH COMPASSION.
MEASURE EACH DECISION BY WHAT IS BEST FOR AMERICA.
ABOVE ALL ELSE, BE A PATRIOT.

Max sat alone, gazing at the gold plaque absent-mindedly. It was his first time in the Oval Office without the web of people that went with the job, and for once, he could relax. His time alone was brief, he knew, but it was his time, and he knew how he would spend it. He opened the concealed drawer and pulled out the gilded diary, turning to an early entry written in the familiar cursive of Thomas Jefferson. It seemed to glow, and in his mind's eye, it spoke to him in a resonant voice, using a dialect that he was certain was Jefferson's.

"*Thy mind is troubled with the concerns of state, I see.*"

Max closed the book quickly, and the image of Jefferson disappeared. He opened it to the same page, and Jefferson returned to his mind.

"*Thou art connected to the universal intelligence as was I, and those who legitimately came to this office before and after,*" said the genius of Monticello. Max was perplexed, and strained to understand what was happening. Without uttering an audible sound, he spoke to Jefferson.

"*Can you hear me?*"

"*Yes, and thee can hear me.*"

"*But how is it that I am talking to you, after being dead for hundreds of years,*" Max questioned. "*Are you a ghost?*"

"*Where does one go after death? The mortal flesh may depart, but the spirit remains in those who wish it so. The diary channels the thoughts of the spirit to those who are fit to receive. Thus it has been and will be until the last word is written,*" he responded with a clarity that resounded in Max's heart.

Jefferson continued his advice with an urgency that Max could feel inside of his mind, prompting him to focus with an intensity that he had not felt before. "You can see those who came before you, who occupied this oval office and who wrote these words." He pointed at the diary, which glowed with increased intensity. "*You need only to be alone in this room and in need of wisdom. We can hear the words that trouble your mind.*"

"There are many issues I would like to discuss, but time is short. You know my concerns, so I will listen to what you have to say," Max spoke tentatively.

"Thou must speak thy mind," Jefferson responded. *"Thou art fearful of enemies in the mist, who may strike from places hidden from your sight. Your concerns are not for yourself, but for our nation. The enemies have different names and occupy a different time, but they have always been lurking, regardless. Thou must resist their attempts to remove thee from favour with thy countrymen."* In their internal discourse, Max noticed that Jefferson's manner of speaking was becoming more contemporary as he spoke.

"What should I do about my enemies?" Max's mind was preoccupied by Pryor, who had disappeared from office the day before the election, and prior to his briefing by Roger Sinclair.

"You have but one enemy, but he wears many disguises. Your single enemy is composed of many parts. When you cut off but one part, your enemy lives on, manifesting in others. There is no single person to defeat. Focus on defeating ideas that threaten your presidency, and the rest will follow." Jefferson stood, examining his shoes. His appearance was evolving in Max's mind's eye. There was no powdered wig, and no leggings. It was the visage of Jefferson, but he sported modern clothes.

"I know not what animal gave its skin to make these, nor what color its hide, but my aching feet are pleased." He bounced around the room in his plastic soled shoes, transformed from the high riding boots he wore in his time. Once he had reveled in his comfort to his satisfaction, he sat again. *"The enemy is an idea, and in that idea there are many linked common beliefs. The key to defeating this gargantuan beast is in numbers of like-minded warriors of your own enlistment, but remember,"* Jefferson shifted in the chair and leaned forward. *"It is as useless to argue with those who have renounced the use and authority of reason as to administer medication to the dead."*

Having imparted as much wisdom as he chose for the moment, Jefferson sat back and marveled at his appearance. "*These trappings are light and airy. Wool can be so scratchy,*" he commented on his new appearance. "*Why is my hair not like yours?*" Jefferson inquired. He touched his red hair, still long and tied at the back.

"*There are a lot of men still wearing your style in my time,*" Max replied.

There was a knock at the door to the Oval Office, and the image of Thomas Jefferson vanished.

Max recovered from his dream state and quickly deposited the diary in its secret drawer. Luke Postlewaite shuffled into the room, looking rumpled and exasperated. Without bothering to sit down, Luke approached the ornate desk and placed both hands on the edge. Peering at his life-long student with the grayed eyes of age, he wasted no time with formalities.

"You're fucking up," he said without the slightest hint of reverence for the office.

"How?"

"You need to get your ass out from behind that desk, get out of this political museum, and go out there and do your job." He paused to catch his breath, and continued. "I have been sitting awake, watching the major news programs, three at a time, Max, three at a time, and they are starting to turn on you." He was agitated, that was definite. "Somovich and Aspect, and Glenda, who is an old friend of mine, to boot, even she has been sniping at you. Your popularity will never be higher than now, Max, and I'm not going to sit back and watch you squander your only opportunity to accomplish your destiny in the way you have been taught." He sat hard in the leather chair and scowled, gasping for breath.

"What are they saying about me?"

"You'll see, you'll see," he muttered, fumbling his communicator to produce each video clip in succession. "You aren't making any news, and they have to report something, so they have turned on you already."

The holographic image appeared above the desk in 4-D. The Willie B. Somovich program, "Willie B Right" came on first, his lacquered helmet hair shining in the studio lights. Music heavy with percussion instruments preceded the appearance of the host, followed by a close-up of Willie's reddened shining face. He was in his element, and gauging from his smile, he had his distorted version of news to tell.

"Max Masterson is in his first weeks of the four-year term in office, and I gotta tell ya, America, he sucks." Canned cheers and applause followed his opening statement as intended. "I want you to know, America, that Max has let us down, and he hasn't made it a month. Our nation's capitol has yet to recover from the Inauguration Day Event, and the rest of the nation, me included, want to know; " Max, are you going to be just like the rest? When you address the nation in two weeks, I want to hear, Hell, all of us want to hear, how are you going to lead this once-great nation? I will open the lines to our callers, but first, a message from our sponsors."

Glen Aspect was the next to chime in, pompously injecting his opinions in a sixty second monologue at the start of The Glen Aspect Show : "Max Masterson is refusing to provide his official birth certificate once more, my fellow Americans. The Freedom of Information Act, the Constitution of the United States, and the American people demand justice. He hides inside the White House, the official residence of legitimate holders of the office of president, and we don't even know if he is one of us." Aspect walked over to a large photo of the White House at night, using his trademark pointer for effect. "Yes, there it is, you see that light on in the Oval Office? That's where he sits, plotting and planning with our enemies to overthrow our way of life."

Aspect had no basis in fact for his allegations, and the sensational charges had been created by his staff of writers less than two hours before the show aired. When he walked into the studio that morning, he had no idea what he was going to say, but the slick and polished monologue had carried the air of truth: Max was adopted, and despite the desperate search for his original birth certificate, all that his campaign staff could provide to the press was a copy ordered from the State of North Carolina where he had been born.

His natural parents were killed in a fiery car wreck on a road near Senator John Masterson's Fairlane estate, and since his rescue as an infant and adoption by the Senator, Max had been his son. There were no surviving blood relatives. His true date of birth had been a mystery to him until the names of his parents had been tracked back to the hospital where he was born. All Aspect needed for conjuring up suspicion was to question whether the newly-elected president was natural-born. It made no difference that his natural parents were American citizens.

It was a miracle that his opponent, William Blythe, and his spin doctors hadn't stumbled upon that strategy to question his background in the mud-slinging late days of the campaign, but they had focused on digging up dirt on Max in an area that they assumed would be fertile; his love life. In the end, they came up with no scandal. No jilted old girlfriends, no perversions and no lapses in discretion. In the end, they only succeeded in elevating Max's electability.

The last commentator had been one of Max's few supporters in the press during his campaign. Glenda Reasoner appeared, dressed in her trademark Caribbean blue power suit, which comprised the bulk of her on-air wardrobe. It existed in many variations, all of the same color. Highly respected in the broadcast world, her image appeared six days each week to millions of devoted viewers in the United States and throughout the world.

"Our new president, Max Masterson, has been a disappointment on this, the first report card of his administration. Our nation is in tatters." The music rose, and the producer broke for a commercial break, a 30 second spot touting the latest male erection drug, Maximo, which showed a dark-haired man with a hairy chest hovered over the reclined nude body of an obviously inspired woman, who pursed her lips in an "O" . The scene flashed to the afterglow, with the woman smiling and winking at the camera, as a baritone voice boomed, "Maximo, for your mutual pleasure." Glenda returned to the image, apparently unaware that her serious intro had been followed by a pharmaceutical commercial for "male enhancements".

"Max Masterson has become soft on terrorism," she began.

Luke turned off the hologram projector, and Glenda vanished. "What happened to all of your training, your Maxims? You need to speak the truth, do what's right for this country, quit worrying about what your critics think. You don't silence your critics, Max. You listen to what they have to say, but you sure as hell don't change your ways because of them. Remember, if you travel with the herd, you are no different from the ass in front of you."

The last comment by his elderly mentor made Max smile. He had heard that phrase almost daily since he had begun his training by Luke and his father. It was a mantra, and it was meant to set him apart. Great presidents were clear in their purpose, and their strongly-held beliefs were woven into history. Challenges were meant to be conquered, and problems were meant to be solved.

"You need to find out who is messing with you, and put them out of your misery," Luke said in a whisper. *That's pretty much like Jefferson just told me a few minutes ago,"* Max thought to himself.

"It's not that easy," replied Max. I have my people working on it, but they have me on lockdown. I can't go anywhere without a formal itinerary, and advance teams. Then they alert the press to where I'm going to be. It's crazy."

"Sneak out. You're good at it. We can get together with someone at CIA to whip you up a disguise, and…"

"No government involvement. You are going to have to do this yourself, and find someone good. Maybe one of your Hollywood friends. I can't trust anyone affiliated with a government agency until I know more. And Luke? This has to be as confidential as our little secret about the tunnel. Nobody, and there are no exceptions, is to know that I am going to go out without security, or the disguise I will be using. "

CHAPTER 55

I suppose we need to talk," said Max suddenly.

"Yes, Mr. President."

"I know you're not used to protecting someone like me."

Armstrong smiled, revealing dimples that grew into creases. He didn't smile much, and the effect was disarming. "Mr. President, I believe that observation will go down in history as the biggest understatement in the history of the English language."

"I know, I'm trying to be good, but it's hard. I don't think like those bobble-heads in this town, and I'm kind of a rebel when it comes to doing things the usual way."

Max stood and walked to the far side of the Oval Office. He was aware that every word spoken in the White House was monitored. Advances in technology had snuffed out the concept of the private conversation. To speak to anyone in confidence in Washington D.C., a person needed to go find a cave somewhere.

"I cannot, and will not, be sequestered in some bunker while the whole nation is under attack. I need to be out there with people. I need to know what they are thinking, and I can't do that by being tucked away and safe. If you make me into some fish in an aquarium, I'll quit. We need to work out something that makes both of us happy." Max paced as he talked, and Armstrong was immediately caught up in his intensity.

"Sir, I have done a lot of tossing and turning about that."

"Well, what do you think? I respect your opinion, and you should never bite your tongue around me. If you feel strongly about something, I want you to tell me."

Armstrong hesitated, longer than he would in most intense situations. His training required immediate, unequivocal action. Recalcitrance was acceptable, but not with an ally.

"Dammit, when we're alone, can I call you Max?" He was perspiring, wondering whether he had crossed the line of authority. He was familiar with the anxious. He thrived on it, but this was new territory.

"Justin, when we're alone, we can use first names. It's more comfortable that way. The only difference between you and me is that I'm the President of the United States, and you're not." It was Max's turn to smile.

"Max, if you don't quit doing all of this crazy-assed stuff, I'm going to end up scraping your bloody corpse off the sidewalk, and after I get done being a pallbearer, I'll be out of a job."Max appreciated the candor. He was tired of the ass-kissers, the people who had the right words for the occasion, but feared the truth and had no ideas.

"Justin, you guys have been trained to whisk me away at the first hint of trouble, like a rabbit who smells danger. You think that if you hide me away, you're doing your job. If you build this invisible barrier between me and all of the possible ways I can die, I'll live to politic another day. That's not how I choose to live. I'll die someday, but not before my time. I intend to make my mark on this world in my own way, and nobody, not you, not anyone, is going to take my mojo away."

"Max, that's what keeps me awake. I have to take all that I have been trained to do, and adapt."

"Now you're talking." Max tapped a hidden latch on the wall, that opened his access to the wet bar. He helped himself to a cold Perrier, and poured three fingers of scotch into a crystal glass.

"Want some?"

"Well, now that you're asking, I'd take a triple shot of Jack, neat."

"Get it yourself."

Armstrong smiled. He knew he was pushing it, and he had reached the limit of the president's effort at being a regular guy. He stood, towering over Max, and helped himself as the president took a long sip and made his way back to his desk.

"Justin, how did you end up guarding me instead of sitting in a trench in some God-forsaken desert somewhere?"

"Well Sir, we Seals prefer water to deserts, and I got a chance to take down a bad guy a few years ago in Pakistan." He took a long sip, draining the glass. "… so they kicked me up the ladder. I kept getting kicked up that ladder until my ass ended up here." He relaxed a bit, but his back remained ramrod straight, poised to move. It was rare when he settled back into the comfort of a chair.

"Look, if we're going to do this my way, and we are going to do it my way whether you or anyone else like it or not, you need to follow a few guiding principles," said Max in a commanding tone. First, I will not give anyone my agenda. Those press secretaries and schedulers are going to hate me for this, but I want to keep everyone guessing about where I will be next. If we deem it necessary, this will involve the use of misinformation, delivered from official and reliable sources, but anytime I go anywhere, we will be vague or outright deceptive. I have no faith that the press can keep a secret, and they will do anything to get an exclusive, so I amuse myself from time to time by messing with their heads. Over the years I have become an expert at doing just that. " Max drained his ever-present glass of sparkling mineral water that appeared on his desk anytime he was in the Oval Office.

"Roger that," replied Armstrong. *He doesn't realize that I have spent all of my free time and some of my duty time researching this president, and the more I know about his methods, the more I admire the genius of his Maxims. It's not reality. It's the appearance of reality... He's got me sold on that one already.*

"Speeches will be pre-recorded and short, and any questions about my words will be explained by my vice-president, my press secretary, and my chief of staff. I will not waste my time answering questions about the message. Understood?"

"Yes, Sir."

"Now, we need to talk about security. Mine. You will not coop me up. I intend to spend more time at Fairlane than I do in this museum, and when I travel in public, we will pull a Max." Armstrong stood, a surprised expression overcame his face.

"How did you know we call it that?"

"I eavesdrop. I know you refer to me as Wizard, and when we entered the tunnel, you radioed ahead and said that Wizard was pulling a Max." He stood from behind his desk and stepped toward the door, signifying that their conversation was about to come to an end. "You were very careful not to broadcast your position, and you earned my respect. We will resume my self-defense class in one hour, and I expect you to teach me how to take down an opponent and disable him like a Seal. I hear that you can do it in four seconds." Max grinned.

"I can do it in three, but I can kill in two, Mr. President."

"You could kill a man in two seconds. How?"

CHAPTER 56

Max and Armstrong traded hand blocks in the basement of the White House, and they had been at it for the past 45 minutes, aggressive and athletic. They sweated and sparred, and they developed a mutual respect for each other.

"Mr. President...Max..." He hesitated long enough for Max to sweep his feet out from under him, and he was lying on his back looking at the lights in the ceiling.

"Well, up until now you didn't earn it, but now maybe you have. I haven't been pinned since high school," he quipped. Max helped him up off the mat, and they chose the opportunity to call it a day. "Max, you will never need to know, because me and my crew will never put you in a situation where that can happen. But I'll tell you," He took a long sip on his water bottle and continued.

"First, you lunge in like you're gonna hit. That's what they expect. But you don't hit, see, you take your hand, and you go past him like you missed. Then you grab the hair on the back of his head, and you pull it forward. Then you drive his nose into his brain with the palm of your other hand. If you don't see his eyes roll back in his head, ya got one hand on the front and one on the back and ya give his head a quick twist. I guarantee he'll be dead."

"Whoa...I don't suppose you practiced that much in Seal training."

"No, we got plenty of practice in the real world. It's guns and explosions that I worry about the most."

◆

CHAPTER 57

The call came in the middle of the night. Only immediate family had that ringtone, Neil Young's *Old Man*. Andrew has chosen it as a reminder of how much Dad hated it. He never knew why, but Dad would turn it off whenever it played on Oldies Radio. "Sings like a girl," he would mutter, and change the station on the satellite radio in his truck. Still, the song was a link to his childhood, and it was only reserved for family.

This time it was Mom, and he answered immediately. A call from Leila Fox from Michigan meant that something was seriously wrong. Most times, she dealt with it herself, whatever crisis arose. By the time Andrew became aware that Mom had resolved a problem without his help, she would always shrug it off and say, "Don't worry about me."

"Mom, what's wrong?"

"It's your Dad. His sugar spiked and he went into a coma. I put him in the wheelbarrow and got him into the truck, and I drove to Battle Creek like a bat out of hell, and you know how he hates hospitals, but he was in no condition to argue with me, and the doctors said…"

Andrew interrupted. If he hadn't, he would have to listen to the story until the bitter end to determine whether his father was dead or alive.

"Is Dad dead?"

"No, Sweetie. He's been in the hospital since last Sunday, and he has been going in and out of that coma, and the doctors are sending him home to die. It's his Alzheimer's. They say that there's nothing they can do for him." She sobbed, and he realized that Mom had finally encountered a problem she couldn't fix.

"When are they bringing him home?" Andrew had already begun the mental process of notifying the president and re-assigning his duties to other members of the White House staff, catching a flight to Detroit Metro, and driving the hundred miles to Marshall.

"He should be here by Noon. They are delivering a special bed, because he has bedsores, and I can't care for him like I used to, so hospice will be coming Monday through Friday, but not on the weekends, and I..."

He interrupted again. He didn't wait for his mother to admit that she needed his help. He already heard it in her tone of voice. It was already Thursday, and he needed to be there immediately.

"Mom, I'll get the first flight out of Reagan and I'll be there as soon as I can."

CHAPTER 58

I'm glad you're here." Sandra Fox hugged her brother, and reached for his carry-on bag. Andrew pulled back, and clutched it tighter. He was particular that way.

"Sandy, how's Mom?"

"Fine as can be expected. She grieved for awhile, and then she put her big girl pants back on and went out and roto-tilled the garden. She says it's better when the ground is still partly frozen, but I know it's because she couldn't think of anything else to do. She needed to go outside and get her hands dirty."

Andrew ran the image through his head. His mother, Leila, wielding the growling machine in her coveralls. When she wasn't tilling, she was planting, and then it was the growing and nurturing. Much later, after the sweat and toil had produced, came the harvesting of the fruits of her efforts. During that time she smiled, but until then, her face took on a fierce determination. She focused on the task at hand. It had to be that way, or it didn't get done. She had no patience for waiting until someone else to accomplish those tasks, and she bristled at the suggestion that she was too old or too weak to do it herself.

Andrew had inherited those qualities, and he had acquired a similar sense of invincibility. Nobody was going to convince him that he was too anything…not too young, too short, too inexperienced, too stupid or any of the negative excesses that began with "too".

"He was sick for a long time, and I wasn't here to help out. I feel like I dumped on you and Mom, having to tend to him and the farm. I feel awful about it," Andrew said solemnly.

"Well, get over it. You had other things to attend to, like taking care of that cute president of ours," She placed her hand on his neck and squeezed his trapezius muscle, as she had done hundreds of times before when they were kids.

"Ouch!"

She increased the pressure before letting go. *You would think that after all of this time, I would have seen it coming.* Andrew's sister was bigger than him, with broad shoulders and a disdain for makeup. He had always wondered about her sexuality, but it had never been high on his list of wonderables. He was too tied up in the Washington gig, that firestorm of self-centered thinking. He had a president to pay attention to, and from the start, his job was more like cat-herding while blindfolded than anything else he could imagine. There was no instruction manual that came with the job; he had to rely upon instinct and intuition to get through each day. He was frustrated, and he was adrift.

Andrew was relieved to be outside of the beltway for a few days. Without hesitation, Max had summoned him to the Oval Office, and Andrew had been the one to inform him of his father's imminent passing. They had shared the grief, and they shed a few tears. He had been embarrassed by his reaction to the news. When Max came around the desk and hugged him, the dam broke, and his eyes poured. Even in this time of national emergency, Max had demonstrated what it was to be human, and he knew that this private moment would not be shared with anyone. His grief would be shared with private dignity.

Max had an ulterior motive in sending Andrew home to Michigan, and Andrew was up to the task. Leila Fox had become an un-official cabinet member to the president. He could trust her to speak her mind. Without realizing it, she had her finger on the pulse of the nation, and her observations had been correct since the first day they met during the campaign. She was the old lady who kissed him on the cheek at the end of his sound bites and campaign ads, making him blush in front of the cameras. It was a tactic that endeared Max Masterson to the voters, and she took silent pride in her contribution to his surprising landslide victory

Leila had the ability to cut to the core of an issue, and if she saw that Max was messing up, she would inform him of that fact in her unvarnished Midwestern way. Andrew was assigned the task of gathering the thoughts and observations that Americans had about the president; to identify what he was doing wrong, and what he was doing right.

The ride from Detroit Metropolitan Airport in Sandra's Ford F-150 pickup was uneventful. The typically dismal Michigan winter had the appearance of a painting of a rural landscape that was done in browns and grays. The bright colors of life were reserved for summer. Andrew stared out at the fallow cornfields, with wisps of snow clinging to lifeless stalks that had remained after the harvest. It was difficult to picture the lush rows of green that would be "knee high by the fourth of July", as they were accustomed to saying in this part of the country, but he could trust that it would happen every year as it had always happened.

There were some things in life that could be trusted, and things that occurred in Washington that could be predicted, but trust was an alien concept inside the beltway. There would always be the next crisis, and there would always be the critics. It was Andrew's responsibility to sort out the issues of importance to the nation from the issues created by political enemies, and to advise Max on them. He was enlisted for that purpose. *I won't let him down.* They pulled onto the road that led to the farmhouse, and he pondered the responsibility that rested on his shoulders. It weighed on his mind, but it would wait until Dad had passed. His first priority would be to care for family, and allow his father die with dignity.

Andrew rushed in through the side door, which opened into the large country kitchen. The front door was for receiving guests, and he knew that Mom would be in her domain, preparing for guests. He gave her a warm hug.

"How is he?"

"Good as we can expect," she replied quietly. "When he's conscious, he still has a bit of the old Dad you knew, but he is not the same man. Hospice just left a few minutes ago, and he didn't like them much. I think they're wonderful, but when they were cleaning him up, he called the young lady a potlicker."

"Oh, no. What did you say?"

"I didn't have to say anything. I guess they get used to it. She was very kind, and told me that she had been called worse names."

Andrew made his way to the downstairs bedroom. It was dark in the room, but he could see his father's white hair in the open doorway. As he walked closer, he could see the outline of the hospital bed, with its frail occupant. His once strong and powerful father was little more than skin and bones. The sight of him so still, smaller than he had imagined, made him think he was too late. A wave of panic went through him. *I didn't get to say goodbye.* His vision became blurry, and he stopped to wipe the tears from his eyes. *I told myself I wasn't going to do this. Big boys don't cry. I don't care. He can't see my tears.*

There was a slight movement. Dad's chest was rising and falling slightly, his breathing so shallow that it had been undetectable. His eyes opened and he stared into his son's worried eyes.

"Hi, Dad."

"Hi, Andrew," Dad replied, and his eyes closed. His breathing stopped, and Andrew moaned with despair.

"He has been doing that for days now," Mom said. She had been standing silently behind her son, assessing but not speaking. "Every time he stops breathing, I think he's gone, and after about a minute, he starts up again. Your sister and I have been riding that roller coaster for a while now. This morning, we couldn't get a pulse, he stopped breathing, and we were sure. Then your Aunt Lois rang the doorbell, his eyes popped open, and his heart started up strong as ever." At that moment, Dad took three deep breaths and returned to his pattern of shallow breathing. "There he goes again. The old coot. He's hanging in there until our 60th anniversary tomorrow, I just know it. He was always stubborn that way." She turned, ladle in hand, and retreated to the kitchen.

Leila Fox liked to talk as she stirred the spaghetti sauce. "I got to worrying about you two when the lights went out at the inaugural. I thought the TV was on the blink again and called the cable company. They told me that there was some explosion in Washington, but that you were OK. I think they just told me that to get me to calm down. They didn't know any more about what happened than the Man in the Moon." She banged the spoon on the rim of the pot, and turned to the task of checking on the loaf of sourdough bread in the oven.

Andrew stood too close for her liking, an intrusion into her exclusive domain. "Get out of my kitchen. I don't need you to stand there gawking. Go out and do something." Andrew knew that if he had done the same as a child, she would have ordered him to go outside and play. He ignored her and retreated behind the breakfast bar, where he had sat on a stool and conversed with her from the time he could talk.

"Max is worried that he is messing up at being president, Mom."

Leila stopped in mid-stir and placed the spoon on the counter. She turned to face her son with a look of solemn concern. "I don't know much about politics. I worry about him too." She paused and bowed her head, and it looked as if she was praying. Tears filled her eyes. "I loved your father. He was the only man I ever kissed… that is until Max Masterson came along…" She blushed with the memory of a kiss on the cheek. "I tried every day to do my best, to please him and to care for our family. It's the only thing I know how to do. I can only see life through my eyes, and how our Max is responsible for caring for all of us. I worry about Max Masterson as much as I do you and your sister."

"Mom, he values your opinions. He trusts you without question," Andrew said in a soft voice.

"Sometimes I stop to think, how that every day we are making memories. I think about that, and I wonder whether I have made enough happy memories for my own children," said Leila. I feel sure that if families would be conscious of the fact that every-thing they do or say may one day be a memory, there would be less quarreling." She shifted from the pot holding the sauce to monitor the progress of the noodles that boiled in the big pot in the back. It was an intense process, cooking. ""You know, fewer harsh words." She stirred and shifted again.

Grabbing the handle to the oven door, she stooped, and in the same motion, acquired an oven mitt on her right hand. After a moment of assessment, the bread was brown enough, and was swiped from the oven in a move so expert that Andrew felt an urge to applaud. When Mom was stressed or distressed, she cooked. It didn't matter whether there were enough mouths to feed; she cooked, and if they didn't eat it, the product of her therapy was distributed to the lucky families down the road.

"The serious conversations in my life are conducted in the kitchen. It's better that way, with the aromas and the comfort food to take the edge off of the seriousness. There's too much seriousness in the world," Leila explained.

"You know, your Max got off to a bad start. Did they ever catch those terrorists? He needs to catch them. If he doesn't, they'll think they got away with it, and they'll do it again," she counseled.

"I'll tell him when I get back," Andrew replied.

Why didn't I think of that?

CHAPTER 59

The next three weeks were a roller coaster of emotion that engulfed and consumed. Dad slipped in an out of the coma in a regular pattern. His breathing would stop for a full minute and then he would take three gasping breaths, followed by another minute of shallow breathing. Sometimes, he would be conscious, but mostly he hovered in the twilight state between life and death. Several times a day, his pulse became so weak that Andrew, Sandy and Leila would gather at his bedside, certain that death had finally arrived. Then, like a cruel trick, the three breaths would bring Dad back from the brink.

"I don't know why it has to take so long," Mom muttered. "I'm not worried about your father. We had sixty good years together, and I will miss him, but we said our goodbyes long ago." She held his hand and squeezed, hoping that her husband would squeeze back. A sign, any glimpse of recognition, was all she needed. It had been days since Dad had been able to swallow, and he had begun refusing food and water. It was just a matter of time, but the lingering of it, that inevitability, was agonizing.

"I worry about you and your sister. I'll be fine. You need to go get some work done. I'll watch him for awhile. Now go. Try to get some rest."

"All we can do is try to make him as comfortable as possible," Andrew replied. Her words didn't require an answer, but he felt helpless. "I haven't slept for days. I try to get things done over the phone, and the White House staff is covering for me, but I can't focus. I can do virtual meetings by computer, but it's like being strapped to a desk as I watch a flurry of activity around me. Mom, I need to call Max." He left the bedroom before the flood of grief overwhelmed him. He retreated to his own room, and sobbed quietly before placing the call.

He was amazed when Max answered after one ring. His image appeared on the screen. He was seated at his desk at the Oval Office, his right hand placed on an ornate leather-bound book.

"I have been anxious to hear from you," Max said, dispensing with the formality of a hello.

"Well, I have been riding a roller coaster I can't get off," Andrew replied.

"Your grieving is just beginning. It takes awhile to get over. When he passes, it will seem unbearable, but it must be; it tears piece after piece away. In the end, you are laid bare to your emotions, your soul. We all go through it, but dying is the end result of living. You will survive this. It's a purging, and hopefully, a replenishing."

Andrew was silent, absorbing the wisdom. He had seen the deep concern on Max's face when he broke the news about Dad, and the same expression had returned. It was a focus that he had never seen in another human being; a form of non-verbal empathy that Max seemed to instill in everyone around him. At that moment, he needed that strength.

"How are things inside the Beltway?" He needed to change the subject before the tears returned.

"Oh, crazy as ever. It's crisis of the day time over here, but things are settling down. I'm sending the vice-president to the UN to make some damn fool speech to the Security Council about how we handled the inaugural event. She likes to make speeches."

"She does indeed. I'll bet that she had it written before you sent her to New York," Andrew said, relieved that he could take his mind off of the realities of life and death for the moment. "Are they putting Washington back to normal?"

"Washington DC has never been normal, will never be normal, but we are recovering in record time. They even got most of the cars towed from the Congressional Parking Garage, and insurance adjusters are prowling around adding up the damage. We'll be fine, for the time being. We are tracking down the perpetrators, and Sinclair will be briefing me at 1:00. As much as I hate to do this, I will need you to draft a statement to the American people that…"

"*ANDREW!*" Mom shrieked.

CHAPTER 60

Three days later, Dad's funeral was held, and the weather matched the mood. It was gray and misty and miserable, with wind that seemed to crawl inside the solemn dress clothes and coats of the mourners. It was a good turnout for such weather. Joseph Fox had lived out his life in the same small town in the house where he was born, and the duty of attending was mandatory. The weather was irrelevant.

Leila had been raised in Marshall, Michigan too, first noticing her future husband in the sixth grade. She stood at the graveside and scanned the faces of the crowd as the minister of their church spoke. When he had concluded, she turned and spotted two unfamiliar faces. An elderly couple in dark clothes stood at the back under an old maple tree, her arm in his.

"Andrew, go up there and find out who they are. I may be old, but I swear I have never laid eyes on those people before." Andrew followed her gaze and saw them. The man smiled, and something about his face was familiar. His curiosity had been piqued, too. He made his way through the mourners, who were intent on conveying their condolences. With his focus elsewhere, they moved toward Leila to do the same. Finally free, he walked up to the couple.

"You have my profound sympathy," the old man said, and extended his hand. His movements were fluid and quick, not the labored and slow efforts of an elderly person. Although the man's face was wrinkled and worn, his eyes were clear, a piercing green that Andrew had seen many times before.

"We thought we would pay our respects, and while we're up here, we thought we would give you a hand picking out your next girlfriend," said the man in a familiar voice. The woman giggled softly, holding her hand over her mouth.

"Max?"

"Rachel?"

"There's a cute one over there," Max teased.

"How? When? Why didn't you tell me?" Andrew was flabbergasted, and struggled to contain his excitement.

"Did you know that there are military jets that hold more than one person, and can get from there to here in under an hour? I suppose you flew commercial," Max replied, ignoring the questions.

"Yeah, and it's a blast to fly," said Rachel, smiling. "Top speed of 2500 miles an hour. I plan to see what she can do when we fly back together."

Their disguises were perfect. The only aspects of their appearance that had not changed was their eyes. They didn't wear wigs, but their hats had a gray-haired fringe that concealed their locks. The transformation from youth to old-age was amazing.

When Andrew had recovered from the shock, he returned to Leila's side. "Who are they?" she inquired. "Don't worry Mom, you know them. I invited them to dinner, and they will be staying with us tonight. You are in for a pleasant surprise."

CHAPTER 61

MAP OF MANHATTAN

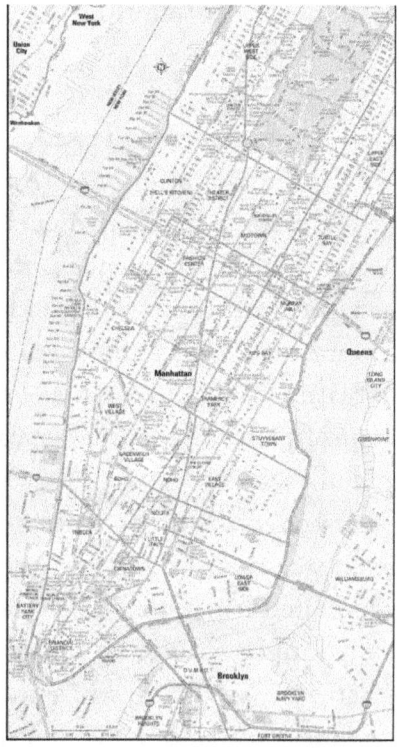

The hotel suite was ornate, with baroque scrollwork and gold accents. The enormous bed weighed over 300 pounds. Its latex mattress promised to provide a pampered sleep to Vice-President Scarlett Conroy, who had traveled to New York for a meeting as Chair of the United Nations Security Committee. The room was a perk of her position, assigned by President Max Masterson as a duty that she would be expected to perform during their term. She didn't mind. In fact, she relished the responsibility.

Scarlett was not only the vice-president. She also held the office of the position of the United States' ambassador to the United Nations. It was an honorary post, but it cemented the world's image of the United States. In addition to Max, she was the face of her country, and contrary to tradition, this vice-president would be busy.

Her day entailed attending long meetings, some of which exceeded three hours. It was capped by her address to the UN Security Council, a report of how the United States had coped with its first experience with large-scale domestic terrorism. She felt inadequate in that closed-door meeting, and she knew why; all they had been able to do was to avoid panic and return the nation's capitol to the status quo.

They couldn't prevent something that they couldn't predict, and prevention was the key. Eliminating the threat was the only way, and they had danced around that subject all day without resolution. Her time in New York had involved twelve hours of private meetings that involved intense discussion on matters that none of them had any power to control, and she was exhausted and frustrated.

She looked out over the New York skyline from the penthouse suite and surveyed the panorama as the sun set low, creating that moment of suspension that is neither night or day. It was difficult just to imagine the sheer size of the 22 million residents of the great city. That didn't include the commuters who entered Manhattan by train, car, and bus each day. She began to see lights inside of the buildings below, exaggerating the vastness of her view.

Savoring the end of a long day, she backed away from the floor to ceiling windows and walked across the plush carpet to the bathroom. As she walked, she kicked off her pumps and stripped out of her stylish politician dress, leaving a trail of discarded clothing and underwear behind her. By the time she triggered the automatic lights of the bathroom, she was fully nude except for her jewelry. Pausing to examine her form in the mirror, she assessed her figure. "Not bad for a politician," she thought, and turned to face the black marble jacuzzi tub of the opulent room. "A bubble bath before dinner will be just the thing to relax me," she surmised, and bent forward to start the flow of hot water.

Out of the corner of her eye, she detected movement on the black surface of the large vanity, and turned to focus on the bowl of the sink near her head. At eye level, a large, black, hairy spider darted forward and she fell back, hitting the floor with a startled gasp. She hated spiders. From her vulnerable angle on the floor, she couldn't see where the spider had gone, and for a sweaty heart-pounding moment, she feared that that it had jumped in her hair.

She back-pedaled on her hands in a crab walk until she was as far as she could travel without bumping her head, and began running her hands furiously through her long auburn tresses. She stopped, imagined that she could feel something moving, and did it again. Once she was satisfied that the spider wasn't lurking on top of her head, she slowly rolled to her knees and stood. She scanned the black marble for the whereabouts of her tormentor.

At the bottom of the sink, the creature twitched and startled her again. If it had remained motionless, she might have missed it. She hoped that this was not the jumping kind, and slowly approached the sink. *If I can only reach the faucet, I can wash it down the drain*, she thought. She was too civilized to grab a shoe to beat the life out of it, and the last time she had seen anything that resembled a weapon, she had been in the middle of the massive suite many feet away.

She gave a frantic flip to the crystal cold water faucet, and retreated two steps away from the flowing stream. She watched as the spider was washed down the drain. She let the water in the sink pour while she went back to creating her bubble bath. Once the water had filled the tub and the bubbles had reached the top in a soothing white blanket, she turned off the faucets and slid slowly into the bath.

The drenched spider began his slow and painful crawl up the inside of the sink drain, its simple mind intent on survival, not revenge. If attacked, its venomous bite would be its defense, but it lacked the ability to do no more harm to a human than a few days of pain, itching and swelling. The shock and worry to the victim would be more than enough to give it an opportunity to escape.

Scarlett luxuriated in the tub with her eyes closed, facing the huge ornate mirror on the opposite wall. Its size gave the illusion that the large bathroom was doubled in size. She ran through her activities planned for the evening and pondered what to wear. She calculated how long it would take to prepare for her appearance at the dinner banquet, giving time to arrive fashionably late. That way, she would have a large audience for her next speech, and wouldn't need to speak as long as usual. She began to consider whether Max's style was rubbing off on her, but abruptly abandoned that ludicrous idea as the warm water relaxed her.

She began to sing, secure in the thought that there was no witness to hear her off-key attempt at imitating an old Lady GaGa song that was stuck in her head. She finished her rendition of "Dance in the Dark" and noticed that the water was cooler than she liked. She opened her eyes to locate the hot water faucet at her feet. From reflection in the mirrored wall behind the faucet head, she saw it. Perched on the counter of the vanity above her head, the spider twitched. This time, she screamed.

Within seconds, the door of the adjoining room burst open and two Secret Service agents entered the suite. With guns drawn they rushed toward Scarlett, who sat in the tepid water with her mouth agape and her body exposed, staring at the reflection of the spider above her head. With one scan of the room, the agents followed her gaze and assessed the threat. Without comment, one muscular agent smashed his hand down on the counter and assaulted the threat with a slap. The spider was the jumping kind. It sprung onto the back of the agent's hand and sunk its fangs in the attacker, prompting a surprised yelp and spicy cusswords from the commando-trained former Navy Seal. The arachnid jumped again, hitting the floor as Scarlett screamed, "Get him!"

Both of her Secret Service agents, suddenly realizing that they were in the Vice-President's bathroom witnessing her in all of her naked glory, turned their backs as Scarlett hurriedly wrapped herself in a large robe. They attempted to corner the escaping spider by moving in a crouch with their arms outstretched, looking like two farm boys at a greased pig contest. Finally, the spider was confined in the far corner of the bathroom and they made their final approach.

Then there was a bright flash and the lights went out.

"Did you get him?" she screamed.

CHAPTER 62

Glenda Reasoner had been missing for twelve hours before the lights went out and plunged The City into ominous darkness. To pull off their grand deception, it was essential that Glenda be kidnapped and detained, together with her field crew. If she popped up in the sea of humanity that would soon be fleeing the city, the scheme would fail. Darkhorse carefully devised the plan to set up their kidnapping while she was on remote assignment to the shipping docks on the Hudson river. The caller who had lured them to this location was reading from a script prepared by Darkhorse, but the junior editor who received the call didn't know that.

The hook that brought Glenda and her crew out of the studios at Rockefeller Plaza was a story that she had reported about on many occasions; the vulnerability of our ports to terror attacks from containers loaded on ships originating in the Middle East, Yemen on this occasion. They were to record footage of cranes removing containers from a ship flying a Yemeni flag, while Glenda expounded on the multiple horrors that could be lurking inside their metal walls.

The location he chose was a commuter parking lot near the docks whose security cameras had been disabled. There would be no witnesses in the middle of the day when everyone was at work earning a living. By the time she and her crew had been loaded into the two white SUVS that concealed the incident from the view from the access road, the kidnapping was complete. Sixty seconds front to back, and they were on their way to Pryor's coastal estate in the Hamptons., with the drugged and bound journalists stowed beneath a cargo cover.

She was to be kept alive in the event her life was needed for some unanticipated reason, but she would soon become dispensable, and she knew it. Her crew would be disposed of long before her usefulness to Pryor had expired. She was known for her feisty demeanor and hard-driving persistence during interviews, and her spirit was her greatest asset, but those qualities would not save her when her time was up.

She woke up hours later in a room that could have been in a four star hotel, with one difference. There were no windows, and the door was locked from the outside. Judging from the disarray of her clothes, she had been placed on the bed by her captors and fondled while unconscious, but her clothes were intact, a good indication that she had not been raped. If she had, her rapist would likely have removed her underwear and not bothered with restoring the dignity of putting them back on. Still, she seethed at the idea that they had touched her.

Glenda rose from the bed and staggered into the bathroom. The drug was wearing off slowly. In her groggy state, she heard the sound of a key unlocking the door. She whirled and stood face to face with Adam Pryor. "You will speak the words I have programmed into the message or you will die," he said, dispensing with the formalities of an introduction.

"I know you…I interviewed you…You're Pryor. Homeland Security…You disappeared…They're looking for you…" She struggled to talk through the mental haze that lingered, but only managed a soft moan. She leaned against the vanity to keep from crashing to the floor. "Sleep it off, Miss Reasoner, and then we will talk about what you will do for me." Pryor wheeled and walked out of the room as Glenda slid to the floor.

The computer was assiduously copying her image, voice pattern and dialect, and soon her life would become irrelevant. Voice recognition technology had advanced far beyond the ability of word processing. Image emulation could dispense with the human component once the computer had inputted and filtered the data from her years of Bull Network broadcasts and live appearances. With a mental command, the operator of the Manipulator System could supply words to her image, change the color and style of her clothing, and broadcast any message. It would be a simple matter to hack into the Bull Network and broadcast seamlessly from a remote studio with their own equipment, seized and sheltered before the blast.

CHAPTER 63

Scarlett and her Secret Service contingent walked down thirty-two stories in the stairwell. In the time it took them to move in the darkness from the penthouse to street level, they could have traveled by elevator from top to bottom and back over thirty times. With guns drawn they guarded the descent from the front and back, constantly trying to get a response from their communicators. There was no static. They were useless, like the TV, and the lights. Their only illumination was from a small chemical glow stick that was part of the survival kit assigned to each agent. They gave approximately five hours of light, long enough, they hoped, to get to a place where they could wait out the night. Once the glow stick was activated by bending the stick and cracking the interior case that kept two chemicals separated, the mixture emitted an eery green light. Unlike a flashlight, the glow could not be turned off and saved for later. They had five hours of glowstick illumination and no more..

Scarlett placed her left hand on the back of the Secret Service agent in front of her, and tried to hold the rail with her right. At each landing, the team would stop briefly to listen for activity, not knowing whether the incident was an attempt on the Vice-President's life, or something much bigger.

Scarlett had enough of silence, and the sound of her voice in the darkness was startling. "I know you boys got an eyeful back there, and if you ever breathe a word of this to anyone, or if I read that some anonymous source just happened to say that I'm afraid of spiders or have a nice rack, you will all be washing dishes in the Senate cafeteria for the rest of your careers, y'all got that?"

"Yes, Ma'am," they replied in unison. The humor of the situation had been lost on them, and they were deep in doing what they had been trained, but the agent in front let out a brief chuckle at the thought. "I heard that," she muttered in her most threatening tone. "I…"

"Ma'am, we're at the ground floor," he interrupted. "Check the perimeter. Standish, you guard the Vice-President. We're gonna go out for a little look around." The three quietly opened the door to the darkened lobby and fanned out. In the distance in a side hallway, they could see light, and a heard a pounding noise. They approached silently and leveled their Glock 9 MMs at the sound while wheeling around the corner. At the end of the hallway, a woman in a full length mink coat, over a diaphanous nightgown stood at an ATM machine. She held a lit candelabra. She screamed.

"I was only trying to get my money out. Don't shoot me! It's my money in there. Damn thing doesn't work!" She pounded on the machine one more time, as if her actions would suddenly make it spring to life and give her comfort. Her makeup was smeared from crying, and their intrusion into her agony produced a new torrent of tears. "I just don't know what I'm going to do," she sobbed. I can't find my husband, and I'm all alone, and it's dark…so dark." She slowly slid to the floor. Her high heels slid off her feet as she plopped to the marble tile.

"Shit," exclaimed one agent, ignoring her plight. The sudden appearance of the inappropriately dressed socialite had sprung him back into survival mode. "Go down to that boutique down the hall and find the warmest ladies' coat you can get your hands on, and some comfortable boots for the Vice-President. Better yet, grab that candle, get Ms. Conroy, and bring this lady with you. It's going to be cold outside."

CHAPTER 64

"Max Masterson, it's not nice to scare an old lady like you did," Leila Fox was busy serving up a dinner for six people that would have fed twenty. "I nearly had a heart attack when you peeled off your face and tossed it onto the La Z Boy chair," she said, while spooning a mountain of mashed potatoes onto Andrew's plate.

"Mrs. Fox, I had no intention of frightening you to death, but that disguise was getting to me. I startled myself when I looked in the mirror after putting it on. Rachel and I had them made so we could get out in public without it becoming a major event. Pretty good, eh?"

"Pretty bad, I'd say," Andrew chided. "Max, you can't go around without Secret Service protection. Not with the country on high alert."

"That's what I keep telling him, but he keeps coming up with ways of getting around established protocol." Armstrong took the rare opportunity to voice his opinion, but he knew that Max would disregard it.

"Fat lot of good that did for Kennedy and McKinley, and don't forget that nut job that shot Reagan," Max responded.

"Max, you keep on doing things your own way," Leila Fox inter-jected. "That is one thing I like about you. But be careful. I don't want you to end up dead like my dear departed Joseph. I can't deal with any more dying until my own time comes."

"Mrs. Fox, I'll try to stay alive long enough to come to your hundredth birthday," Max replied.

Armstrong's communicator alerted him. He had been in contin-uous contact with Secret Service to monitor anything that arose while he was away from the White House. "Mr. President, another device has been detonated in New York City, and we have lost contact with the Vice-President. We need to leave immediately. Sorry for your loss, Ma'am."

◆ ◆ ◆

Max, Rachel, and Andrew flew back from the Midwest, with Rachel as pilot and Armstrong as co-pilot, with Max and Andrew free to strategize in the jump seat during the hour-long flight back. Andrew shared his mother's advice that had not been repeated by her at the gargantuan dinner she had prepared for after the funeral. There wasn't much left to advise, and Andrew was relieved that Max had been free to ask questions without his acting as an intermediary. Neighbors had prepared dishes for the wake at the community center, and what wasn't consumed by the neighbors in the middle of the day remained on tables that lined the dining room. They had carried as many leftovers as the cargo hatch could hold, and Andrew knew that his mother's home-cooked meals would be devoured by the White House staff before the sun set.

"Mr. President, we have a problem." Andrew Fox and Roger Sinclair stood in the doorway of the Oval Office, their faces grim.

"Good! If we didn't have any of those, I'd have nothing to do, other than look at what they did to New York. When is this going to end?" Max sat confidently behind his desk, reviewing the evening's reports on his monitor. Shortly after dark, a burst of gamma radiation had burst from the top floor of Trump Plaza in Jersey City, taking out most of New York City's electronics, on the far side of the Hudson River. The power grid fell shortly thereafter, plunging the city into blackness. All transportation was shut down, and reports from outside the blast zone had indicated that a geostationary satellite which transmitted all communications for the greater New York and New Jersey metropolitan area had been rendered useless. Nobody was moving, and nobody was talking. The electronic components of every cell phone and cellular tower had become fused by gamma radiation.

Sinclair chose to ignore Max's sarcasm and reported what he knew. "The same folks as the ones who disrupted your inauguration are responsible for shutting down New York. This time, they did it on a much larger scale. They put the bomb on the highest floor of a building so that it would spread over a larger area."

"What are they capable of?" Max inquired, his eyes glued to the screen. "We don't know how many of these things are out there or where or whether they intend to do it again."

"It's more complicated than that," said Sinclair. "We have been unable to communicate with anyone inside of New York City for more than two hours, and the Vice-President was last heard from about an hour before the blast. She and her Secret Service contingent of four agents were in her hotel, and they planned to attend a social function and dinner at the Waldorf Astoria hotel later. She was scheduled to give her speech to the UN tomorrow morning about our response to domestic terrorism. We haven't been able to raise Secret Service or the hotel, and we fear the worst."

"Don't go there," said Max.

"I don't have to go there. It's already here," replied Sinclair. His concern for Scarlett's well-being had caused his eyebrows to knit together, despite his controlled effort to remain calm. What the words didn't communicate was more than projected on his face.

"Retaliate."

"We can't. They're here. Among us," replied Sinclair. "I have been trying to tell you all along. Unless we find out that there is a central command that is running this terror operation and can bomb the hell out of them, or we can find the head honcho and put him away, we have to do the prudent thing and continue to run this government. We have the FBI investigating whether other bombs of this type have been found, and CIA is checking for links to foreign terrorists. They must have obtained the bomb-making material somewhere, and my guess is that it came from somewhere outside the U.S."

"Are we still in COGCON 1?"

"No, once we got through Inaugural Day and assessed the damage, we stepped down security. At the time, we looked at it as an isolated incident," replied Sinclair. "Everyone is back at work here in the Capitol, thanks to our hardened power grid and Faraday shielded electronics. It's the civilian population that we failed to protect..." Max interrupted.

"We are back at COGCON 1. You know the protocol. To insure the continuity of government, we must go in there and rescue the vice-president, and we need to do it now. The longer we wait, the worse it will be, and I seriously doubt that her security detail is sitting in a dark, cold hotel fretting about what they are going to do next. How are we going to find her in a city of 24 million people, all of them traveling on foot?"

"We are already on the way," Andrew Foxannounced. "Two Helos are over New Jersey at the moment. We can watch it all on the monitor. Dawn will break in another ten minutes, and we will be able to see what is happening out there. Right now, the only visuals we have are what we can see from the searchlights and night vision electronics, and most of the city is huddled indoors trying to stay warm. There aren't many people out on the streets yet, but my guess is that they will be, once the sun comes up. They have nothing else to do if they want to survive."

Sinclair interrupted. "Always assume there is a second bomb. And after the second, a third. We are dealing in unknowns, but if we put a lot of people in the air…look, a lot of people are going to die. This blast was ten times the size of the Inaugural Event, and we don't know how many there are. Our shields have not been field-tested, and we don't know if they will…

"I don't care. We have to do something, and fast. They are to retrieve the vice-president, while we figure out what to do next." Max sat down hard and wrung his hands.

CHAPTER 65

I don't know, I just don't know," said the woman as they emerged onto the street. Brown boots. They don't go with my Chinchilla." Scarlett had managed to find a full-length mink with a hood, and the same brown boots in her size, but the rescued woman was having a fashion meltdown. She desperately clung to the arm of one agent, who, despite desperate efforts at shaking her off, had resigned himself to the idea that she would be along for the desperate journey.

"Are we going to find my husband? He had a dinner meeting with some clients at the Russian Tea Room. He told me to make myself look pretty and to wait…he said he wouldn't be long…" She broke into tears. They didn't respond.

There was no moon, and clouds covered the stars. They were in total blackout. The streets of downtown Manhattan were abandoned, but they could see the twinkling of fires far off in the distance. Although the temperature was below freezing, people were gathering in the streets in the residential section miles away, and they made their way in the direction of the lights.

Scarlett, her Secret Service Detail, and the bereft socialite made their way in the direction of Central Park. The going was slow, and by the time they had traveled ten blocks, they were cold, wind-blown, and craving shelter. "We need to get inside. And soon," announced Scarlett. "What I wouldn't give for a roaring fireplace right now."

"Why didn't you ask? My friend Mitzi has a huge fireplace. She lives near the park, right over there." Scarlett and all of the agents looked at the woman with amazement. "Do you know the address?" they inquired in unison. "Well, we don't just sit in our hotel and order room service," she said defensively. "Whenever we visit, oh, about three, no, four times a year, we get together with our Palm Beach friends who have properties in the city, and we compare tans and complain about the weather, and Mitzi just separated from her husband, you probably know him, he's a big…"

"Can you introduce us to Mitzi right now?"

"Well, I usually call first…Oh, I guess I can't…She might have already gone back to Palm Beach. She told me how much she missed us and couldn't wait to lounge by the pool. It would be gauche to drop in unannounced. It just isn't done."

"Miss, what is your name?"

"Britney. Britney Shalowan. From the Palm Beach Shalowans," she replied, suddenly becoming sheepish.

"Britney, do you know who I am?"

"No, I'm thinking that you're somebody famous, because you look familiar, and I would never forget hair as gorgeous as yours."

"Hon, I'm Scarlett Conroy, the Vice-President of the United States."

"Oh, Hi, I was going to vote for you, but Biff, that's my husband, Biff said that I had to register before I voted, and I had a manicure that day, and you know how hard it is to get in. My manicurist schedules them four months in advance…Can you believe that? Four months!"

Scarlett smiled for the first time that day. "Britney, darlin', would you be so kind as to take us to where Mitzi lives? Now, you don't think she would mind if you brought the vice-president over for a little visit, do you?"

"I guess it would be OK, but what about them?" Britney looked at the four burly agents, who silently monitored the perimeter for signs of danger.

"Oh, I'll vouch for them. They are perfect gentlemen," replied Scarlett, recalling her moment of high exposure the previous evening.

They knocked on the ornate wooden door to the upscale Manhattan flat of Mitzi, but there was no response. Without seeking permission, one agent kneeled before the door and produced a tool kit the size of a credit card from an internal pocket and inserted a thin metal device into the keyhole. In less than ten seconds, they were inside the room as two frightened models, bundled in the warmest clothes they could find, looked on from the end of the hallway.

It was their second day without shopping for eyeliner and lingering over a Grande Caramel Macchiato from Starbucks. They looked and felt miserable. Scarlett had the fleeting thought that they would need to cope or die, and they were as suited for survival as a butterfly in a hurricane. From her briefings and research on EMP incidents, she knew it would be months or years before New York would again become habitable for people with their sensitive fragility.

She stared at the shivering women and tried to imagine how ill-suited their lifestyles were for survival, starving and drugging themselves to stay thin enough to provide bony support for the latest designer clothes. They would cling to the familiar and perish, she surmised. She silently wondered whether they would want to survive in a world as harsh as the one that awaited them outside their front door. Attending to the task at hand, she made a mental note to leave the door unlocked when they left.

The Secret Service agents immediately checked the spacious residence for the presence of Mitzi or anyone else, and once they were satisfied that they were alone, they began the task of making a fire.

Mitzi had left enough wood in the bin to look "rustic" even though her tastes bordered on Art Nouveau. She bought the brownstone built in the 1920's for a steal during the real estate crash in 2012. The large fireplace was a centerpiece for entertaining, with a mantelpiece made of granite and matching stone panels that rose two stories. She had dabbled with the idea of converting it to gas or electric, but the thought mortified her frequent guests, who enjoyed milling around the warmth that it provided during her infrequent visits in the Winter months.

This year, Mitzi came for Christmas and was gone before Valentine's Day, longer than her usual stays. She had been anxious to return to Palm Beach shortly after she had arrived, but problems with her trust fund had delayed her return while dealing with lawyers and other "annoyances". The management of her wealth was her only business activity. The rest of her time was spent immersed in the elite society that remained separate and insulated from the rest of the world. The longer stay in New York had compelled Mitzi to stock up on more wood for the party fire, but most of it was gone by the time it was needed for their survival. A few hours at most, and then they would be scrounging for wood if they wanted to stay warm.

Britney was clearly unhinged by the unannounced and unintended intrusion into Mitzi's home. She walked around aimlessly, bundled against the cold that seemed to seep inside of her clothes, muttering.

"This won't do. It just won't do. What will I tell her? I'll certainly be vilified for this when I get back...Will I get back? Oh my..." She crumpled onto the plush couch and began to sob. Her world had fallen apart in a momentary flash.

"I figure we have about a half-day of wood there, and then, we'll have to start using the furniture," surmised one agent. Let's see what she left behind for us to eat." They scrounged in the massive kitchen, unused mostly, with a double-doored refrigerator that shined with stainless steel that matched the massive electric stove and cupboard doors. It contrasted starkly with the black granite countertops that lined the walls. The refrigerator held bottles of Perrier, but no food. The freezer was the better provider. A dozen thick steaks in butcher wrap sat partially thawed, along with two large cartons of mint chocolate chip Hagen Das ice cream. The cupboards provided caviar and smoked oysters in large cans, along with crackers, olives, and midget kosher gherkins in jars. "We're gonna eat like high society for awhile," surmised one agent. "I love those little pickles."

"Take one of those cartons of ice cream to the hummingbirds down the hall," commanded Scarlett. "If they want to show their gratitude, don't hurry back. They looked like they needed a little warming up." "Yes Ma'am," said the youngest. He grabbed the carton and three spoons and eagerly departed. Two minutes later, he burst back into the room. "That just made them colder. I'm wondering whether the Lady of the House left behind any furs that they could borrow." He bounded up the stairs to the master bedroom and emerged with two full length blonde mink coats. "When a man gives a woman a mink, he's about to get lucky," They shook their heads and watched with amusement.

"This won't do. This just won't do," protested Britney.

On the street, the usual hangers-out were restless. Most were drunk or stoned. Awake, they sat leering at the families, watching. They were like a pack of wolves, snarling and circling, waiting to attack. They wouldn't go after the families, who tried to stay in the center of the street, fearing that they would get plucked off the sidewalk and dragged into the shadows, where an uncertain fate hid. It was the fear that propelled them in a half-run toward the park, looking down alleys with sideway glances, shuffling, maneuvering through the acrid smoke.

The buildings were beginning to burn. Some may have been started intentionally and others the result of fires built in places that were the wrong place, but there would be no investigation, no news reports or onlookers in the street. There was no way to put them out, and nobody cared. In survival mode, you protect what you can save, and delaying the inevitable was a waste of time.

CHAPTER 66

Max watched on the monitor as the Helos flew low over the treetops of Eastern New Jersey, and as they approached their destination the growth of green gave way to the densely populated areas near New York. The pilot explained that they would first enter the hotel from the roof, where a helicopter pad was available, but that they didn't expect that anyone remained in the building. With no power to heat and light, it would be uninhabitable once the temperature inside the building dropped below freezing.

The pilot and rescue team were going to rely upon the survival training of Scarlett's Secret Service agents, and they would be leaving signals wherever they traveled. The remote camera revealed a darkened city in the distance, still disabled and silent. The Statue of Liberty could be seen as they approached from the New Jersey side of the Hudson, and as they flew closer, the details of the magnificent statue became more visible. Then, there was a brilliant flash, and the cameras went blank.

"They blew it up, those rat bastards!" Max turned to see his trusted security advisor, Roger Sinclair, standing behind him, watching the monitor with an intense gaze. "They took out our eyes, and destroyed Lady Liberty. Evil." Sinclair shook his head.

"If anyone could find these cowards, it's you." Max stood and faced his security advisor, his eyes drilling into his mind, seeking meaning. Sinclair was un-nerved by the sudden intrusion, but recovered quickly.

"I know who did it, and I know why. I just don't know where."

His words resonated with every person in the room. They no longer stared at a blank screen. The focus shifted to him alone. He explained quickly and concisely. "The people who did this are Americans." He paused, took a deep breath, and continued. "When they detonated the first EMP device at your inauguration, it was a warning. They wanted to embarrass you, to cut off your strongest ally, your ability to communicate. They had no interest in destruction. They only sought to control you and the threat that you pose to them. If they can't control you, they will lose the dynasty that they have created."

Max stood and stretched. He was weary from the long hours of monitoring the events in New York. They had been down in the Situation Room for most of the night, and they wouldn't rest until there was a plan and a solution, he realized that. They were problem solvers, and there was no political solution that could resolve this situation. They had to determine the reality, seek out the source of the problem, eliminate it, and deal with the damage. There was an awkward , silence, but none of the room's occupants dared to speak. Suddenly, Max spun and faced Sinclair.

"You told us that they are Americans. I want to know who." He walked across the room and gave Sinclair a piercing glare.

"Pryor. He stole these devices and deployed them. I'm still trying to determine how many and where they have been deployed, but my source has disappeared on me and I haven't been able to determine where Pryor may be at the moment. In fact, we have been looking for him since the day before the election."

CHAPTER 67

Max retreated to the Oval Office for a reprieve from the tension. He needed the time alone to sit for ideas and to plan. The revelation that his father's nemesis was the common thread of evil in the recent incidents was mind chilling, and the overwhelming wave of revenge had begun to wash into his thoughts along with the weariness. *This is not going to be easy. He has had years to consider his plan. If he can create despair, if he creates fear, and then uncontrolled terror . . . after that, the desperate will do anything to make it end.* He settled into the plush leather executive chair and cherished the brief opportunity for solitude. Without conscious effort, he reached into the concealed drawer and withdrew the presidential diary and placed it onto the expansive walnut desk. He paused to collect his thoughts, and for the first time in his short time in office, he worried.

Running his hands along the ornate book cover, he pondered the challenge before him and the country. His consternation was compounded by the very personal vendetta that was unfolding. Pryor had years to plan, and Max had days to react, or appear impotent as a leader . . . *I need to react, and to win this battle, or he will eventually own the minds of America. If they lose faith in my ability to lead, to protect, then I will be reviled for the rest of history.* Gradually, the book glowed, and he opened it at the halfway point, where the pages glowed brightest.

"I was governor of the Empire State before I sat in this esteemed place, born and raised in the city which your enemies have plunged into darkness," said Teddy Roosevelt, sitting in the chair in front of him. He was dressed in his famous Rough Rider uniform, his sabre at his side, hanging from a wide belt. As Max watched in amazement, the uniform morphed into khaki hiking clothes, and the sabre shortened into a cell phone that hung from a much thinner belt. The hat remained, but the knee-high riding boots had become hiking boots.

Max chose not to respond, knowing that his time with the departed president was short and it was time to listen. He was getting used to this welcome intrusion, and he needed wisdom and guidance.

"You are faced with a challenge that requires decisive action. Your own countrymen have attacked your family, and have harmed our fair nation in nefarious ways, all to get to you." Roosevelt shook his head in disgust. *"Much has changed since my day, my boy. In my time, we knew what it meant to be American. We knew the privilege and honor that attached to our birthright and it was us against them. We would no sooner harm our countrymen than harm ourselves, and traitors were dealt with harshly."*

Max spoke with his mind, and his voice broke with the tension. *"Mr. Roosevelt,"* he began.

"Call me Theodore, Son. They all called me Teddy, but I dislike that reference intensely. Theodore will do."

"Theodore, I am torn between thoughts. Personally, I want to find this cowardly bastard and snuff the life out of him with my bare hands, and then there's the part that wants to rid the world of the evil that he represents. He, or they, killed my mother, attacked my

father, and made me an orphan for the second time in my life. I'm seething."

"My boy, when confronted with a dilemma, you must always take the high road first. Do what is best for the nation. The personal aspect you must leave in the hands of your maker. Take care that you do not appear weak to the people, or they will turn on you . . . " He paused for effect. *". . . And never seek shelter when you should lead the charge."*

There was a knock at the door, and the image disappeared. Andrew Fox popped his head into the room and gazed at Max with a concerned look. "Are you OK?" he inquired.

"Oh yeah. Just sitting for ideas. We need to move quickly in a very visual way," replied Max. Andrew looked puzzled, but dismissed it.

"I just wanted you to know that we got some of the satellites at the periphery of the blast zone back online, and they can't give us much detail from that distance, but I thought you would like to see this." He shoved a night photo of the eastern seaboard across the desk with a flourish. It clearly showed the hole of darkness that extended up and down the Atlantic coast for hundreds of miles, but there was one exception: A bright pinprick of light shone brightly on the edge of the darkness. "What's this, how can someone in a massive blackout have electrical service?" Max inquired.

"We don't know for sure, but that dude has power when his neighbors don't, and from the looks of it, he has a lot of it," Andrew replied.

CHAPTER 68

Max returned to the situation room from the Oval Office with handwritten notes and a determined look. His inner circle of trusted advisors included Roger Sinclair and Andrew Fox. They waited for direction. Sinclair spoke first. "Max, we have created a no-fly zone around the city. There is nothing moving right now, anyway. The communication satellites have been dead since the blast, so nothing has been coming in or out of the area for the past few days; but they are leaving on foot, bicycle, or anything that can move. Some people commandeered a sailboat and sailed until they could see lights on in homes on the coast, and then they docked. There are reportsof widespread lootings and killings, mainly for food, and when they heard that plague was spreading, they got out of there."

This was news that they hadn't considered. Plague, the scourge of Europe in the Middle Ages, was a disease that spread from victim to victim like wildfire. Fleas carried the disease, and the rats carried the fleas. It was capable of killing millions in a short time, in a pandemic that could be easily be prevented by maintaining hygiene and staying out of contact with the carriers of the disease.

Max stood and crossed his arms in a defensive stance. He stared at the blank screen in silence, deep in thought. "How do we know that the rumor is true?" He knew the answer to his question before he spoke. It was the most basic of Maxims.

It's not reality. It's the appearance of reality. If people believe that plague is spreading throughout Manhattan, they will do anything to get away.

"One woman said that as soon as she saw a big rat attack the family dog, she and her husband packed up the kids and what canned goods they could find, and headed for the docks. She said that there was a line of people streaming out of the city by foot, and the bridges were packed. The Lincoln and Holland tunnels are flooded, and mass transit is disabled, so it looks like their options are limited. Fires are spreading with no way of putting them out, and soon we will have a ghost town bigger than your imagination can conceive. They did a lot of damage with two EMPs, and we have no way of knowing if there are more."

"There are more," said General Robert Bradbury, chairman of the joint chiefs of staff. He had entered the situation room quietly, and stood listening to Sinclair's report. "I have ordered our National Guard to begin searching every tall building in major cities, focusing on private residential high-rises in strategic locations that can do the most damage. We found one in Copley Place in Boston, and another in Chicago at the Trump Tower. Minutes ago, they found one in Seattle at the Columbia Center. Funny thing, though. The devices in Seattle and Boston were found in plain sight, and both were dummies. From the outside, they looked like they were rigged to explode, but when we finally got them out in the open and got inside the guts of these things, they were hollow. No tritium, no trigger, just enough uranium to set off our detectors."

He paused to allow time for them to absorb the newly discovered situation and went on. "The one in Chicago, though, was a live one. It could have shut down the city. We traced its place of origin to the Ukraine, and my people are looking into how they got into the country. It looks like Homeland Security intercepted about a dozen of these babies a few years back, and then they disappeared."

"So we had them in our custody and now we don't. Splendid," said Max with a sarcastic tone.

Bradbury went on. "This could become a national disaster if we don't do something soon. I feel helpless. We are good at blowing up our enemies, but terrible at eliminating a threat that lives inside our borders. The combined might of our armed forces can't rid the country of this cancer, Mr. President."

"Not for long. Send in the drones and find out what's happening in there, and get my vice president off that island . . . now," Max said matter-of-factly. "Do you have any way of rigging a drone with AV equipment, so I can talk to people from here? Right now, they are totally cut off from the rest of the world. We need to get mass transit moving soon, or a lot of people are going to start killing each other for food." Max paced in silence, deep in thought, his hands clasped tightly behind his back.

"Sir, how do we get those people off Manhattan? I'm not concerned about Long Island, they can handle it, at least for a while. But the city? There are millions of people who can't get through the day without their coffee and a prune Danish, and they're stranded, sir . . ."

Andrew Fox had come from the Midwest, and had learned how to live off the land. His only trip to New York City was his high school graduation trip at the end of his senior year. He was intimidated by the speed at which the people moved in herds, intent on their individual purpose. He had remembered wondering what they all did for a living, until the enormity of the question overwhelmed his mind. It was too big to think about, and his limited experience shut it out of his brain. He had gone back to gazing up at the size of the buildings until his neck hurt, and then it was time to go home.

"How many people are we talking about? I know that there are a lot of commuters, but the detonation was at 7 p.m. . . . Didn't a lot of the commuters already leave for home?" Andrew was quickly becoming overwhelmed by the logistics. *To think I only had to look out for myself a few months ago, and now I have to figure out a way to transport millions of people.*

"I already checked on that. There are about two million permanent residents who were probably on Manhattan Island at the time, and who rely almost totally on the subways and buses and taxis to get around. I'm guessing that there are close to eight million commuters each day, and that most of them had already left the city for home, but you can bet that some of them were just wrapping up happy hour when that thing went off. Let's assume there are about three million people who need to evacuate," explained Roger Sinclair.

"How about trains? Doesn't Grand Central Station have some old locomotives they can hook up to a bunch of passenger cars? Every old movie I ever saw has some guy kissing a girl at the train station before he goes off in one of those passenger cars . . ." Andrew was feeling the enormity of the task.

"I want Andrew to look into running passenger trains in there to get them out of the city, and we need to set up a supply line for food and water. Better yet, don't feed them until we get them out of there, or they might hunker down and refuse to leave." Max paced, his lips pursed in deep concentration.

" Don't we have any old locomotives mothballed in a warehouse somewhere? We'll need to run trains from . . . where, Grand Central? Union Station? Someone check into that. Let's move on this. The longer we wait, the worse it will get. People who don't have anywhere to go can be kept in temporary housing, and I want the National Guard to set that up walking distance from the most accessible rail line outside of the dark zone. Let's do it." Max slipped seamlessly into the role of Commander in Chief. He had been trained since childhood to be president, and it felt natural.

"Sir, don't you want our military to move supplies into the city?" responded Vincent Bowles. The undersecretary of the Department of Homeland Security was a holdover from the previous administration under then-president Warren Blythe. In the scramble to fill high government positions in the Masterson administration, Bowles had filled the gap left by the previous director, Adam Pryor, as efficiently as plugging a dike.

"Mr. Bowles, I don't know what planet you're from, but I want you to consider this: We have a dead city that is cold, and people are going to be lighting fires to keep warm. When people play with fire, they tend to burn things, like buildings. When one goes up in flames, they call the fire department. Only now, the phones don't work, and even if they did, the fire trucks can't get there to put out the fire. Even if they could, if the high-rises start to burn, there isn't an extension ladder long enough to get to the top floors. I expect that it's only a matter of time before we have the biggest conflagration in history since Hiroshima, and I'm determined to save as many people as possible. We have to get them out of the city."

CHAPTER 69

He had walked in silence along with the rest, unaware of his destination. He was wearing the work clothes of the white-collar world, a gray pinstripe suit covered by an equally gray topcoat, designed to keep its occupant warm long enough to step from a cab into his office building in downtown Manhattan and return to a waiting cab at the end of his work day. He wore Florsheim patent-leather shoes, standard footwear for businessmen of his type. The only barrier between his feet and the thin leather shoes were silk socks. He had walked in the midst of the crowd, headed west to somewhere else, and had traveled ten blocks before the blisters began to form. Now his feet were swelling and his wool topcoat was letting the February winds in. He was hungry just like the rest, and cursed himself for staying behind at happy hour instead of taking the commuter train back to the comfort of his Connecticut home.

In the three days since the detonation, the shelves in the stores had been stripped of everything edible, and those who had chosen to remain in the dark and silent city had begun to kill each other for food. Even the rats were coming out of their hiding places, some as big as cats, and aggressive. When word-of-mouth rumors began to spread that bubonic plague had been diagnosed in a neighborhood in the lower east side, he decided that it was time to get out. To the east was Long Island, and then the Atlantic. A dead end.

West was the only practical way to go, and the bridges over the Hudson were already full of foot traffic. Those lucky enough to own a bicycle had already evacuated ahead of the crowd of city dwellers, wary of those who would attempt to knock them down and steal their ride. At this point, walking was the only option.

It was the families who began the exodus. The fathers sensed the danger, the mothers gathered up what they would need to survive, and the children asked questions about the unanswerable unknowns that festered inside of all of them. Many wore three layers of clothing, but others tried to lug suitcases. Some toted their essentials and children in shopping carts pilfered from the supermarket.

The bridges were full of pedestrians, all leaving the burning city for the promise of something better. Some had a destination in mind; relatives in other parts of the country who would take them in, no matter how tense it could be. They were absorbed back into their extended families for the duration of the "event." They were the lucky ones. They got out when they could, before the harsh realities of their situation threatened their survival, falling into the comfort that family could provide. Years later, people would recount the "event" as a life changer. In some ways, the survivors were made better for it. Getting out of the city was the difference between life and death for them, and they were spared the horrors that remained behind in the darkened shell of Manhattan, illuminated at night only by the tall buildings that burned out of control.

The Lincoln Tunnel and the Holland Tunnel were both flooded. The powerful pumps that maintained them under the Hudson River failed when the grid fell, and the river was slowly reclaiming its territory. His only option to escape the city was the George Washington Bridge, and from his office on the upper west side, it was the closest.

The wind came out of the Northeast, cold and gusty. He could feel it cut through his topcoat, and his shivering increased in intensity until his bottom lip quivered uncontrollably. He wasn't alone. He walked in step with numerous other evacuees, bundled the best they could.

"Where ya from, man?" A stocky, square-jawed man with a prodigious growth of stubble on his face peered at the businessman from a snorkel jacket that had seen better days. Without pausing for a reply, he said, "Managed ta get this one from the Goodwill store before they stripped it clean. Yer gonna freeze yer ass off in that getup," he said, displaying his keen sense of the obvious. "First chance ya get, find yourself one 'a these. Toasty in here. Yessir!" He picked up his pace as the businessman slowed near the center span of the bridge.

He paused to rest, and looked south. From this vantage point, he could see the length of the Hudson down to the Jersey side, where the Statue of Liberty stood like a green speck in the distance. It was many miles off, but it was unmistakable. Between gusts of wind, he could hear the thrup-thrup of the rotors of helicopters. Two black specks moved into view, traveling low and moving fast. It was the first mechanical sound he had heard since before the blast, and for a moment, he had an adrenaline rush of hope. Then there was a bright flash, and the green speck on the horizon wilted in a glow and then collapsed. He stared at Lady Liberty until the glow subsided, and turned toward his destiny. *There has to be a workable commuter line somewhere, and I intend to find it. Anything heading north. I won't be picky. Once I get home, I won't be coming back.*

CHAPTER 70

"Have you noticed anything about Glenda's broadcast that isn't right?" Bill Staffman was monitoring broadcasts on the major networks as Andrew Fox worked on the leftover pizza from lunchtime the day before. With a little salt and some red pepper, it would make great breakfast food, he thought, remembering his college days and all-nighter munchies. It wasn't time for breakfast, but he hadn't had much to eat since the latest incident in New York, and they hadn't left the building for a day and a half.

"No, she looks the same, everything looks the same," replied Andrew.

"That's just the point. That studio is in New York."

"Holy shit . . ."

"And another thing. She used to have a lot more personality, you know what I mean? She used to cut up a lot more, and she used to be a whole lot easier on Max. Now she just reads the news and gets off."

"Now that you mention it . . . yeah, there's something mega-weird going on there," Andrew surmised. "Run up her last broadcast. I want to look at it with new eyes." He dropped the crust into the pizza box and walked toward the wall that served as the broadcast screen. "Make it big." Glenda Reasoner came up, her image as large as the wall.

"In the latest disaster of the Masterson administration, now less than two months old, Max Masterson's popularity rating has plummeted from an all-time high of eighty-three percent to seventy percent, and I predict a big fall after the events of the past twenty-four hours. New York is burning and people are dying, underscoring the failure of our president to lead." The image of people screaming and running had been inserted, and then the camera brought the image of Glenda at her desk into focus.

"Focus on her hands," said Andrew.

Staffman manipulated the image, and as Glenda spoke, they watched in high-definition.

"She was doing something with her hands. My memory works that way. When I remember an image that doesn't look right, it comes back to me in virtual detail. It's a blessing and a curse," Andrew revealed.

"Are you sure it isn't just the stale pizza?" Staffman was skeptical. He didn't appreciate that some kid from the Midwest had taken a position of high importance over him, a long-time loyal trooper. He appreciated how far he had gone, but in the Washington environment, the pecking order was everything.

"No . . . Look."

Glenda was tracing letters with her left hand.

"H," she traced, casually, but clear.

"E" came next, so subtle, but unmistakable.

"The Masterson administration has failed the American people. At a time when we as a nation would support our president, he has slipped to mediocrity."

They weren't listening to the words. It was her hands.

"L," she traced.

"America should run this charlatan, this nonpolitician, from our highest office, and bring in someone who can bring us back to our essence. We need to support the way things are, our status quo."

"P," she traced before the clip had finished.

"Kid, you are amazing," said Staffman. He reclined in his chair, and contemplated the next action. "You can inform the president, and I will inform everyone else that we are being played."

CHAPTER 71

They began burning the Chippendale furniture when the small supply of firewood ran out. It wouldn't matter soon, anyway. The city was burning, and the smoke hung in the air as a constant reminder. Before long, fire would indiscriminately consume the building and everything in it. "I want an evacuation plan, and I want it now," Scarlett announced to the room.

"Madam Vice President, it is protocol to remain in place and secure and wait for extraction," Agent Jones said.

"Well, Jones, what is protocol for extracting the vice president from a burning building in a city without any shred of hope? They can't put out a fire without water or power, and I have no intention of being a casualty, is that clear?" She seethed at the thought that rescue efforts had not taken her away from her misery, and she was not one to give up and wait for something to happen. She would lead.

"Bailey, find yourself a bike or something, and go over to the Hudson and scout our situation, and report back to me. I need to know what's happening out there."

Bailey nearly flew out the door in search of transportation. Five minutes later, he returned with a mountain bike in his meaty hands.

It was a woman's model, with a frame much too small for his large size, but the tires were full.

The smallest agent, Manley, stepped forward. He was the obvious choice, and the only one who spent his weekends grinding out the miles on his racing bike. Scarlett wasted no time. "Fill your water bottle and go find a way to get us out of this city, now!" She pushed him toward the door as Bailey scrambled to fill the water bottle with Perrier that was stocked in the pantry. Manley adjusted the seat to the top setting and in less than a minute, he was expertly tooling down the road toward Central Park.

His first objective was to cycle across Central Park away from the advancing flames, and if he didn't encounter the rescue crew, to head west to the river and see what he could see. *There has to be a huge effort to recover the vice president, but without a point of reference, they are either back at her hotel, or they are scratching their heads trying to figure out where we are right now. I'm betting that they are narrowing down our options to Central Park, anywhere but in the path of the fire. That's where I'd go, and that's where anyone with any sense would be headed.*

There was a large group of people milling around in the park. At the Delacorte Amphitheater there was a man on the podium, talking loudly into an old-fashioned megaphone. He was too far away to hear, but Manley could clearly discern that he was an emergency management official of some sort, instructing them of their options and urging them to leave New York. He rounded the curve of trees and saw it at the East Meadow; a black helicopter, definitely part of the rescue operation, its blades stationary and surrounded by a cordon of individuals holding weapons. He increased his pace until his legs burned. He continued pedaling down the hill, where the helo bearing the American flag sat like a large insect.

"Coming through!" Manley performed a skidding sideways stop at the end of his approach, spraying slush and mud in a high arc of the back of the crowd. Without waiting for the inevitable protests, he launched himself into the mass of people and propelled his athletic body toward the helo. His approach was a complete surprise, and for a brief moment, the crowd parted, leaving him facing the muzzles of automatic weapons capable of ripping him in half in less than a second.

"Secret Service! I'm here to take you to Hairbrush!" They had to believe him . . . he knew the right words. Hairbrush was Scarlett's classified name, and it granted him immediate access. "You need to get this bird in the air and let Washington know that we have her safe and sound," he said, launching himself into the helicopter.

"We can't do that, sir," said the pilot. "We kept her flying after the second EMP went off, but it knocked out all of our communications. We'll be flying blind . . ."

"I don't care. Our first duty is getting Hairbrush to safety, and we will serve her or die trying," he responded. His urgency was contagious, and the helo's blades began spinning. Manley directed them seven blocks away to the town house.

While they were in the air, Manley noted that the fire had spread and there were people running in the street toward the train station, where a black locomotive attached to passenger cars, all apparently snatched from a museum, was boarding refugees fleeing the city. Judging from the number of the waiting evacuees, it would not be enough. Smoke billowed across Manhattan like a gray curtain, changing the day into night for long minutes. When daylight was able to poke through the haze for a moment, the waiting crowd's enormity was revealed.

The fire had begun at the source. The buildings across the Hudson that were closest to the Statue of Liberty sustained the most intense bombardment of the EMP blast, and the electrical charge caused sparks. The buildings were old, and the fire was inevitable. The wind coming out of the west spread it like a forest fire, moving in a wave toward the East River. *Soon, anything that can burn will go up in smoke. We need to get to the Vice-President, and fast.*

◆ ◆ ◆

They flew low enough to witness the chaos below. People were fleeing by train and on foot, all heading west off the island, with the spreading fire hastening their departure. These were the New Yorkers who had hunkered down, waiting for it to be over. When the lights didn't come back on, and their apartments got cold, they had panicked. The glow of the flames came from the west, a constant reminder of the urgency of their mission. Their destination was well-marked. While Manley was on his reconnoitering mission, the rest of the vice president's Secret Service contingent had been busy. In the snow-covered street outside of the townhouse, a large arrow had been created with fireplace ash.

Scarlett and her protectors heard the helo simultaneously. Without the need to voice the words, they moved as one toward the door. As they left the building, the fashion models stood at the top of the hallway stairs, crying and begging, "Take us! We'll die here!" Scarlett paused and scanned the pitiful sight. Their makeup was smeared from constant crying, but it failed to diminish their fragile beauty. A wave of pity came into her mind, but in a flash, it was gone. They were in survival mode, and the first obligation was for the continuity of government to be assured. "You're on your own now," Scarlett announced in a solemn voice, and then they were gone.

CHAPTER 72

On a dock on the Hudson sat the other helo, surrounded by the remaining members of the rescue team. The blast at the Statue of Liberty had fried all means of communication even though the internal controls were well shielded from the gamma radiation. At least they were able to stay in the air. Without the shielding, both aircraft would have been at the bottom of the river, their occupants entombed beneath the brown water. The helo carrying the vice president landed briefly to redistribute passengers before a high-speed flight to safety.

Once the helos left Manhattan and crossed the Hudson, the scene below became surreal. They flew directly over the Statue of Liberty, or what was left of it. The second EMP blast was much smaller in scale, apparently. It was enough to melt the copper arm holding the torch, and the interior structure was fully exposed. The metal skeleton was glowing, and the super-heated mass was slowly collapsing in a melted heap. Lady Liberty's face looked toward the sky from the ground, cracked from crown to jaw, the last recognizable feature of a noble countenance. It provoked a profound sadness in Scarlett, and the image lingered in her mind long after they had left the disaster zone and flew toward Washington.

"Do we have any way of contacting anyone to let them know our situation," inquired Scarlett. "No ma'am," replied the copilot, his hands tenuously cupped to the vice president's ear to make himself heard over the thrup-thrup of the helo. "We managed to rig our transponder to get it working, so they know we're alive and moving, but the gamma radiation must have been intense . . . we think it got past the shielding at the antennae and fried our communications. We can't transmit or receive a signal, and nobody thought to bring spare parts. We're flying on instinct and dead reckoning, but don't worry ma'am, we'll get you home."

"Marine, quit ma'aming me, and tell me what happened," she snipped.

"Well, it used to be called Radioflash. Starfish Prime. Operation Fishbowl. Knocked out streetlights in Hawaii from eight hundred ninety-eight miles away. Set off burglar alarms, destroyed microwave links back in the nineteen fifties . . ."

"You're talking gobbledygook to a reasonably intelligent woman who happens to be a heartbeat away from the presidency. Give it to me straight and talk so I can understand what the hell you are talking about!" Her scolding tone intimidated him, but its effect made him focus.

"It's basic physics that they taught us in flight school, ma'am. Those devices weren't made to destroy buildings and people. They mess everything up with gamma radiation. You saw the effects of it on Inaugural Day, but that was a baby compared to the first one that toasted New York City . . ."

"How did it do so much damage?" She needed to be briefed so that when she got back, she would sound like an expert. It was expected of the commander in chief, and she had no intention of looking like a damsel in distress. She would surely be called upon to make a statement to the press, and she wanted to look and talk presidential. Her status as vice president was merely a resting place on the ladder to the presidency, she reasoned. Besides, the way Max had always exposed himself to danger meant that she may assume that role anytime.

"Well, the way I understand it, EMP bombs cause damage three ways. There's the E-one pulse . . . it's a brief, intense electromagnetic field. Electrical breakdown voltages get exceeded."

While he continued to explain, Scarlett searched for the comb and makeup she had scrounged from the Palm Beach socialite's apartment. She silently cursed herself for ordering Britney onto the other helo. She lacked a mirror, and had to be satisfied with her reflection on the window. "Go on, I can multitask," she ordered.

"Then there's the E-two pulse . . . it's like lightning. But the third is the most damaging over a large area. The E-three pulse is very slow, and it moves the earth's electromagnetic field out of the way. It's like a geomagnetic storm from a solar flare. It causes electromagnetic-induced currents in long electrical conductors and shuts down the grid. It pops transformers on power lines and there's a cascading effect . . . it will take a long time to bring the city back to life, or what's left of it."

"One bomb did all of that?"

"Yes ma'am, and when the buildings started to burn, we had no way of putting out the fires."

Scarlett absorbed the enormity of the situation, and reflected on how America could prevent a repeat of the disaster that was raging below them. It was obvious that the first order of business was to eliminate the threat.

◆ ◆ ◆

One hour later, the helo carrying Scarlett landed on the White House lawn, and she walked in with a plan.

CHAPTER 73

Scarlett strode through the front door of the White House with purpose, not waiting to speak to the cluster of anxious aides that had assembled to ask questions and take direction from her. In the past, Scarlett was known to burst into a roomful of subordinates, peppering them with orders in brisk succession. That day, she made her way past the assemblage without a word, ascended the steps to the second floor, and entered the queen's bedroom. Locking the door, she turned to face Roger Sinclair. "I assumed you would find your way here eventually," he exclaimed. She fell into his arms and sobbed. "I thought I would never see you again. We almost didn't make it out of there alive."

"You were surrounded by the best, and I knew you would be well protected. I didn't worry that you would get out of there until the second blast at the Statue of Liberty knocked out our eyes and ears. We knew that both helos were intact, but we had no idea what was happening on the ground. I warned them that they could expect a second bomb, and now we have found more." She held him tight and kissed him deeply, prompting his arousal. Immediately, he began unbuttoning her blouse. "Oh, baby, I must look a mess. I haven't bathed for three days," she protested.

"I know that, darlin', that's why I drew you a bath. You don't mind if I sit on the edge of the tub while you luxuriate in the bubbles, do you?"

"I prefer, in fact, I command, that you join me," she said in her most sultry voice, taking his hand and pulling him toward the sitting room. "You really know how to treat a lady." He undressed her with urgency, and she expertly unbuttoned his dress shirt, pulling it down over his shoulders when she was halfway down his chest. It was a game they played, the effect was to pin his arms to his body, rendering him helpless. She then worked on his belt buckle, and pulled his pants down around his ankles. He smiled in anticipation of things to come. Scarlett had total control of the situation, and he willingly played the role of helpless male.

"I see that you missed me," she teased, making an effort to avoid the prominent erection that tented his boxers. She wanted to delay his satisfaction, and prolong his excitement. It was better that way. Hooking her hands inside the waistband, she drew him in the direction of the bathtub full of bubbles. He took stutter steps. Scarlett laughed in delight at his predicament. "You can brief me on the State of the Union, and I promise not to interrupt, Mr. Sinclair, or you can wait until we have concluded our bath. Which course do you recommend?"

"The only union I intend to brief you about is the state of our union, Vice President Conroy, and that is for your eyes only."

"In that case, sir, I will release you from your confinement, so that you may have your way with me," she joked. They made love with desperate passion, splashing water and bubbles in ripples across the tiled floor of the bathroom. "We seem to be defiling the queen's private bathing quarters," Roger remarked. "I won't tell her if you won't," she giggled. When Scarlett was alone with him, the hard persona of her position was put aside, and she was free to be a woman. It was something she craved, the playful banter and the physical release, and her secret lover held the key to her satisfaction.

Hours later, they entered the Situation Room from separate doors, their hair still wet. "It's about time you got back here," said Max, winking.

CHAPTER 74

The drones flew into the dark zone as the sun was setting. The video images were disturbing and terrifying, showing a massive column of smoke from a distance of twenty-five miles. As they approached the Manhattan skyline, the sun had sunk below the horizon, and the flames became visible. Some of the taller buildings were totally engulfed. The orange of the flames reflected on the windows of adjacent buildings, magnifying the glow and illuminating the empty streets. Other than the flames, the only other light in the darkness was where the activity and the people were located; Grand Central Station was well lit, and Union Station, too.

Andrew had secured four locomotive engines and as many Amtrak passenger cars as they could pull, all from railroad museums and rail yards throughout the Northeast. Large portable lighting systems had been brought in as well, and from the air, the islands of activity stood out from the darkness. Those who had not made it off Manhattan, by foot or by their genius for survival, huddled inside and in the cold, waiting to leave. Old locomotives, pre-electronics, some dating to the early twentieth century, were brought in along old railroad lines from New Jersey and were transporting the evacuees off the island in a continuous loop. After that, if they had no family to take them in, or the funds to stay elsewhere, they stayed on the train until the end of the line, where temporary housing, not much more than a tent city, awaited. The end of the line was where those who had the least would suffer the most. In keeping with Pryor's philosophy of survival, the Masterson administration, and Max Masterson alone, would be confronted with the failure that Adam Pryor had designed.

When the sound of the old locomotive became recognizable, the hunkered-down occupants of New York were drawn to it like moths to a flame. The steam whistle was insistent, and couldn't be ignored. They packed up what they could carry, some with backpacks, but most with large suitcases more designed for air travel than evacuation.

◆ ◆ ◆

"Whoever is left when the fires are done, and the rats take to the streets, and the food runs out, those are the fools. I can only focus now on the people of Manhattan who want to live," Max declared to those present in the Situation Room. General Bradbury looked on with the others, recalling evacuations in wars that had failed, and the frantic change of regimes that had led to thousands of innocent deaths. Turning to Max, he crisply saluted. "Mr. President, back when we were in the big buildup with the Soviets, a few well-meaning military tacticians and engineers built these devices to destroy the infrastructure, so we could march in and take over without killing people. It looks like we failed. All of us." It was disconcerting to see the career military leader look so helpless.

Bowles took no clues from his earlier dressing-down by Max. His ego kept him from remaining silent, "A lot of people are going to die. The weak and innocent and the sick will go first. Those who have the least will suffer the most." General Bradbury left the situation room without another word, followed by Bowles. Shaking his head, Max returned to the task of leadership.

Bowles will not be returning. I have heard those words before.

CHAPTER 75

Daniel Stableton's family had farmed the rich soil of the valleys between the Delaware and the Hudson River for five generations. They were dug in, and weren't going anywhere. The valley was where they lived, and the twelve children born to his parents, Edna Maude and Clifford, had not wandered far from the 160-acre homestead that had produced the large family. Before them, Daniel's grandmother, Nora, had produced another batch of twelve kids, and died in childbirth while trying for a baker's dozen. That was the way life was away from the city, sixty-five miles away. Some of them had moved closer to town. Liberty, New York was twelve miles to the west, but most, if they hadn't found a way to go off to college after high school, had remained home.

Unlike the city dwellers, they were as self-sufficient as any family in the twenty-first century. They weren't on the grid. A hydro-generator supplied electrical power from the dam, sufficient to provide for their needs. A solar charging station kept a bank of deep-cell batteries charged at all times, and their tractor and ATVs were plugged into the charger when they were not in use. They grew their own crops for the most part, supplementing their harvest with store-bought items when they had to, but they seldom spent money on things they saw as frivolous.

All family meetings were held in the kitchen, where the round table had a chair for each member. After Mom and Dad, everyone had equal say about family matters. Dad would announce the issue, and Mom would express her concerns. Then they went around the table, from oldest to youngest. "We have a crisis," Dad began. "You know that they just brought the people from New York City out to the Torgesson's farm to live until they can go back home. They may be there for a while. You saw what happened to the city when the power went out. The buildings are still burning." He scanned the faces of his four children, who sat silent and serious. They had always been his pride and joy, and they not only spoke and acted as a family, they thought alike. There would be no dissension.

"I have never thought much of city folks," Dad continued. "They aren't like us, and you can't trust 'em." He stopped and sipped on his coffee.

"We need to look out for our own and save what's ours. What I'm sayin', is that they will take what's ours if we don't watch out. We need to be vigilant." He turned toward his wife, the organizer. She ran the family, as her mother had done before her. It was her purpose in life, and she took her role as matriarch competently and naturally. She could be nothing else.

"Kids, we need to get busy. Boys, you are in charge of protecting the livestock. I want you to move them from the pastures closest to the tent city, away from anyone who would mess with them. Girls, you will stay here and watch what is happening from your bedroom windows upstairs. Anything that is out of the ordinary, you need to tell your Dad and me. We all need to work together to make sure that bad things don't happen."

Betsy was the first to speak. She was the oldest and the most opinionated. At her sixteen years of wisdom, parents were invisible until the realities of living intruded. The presence of hundreds or thousands of strangers from the city was enough to take her out of her adolescent world.

"Mom, can't we just tell them to go away? They don't belong here. Jeremy told me that he saw some of them in town, and they were scary. They're not like us . . ."

"I know, honey. Until we figure out what's happening, your boyfriend will have to settle for visits at the farm, and you and your sister will be here. We can't chance what they're going to do, and I don't want you to venture into town. For now, we need to stay here."

"But Mom . . ."

"You can shop on the internet, but my darling girl, if you don't seek my approval of what you're buying, you and I are going to tangle."

Dad hollered in a voice they had not heard, and in a tone that frightened them.

"Pay attention! We are a family, and you will do as you are told," he boomed. His intensity was startling. Everyone, his wife included, sat and listened.

"You, each and every one of you, will do as you are told. We are in survival mode. We don't know what they will do, and what they are capable of." He had their attention.

"Boys, you will take your hunting rifles. You can sight the situation through your scopes. If anyone threatens our livestock, and I expect that they will, you will shoot them down. Do you understand me?"

"You mean, I might have to shoot somebody?" Rory was the next in line of consanguinity, and it was his turn to speak.

"You got your first buck with that gun. I know you can shoot. I don't want you to have to, but if it means us over them, yes, son. Don't ask me for permission. You shoot."

"Dad, I . . ."

"I'll be there for you, Rory. I'll take the shot if need be. But if I'm not there for some reason, you need to decide."

Rory took stock of the situation. "Dad, shooting a deer is a lot different from shootin' a man. I don't know . . ."

"I know, son . . ." He walked across the kitchen and hugged his son, so young; and on the precipice of being a man. Behind him, the rest of the family converged. They were together in mind and spirit, and the group hug was comforting and warm. They held each other for a long time, not speaking, just holding. Finally, Dad broke the silence and spoke.

"This is a tough time for all of us. We didn't bring this on, but we have to deal with it or stand to lose all that we have. We need to protect what's ours, and by God, that is what we will do."

CHAPTER 76

Fabio was surrounded by the only members of his neighborhood gang that decided to leave. The city was on fire. People were talking about some plague that came from the rats, and the power was out. The trucks that brought food had stopped coming. The cars didn't work. His apartment didn't have heat, and he had eaten all of the leftover Chinese food that lingered in his refrigerator. He relied on Guido's or Chin Ho's, the restaurants down the street, to fill his belly most days, and they were closed. He had decided to hop on the train when his neighbors, the Sovieros, locked their apartment next to his. They walked out into the January sun with their winter coats and what they could carry.

"Where ya goin'?"

"We can't stay here no longer," said Anthony, who huddled in the middle of the street with his wife and two young children. "You need to think about what's about to come. Once that fire hits our building, where are you gonna go? It can only get worse. People been talkin' about them rats, the Gambian ones, that's bigger than a cat. No way we gonna stay here with the rats and the fire and all. You need to man up and get outta here while you can. We're taking that train." They turned and walked away, toward the train station that emitted the whistle every few minutes. It was the only sound other than the crackling of the fire that was aggressively consuming the building at the end of their street.

The city was dead, and those who tried to cling to the way things used to be would die along with the past. Fabio stood in the empty street, watching his neighbors disappear in the distance. He realized that he had never been anywhere than the city, and the thought of leaving New York was frightening to him. All he had was the city, and now it was like a lifeless corpse. All that he had and everything that gave him comfort was going up in flames. There was nothing he could do about it, and he had to go.

"Come on," he announced to his only remaining friends, Arthur and Frankie. They had considered themselves a gang, a mutual protection society created in childhood and a stronger alliance than his loose-knit family. When their parents passed away, the gang became the only family they had, and their loyalty to each other was a bond that could not be broken. They retreated to their apartments and gathered up their possessions of value and clothes they thought they would need, and appeared in the street a few minutes later. It turned out that they were traveling light. There wasn't much to save.

"Frankie, you can't take your Xbox. The bomb broke it. It don't work no more," explained Fabio. "Bring what food won't go bad, and some clothes, and the warmest coat ya got."

"But Fabio . . ."

"Ya can't bring nothin' that runs on electricity, understand? It ain't no good no more."

"OK, I'll just bring what you told me . . ."

"Hurry," said Fabio, as the roof of the building next to his apartment erupted in a roar of flame and smoke.

CHAPTER 77

Bradbury stood in his Pentagon office facing the split-screen monitor that occupied one wall. The doors were locked, and his staff was given strict instructions that he not be disturbed. His orders would be followed without question. Like the general, his staff had risen through the ranks, and disobeying the command of a superior officer would have resulted in a busting of rank. The interior of Pryor's massive great room occupied the left side of the screen, and the right side showed a glitzy high-rise hotel in Las Vegas. In the great room stood Pryor, dressed in an ornate military uniform, more grand than the general himself. *He has become a military man now, has he? I'll have to have a few tense words with the Society about this. We have a madman steering the ship.*

There was another presence in the room. He could see the back of the man's head and that he had dark hair, but that was all. He held a cell phone in his left hand. "Mr. Pryor," the general began. "I informed you at the last meeting of the members that when it came time to impose martial law that you would have my full support. The combined forces of our military would be under my control, and the commander in chief would be removed from power until order is restored. I conditioned that support upon the premise that there would be no collateral damage of American citizens." General Bradbury paused, anticipating that Pryor would loudly protest his opening comments, and he was right.

"General, I want you to see how we deal with deal breakers. If you will focus your attention on the tall building on the right side of the screen, you will get an understanding of our situation." Pryor ignored Bradbury's comments. He was wallowing in his megalomania; his illness had rendered his mind incapable of entertaining a thought that differed from his own.

That son of a bitch thinks that dressing up to look like me makes him a military leader. If he ever served, it was stateside behind a desk. He never looked into the eyes of a man facing death at his own hands. He doesn't have the guts or the discipline to pull the trigger himself.

"Before we begin, I want you to understand the events that led us here. What you see is the tallest residence in Las Vegas, the Apex. In the penthouse of that building is a traitor to our cause, along with his crew. We know him as Bob, and we have been sending him around the country installing our little EMP bombs for us. This one is just a dummy device, with a big surprise. This will be his last assignment, for poor Bob couldn't keep his mouth shut and do as he was told. He tattled on us, general, and we can't have that, can we?" Pryor nodded to Darkhorse, who punched three numbers into the cell phone. A second later, the top of the building exploded in a bright fireball.

Bradbury took the explosion as his opportunity to terminate the connection.

The duty of a soldier is to live and fight another day. If someone doesn't take him out before I get the chance, I'll personally kill him with my bare hands.

CHAPTER 78

I'm hungry, and I need meat." Fabio and his cohorts sat huddled in the canvas tent, a remnant of wars past. It had been preserved for unknown future use by government bean counters, who could qualify the old relic as "in use." That way, the drafty shelter could be checked off on audit forms as useful, and the taxpayers could see their money in service. It didn't keep out the cold, though, and whenever the wind blew, it was as comforting as a miniskirt in a blizzard.

"We been here for a full day, and all they fed us is granola bars and water. The coffee sucks, and I ain't seen no real food since I left the city," Fabio complained loudly to whoever chose to listen. Most people came to the food tent to fill their bellies and trade gossip. He came out of boredom and the need to cause a ruckus.

He was still their leader, despite their change of location, and they shared the misery. The people who came by train to this temporary home had nobody they could rely upon to take them in; no relatives, and no money to pay for their keep. They were America's orphans, transported from the familiar to a place they didn't want to be. Fabio thrived on his mini-leadership status. He ventured out of the tent with Arthur and Frankie in step, intent on creating enough mayhem to set himself apart as a badass. He brandished his switchblade, sharpened until it doubled as a razor. Whenever it emerged from the internal pocket of his leather jacket, it provoked fear in anyone within slashing distance.

"I am the master of my world, and you are my slaves!" He spun, the blade extended at arm's length. The crowd backed away in silence, and he stood in the middle of the clearing, the sun gleaming off the metal of his weapon.

"Put that thing away or put it to good use," exclaimed a voice from the back of the gathering.

"Who said that?"

"I did." The crowd parted, and a man in his late seventies stood alone, a defiant look on his face. He wore a black ball cap that signified he had seen combat in Vietnam, and his tattered khaki coat bore the insignia of the First Battalion, Ninth Marines. The symbol on his patch was the Grim Reaper. His battalion was known as The Walking Dead for the high number of casualties sustained in jungle combat, and he had survived. That feat had officially qualified him as a badass among his fellow marines, and he had proudly carried that reputation throughout his long life. He was a man that Fabio was ill prepared to confront.

"I already have a few scars I picked up in Laos, and I'm willing to bet that I can wrestle that pig sticker out of your hand and poke a few gushers in you before I'm down and out," he announced.

"You think so, old man? You think so?" Fabio moved forward and swept the knife in a menacing arc. Many of the observers backed away from the threat, but the unarmed marine stood solid with his arms at his sides.

"I ain't gonna stand down to no punk with a knife who never had cause to use one except to clean the crap from under his fingernails." He moved closer in a menacing motion, into the range of the knife.

Fabio took two steps backward, and several people laughed. He was all bravado, and the marine had determined early that his opponent had no expertise at hand-to-hand combat. Worse for Fabio, the young man had no desire for anything more than intimidation, and the old marine could see it in his eyes.

"I'll show you, I can use this to cut you up, but I won't bloody it up on some old vet. You'll see. I'm gonna get me some meat."

"Hunting with a four-inch blade? You intend to sneak up on Bambi and cut his neck?"

Fabio sputtered. Without words and lacking the ability to respond, he had been stripped of the small amount of control he maintained. He had nothing.

The laughter spread, and Fabio fled, followed by his two obedient stooges. They ran until they were out of breath and the sound of the laughter had dissipated in the whipping wind. "I'll show them. They'll see," he proclaimed. Arthur and Frankie stared at him, needing guidance and getting none. They shivered and waited, without a plan and without a clue.

CHAPTER 79

Thirteen-year-old Rory Stableton looked through the sights on his .30-06 rifle at the tent city. His companion was his eleven-year-old brother, Jonathan. Both boys carried a backpack containing peanut butter and jelly sandwiches their mom had prepared before dawn, along with an apple and fresh brownies that still emitted the comforting aroma that had lured them to the country kitchen the night before, long before the baking was done. It had worked every time, that luring scent. It comforted them, the familiarity of it, and they moved confidently toward the stone wall that would be their post. Before the sun came up, the boys were off on their assigned tasks, intent on their mission.

Between their observation point at the top of the hill and the canvas home of displaced New Yorkers, was the winter pasture of the Stableton herd of dairy cows. Beneath a thin layer of snow, there was the leftover hay of summer, once six-feet high, that now lay brown and flat on the ground. In the organic remains of the previous harvest season was food for the production of milk, and with it, the start of cheese, and the nutrition the cows needed to survive the fallow months before spring. There were thirteen of them, placidly grazing in the sun. It would only take a ring of the dinner bell at the cow barn, and their simple minds would lead them ambling slowly back to shelter for the night. But there was no time.

Off in the distance, Rory sighted three dark figures closing in on a yearling that stood at the low end of the pasture. They were still over a hundred yards apart, but he could see the sun glint off metal in the hand of the leather-jacketed figure in front. He was in a crouch and moving slowly toward the small herd of Jersey cows.

Rory looked down at his little brother, who was trying to quietly swallow the last of Rory's brownie. He had already finished his own, and the guilty look on his face was enough to convict the young boy in any court in the land. Normally, Rory would have taken the opportunity to thrash him and take back what was left of his lunch, but he didn't care about that now. He needed guidance.

"Johnny, get the phone and call Dad."

"Where is it?" the boy replied, his speech garbled by the prodigious amount of brownie that had not left his mouth.

"Look in your pocket, you ass."

"I'm tellin'," he responded.

"Johnny, if you don't hurry up, that guy down there is going to kill one of our calves, and then I'm telling on you . . . hurry up, you turd."

Fumbling on the outside of his pants, Johnny felt the familiar outline of the cell phone. He pulled it out and quickly handed it to Rory, who flipped it open and said, "Dad."

CHAPTER 80

Fabio stood in a half crouch, his knife in his right hand.

"Here, boy." He slowly crept toward his prey and whistled.

"Fab, I don't think that's a boy cow. It has those milky things down there. I remember them being bigger on TV . . ."

"Shut up, Frankie. Here boy." He took another step in the calf's direction, prepared to run at the first sign of aggression. It was the closest he had been to a living animal that large outside of a zoo, and his heart was pounding with adrenaline. The heifer raised its head and continued to placidly chew its hay.

"Look how big its eyes are. I never saw such big eyes . . ." Arthur had expressed what his cohorts were thinking. "Are you gonna kill that cow?"

"Both of you just shut up."

He didn't move forward, deliberating his next move. "I'm going to cut us up some steaks, and then we'll be eating better than those assholes down there. Then who's the hero?"

Fabio took another tentative step toward his prey.

"Maybe you oughta milk it."

"Do you know how to milk a cow, Frankie? I sure don't. Why

don't you just crawl under there and start milking, and when you're done pulling on those tits, I'll get me some meat."

"I'm not touchin' those things."

Fabio turned his head, intent on continuing the ludicrous argument. "You freakin' idiot. You'll scare it away." The young milk cow sensed danger in his voice, and raised its ears. They froze in their tracks and stepped back. The trio moved backward in synchronized movements, holding their arms in a mock surrender posture.

Arthur had never been out of the city, and his gaze was intent on the animal's eyes, just like he had seen in countless movies when the main character encounters a wild animal in the jungle. If he had been paying attention to where he was stepping he wouldn't have stepped into the steaming pile of cow manure. The scent hit his nostrils and he yelled, pulling his leather-soled street shoes up in an attempt to extract both feet at once. He succeeded until gravity took over, and came back to the ground in a stomp, still in the center of the cow pie. The manure splattered all over the jeans of Fabio and Frankie, who immediately concluded that he had done it on purpose. They took off in his direction, startling the calf, who began a quick amble in the opposite direction and the protection of the herd.

CHAPTER 81

"Dad, Dad!" Rory had entered panic mode, and Johnny was already hysterical. "He's getting closer," he screamed.

"Tell me what you see. How many are there? Do they all have knives?"

Rory looked through the sight of his hunting rifle at the unfolding emergency over two hundred fifty yards away. "Three of 'em. First, two of them were chasing the third man around, and then the one with the knife started chasing the heifer again."

"He's gaining on her!" Johnny was standing erect, his young eyes intent on the chase.

"Set your sights on the one with the knife. Can you make the shot?"

Rory had become proficient with the hand-me-down .30-06 rifle, having bagged his first buck when he was the same age as his little brother, but this was a person, and he was running, and they were now six hundred yards away. He had never intended to do any shooting, just looking through the scope while his sisters used the only two pairs of binoculars from their bedroom windows.

"I don't know," Rory replied. He's about six hundred yards away at the low end of the pasture, and he's moving fast."

"Don't hit the heifer, but peel off a shot behind her. At least they'll know someone's shooting at them." Dad didn't think that there was much chance of Rory hitting anything at that distance. Even in controlled conditions and without a crosswind, a bullet would drop over two and a half inches over six hundred yards, and the ground was the most likely target. Rory took aim and fired just as the man with the knife came within the last ten yards of the now-frightened Jersey cow and lunged.

The bullet tore through Fabio's neck, sending fragments of tissue and blood in a pink spray over his companions. The impact threw his body face forward in midlunge and he hit the hard ground with a thud, slicing his cheek on a frozen cow pie before the report of the gun was heard. While the boys ran at full tilt back to the house, Frankie and Arthur stood agape and watched as Fabio's lifeblood leaked onto the frozen ground, not only from the neck wound, but from the knife that had pierced his torso. It was still in his hand.

"Let's get out of here," Frankie said, his voice shaking. They ran.

CHAPTER 82

Word traveled fast. Instantaneously, in fact. America had reached the stage where the government received the news in the same time as everyone else, and Bill Staffman and Andrew Fox kept an impressive assortment of news sources running 24-7 in the White House press room. It was their job, to monitor the wall of information and advise the president on breaking news. The crisis in New York had dominated the world for days, and sparse images of the burning city were interspersed with stories and interviews of evacuees.

When the story of a New Yorker being killed over a milk cow by a local upstate boy became known, the collective anger was at an all-time high. It pitted city against country, and country was outnumbered. The metropolitan point of view was that it was just a cow, and nobody, especially a New Yorker, should die over a cow. The rural view was basic, and expected; they had the right to protect their own, and these interlopers from the city had no right to be there in the first place. The reality of the situation was this: The boy didn't intend to kill, just to frighten. His father instructed him to frighten, not kill. The perception of that reality could never be reconciled between urban and rural, but with a little tweaking, they could all blame it on the president. It was the American way.

Bill Staffman was the first to brief Max on the situation. He had been there from the start of the campaign, dealing with the press on a daily basis while Max made himself unavailable. It was a war of words, and Bill had become a master of taking away and giving back, supplying sound bites on political issues that were so short that Max's every word was used on a 24-7 basis in continuous loop. While the other candidates' words were filtered, sliced, and spun to create a product that appealed to their viewers, the world heard the essence of Max's message.

"Mr. President, we have a problem."

"Good!"

"Why do you say that?"

"I needed something to get my mind off the other problems," Max quipped. They both laughed heartily. "If you came in and told me we had a *big* problem, then I'd have to start worrying." They laughed again, and it was therapeutic. The tension around the White House had steadily increased to near panic level, and a little dark levity at the right time worked wonders to improve morale.

When Staffman had fully briefed the president, Max insisted upon a full report of how the media was spinning the incident for their respective audiences. "How is Glenda spinning it?"

"That's the strangest of all, sir. She's calling it a lack of leadership. Apparently, this disaster has become your fault."

"Listen. I've got to get out there. I can't fix this unless I can be seen doing something about it."

"Planning on giving the Secret Service a few conniption fits?"

"Yep. Send Armstrong up here."

Sixty seconds later, Armstrong appeared. "I'm thinking of taking a little road trip," Max began. Armstrong groaned. "With all of the respect in every molecule in my brain, Mr. President . . ." When his chief Secret Service agent used formality, it was his way of getting Max's attention. "Go on, say what you have to say, and then I'll tell you what I'm going to do," Max responded, anticipating that he was about to hear every reason why it was a bad idea.

"We just recovered the vice president, and now you want to go on some damn fool . . ." Armstrong sensed his words were bordering on insubordination, and toned it down in midsentence. "Mr. President, the American people need to see you leading from here, and not placing yourself in harm's way."

". . . but I was going to go in disguise . . ."

"Well sir, that's all well and good. Then you can give up the idea of traveling in disguise for the rest of your term in office, and I can go back to protecting you in the conventional way. Everyone, and I mean the press, your enemies, and eight-year-old kids on the street will be trying to catch you at that game." Armstrong was right, and Max knew it.

"OK, I'll take that advice. But how do you suggest I get my message to the people?"

Staffman took the opportunity to speak first. "That's what I came up here to brief you about, Mr. President. We have pieced together some footage of you and Rachel, some stuff that we had left over from your inaugural, and with a voice-over and some tweaking, you can deliver a message of hope without going anywhere. We rigged some drones with holographic projectors. I know that you have used this cutting-edge technology to your advantage before. We can send them anywhere we want, spreading the message. We can take that same image and message and broadcast it around the world through every media outlet that will run it, and Max, they *will* run it."

CHAPTER 83

The drone appeared on the horizon. Its compact engine provided the only mechanical sound that many of the inhabitants of the tent city had heard in days. They emerged en masse from tents and walked toward the hovering drone. When they came within listening distance, the hologram of Max and Rachel appeared on the ground in front of them. He had used a similar device on the night before the general election, but the image was indoors, under controlled lighting conditions, where the viewer was unable to discern whether the image standing on a stage was real. This attempt was outdoors, and although the day was slipping into the gray of evening, the image projected from the drone had a translucent effect.

"You create your own reality. I want you to create a winning reality."

Max sat on the hood of his Corvette. By word of mouth and the sound of his engine, the crowd assembled on the large expanse of field surrounding his chosen location. Rachel was at his side, dressed in her flight suit and jacket. He took the extremely dangerous course of dealing with Americans in a crisis situation without anyone to protect him from the wrath of people who had, most likely, voted him into office. If he failed at his message, the end result might lead to panic and the end of hope right then, right there. If they didn't listen now, in their time of need, they were doomed to life as a nation of complainers. He needed for them to dig deep into their heritage as Americans and triumph over adversity.

"Crowd up close, so you can hear me," he announced in his loudest voice. He wore a winter jacket with no adornment other than the presidential seal in gold. They only saw the man with the most recognizable face in the world, sitting on a convertible Corvette in the middle of the winter, wearing a jacket and freezing his ass off, just like the rest of them. He was only there in their minds, but he had brought the world before "The Inaugural Event" back to their consciousness, and the image was comforting.

"I can tell you without any doubt in my mind, that you will survive this. This is not the end of the world, or the end of the world of your children or of your grandchildren. We will survive, and survive well." The crowd cheered. They were in desperate need of hope. Despite the efforts of volunteers to find relatives, family, to take in these people, the residents of the tent city had nothing and nobody for the time being, and they were acutely aware of it.

"I'm waiting here with you for the help you need. Whatever you are going through, we are going to make the bad parts temporary." They cheered again, and for the moment, he was their only hope. They were cold, uncomfortable, and hungry. It was clear that they did not want to be there. They would be his toughest audience, because in life, New Yorkers take pride in being the toughest audience of badasses that a person can confront.

"You are all you've got. You can't expect me to wipe your ass for you. The government cannot and should not provide for your every need," Max began.

"Here it comes," shouted a middle-aged man. "Now he will be telling us to be patient."

"I want you to be patient," Max responded. At the same time, I want you to appreciate that we are doing the best with a bad situation. You will not starve to death, and we are going to feed you better from now on. We have found several chefs from the City to help us with that, and we will be bringing good food to you in a New York minute."

"We are a free people, free to succeed or fail, and we will not fail."

"Quitting is not an option. Failure is not an option. The only acceptable choice is to survive, and to persevere until you are back home, in your own bed, and not in fear."

"In a few minutes, there will be helicopters that will land in that clearing right over there, and we will try to take care of your needs. Who's hungry?" The crowd cheered.

Max continued, "I've got government cheese . . ." The crowd moaned loudly in unison. "I know, I tried some of that a few days ago. How can you eat that stuff?" Max smiled, and a cheer rose. They stamped their feet, and the relief was palpable.

"OK, OK, I get the message. How about if I told you that we're flying in a team of New York's best pastrami sandwich chefs, and we're making pastrami sandwiches for everyone!"

Pandemonium ensued, and for the next twenty minutes Max sat with Rachel in his arms from hundreds of miles away, confident that he had done the unthinkable. They could see the crowd's reaction from monitors placed out of the camera field. She smiled. His core purpose in being there, his image at least, was to keep them alive. Now, he had hit upon the keys, just one of them, to keep them happy. All he had to do was deliver.

Out of the crowd, entertainers trickled in, making their way to the front by elbow and nudge, until they were able to attain enough free space to do their thing. Most likely, they were displaced from Greenwich Village, unable to make a living in a dead city without power, without cars, and absent the people who populated it. They provided a small distraction while Max waited for the government helicopters to arrive.

"Tell me what you need, and let's see if we can deliver!" Max hollered in his loudest voice. To come in with amplified sound in their situation would make him look like he was depriving them of the comforts they craved, and it would defeat the purpose of his visit. "I'm cold!" The crowd murmured in agreement.

"We're gonna fix that," Max replied. Do you want to know how?"

"Yes!" They all wanted to know how the president of the United States was going to swoop in and make them comfortable again. No president had ever done that before. Max was ready.

"A long time ago," he began, buying time, but the message needed to be told. "A guy who lived on Long Island made a machine that gave us free energy. He was from Croatia, so he wasn't born here, and he had a hard time. A lot like some of you." The crowd became silent, and as the sun descended over the hills in the distance, making purple and orange highlights on the clouds, he began a story that captured their imagination. For the moment, he was the only entertainment in their lives, and they clung to every word.

"His name was Nikola Tesla. He was what most people would call a genius, but he was just like you and me. He followed his dreams."

"You know all of that talk about an energy crisis and how we are going to run out of power? That's bullshit." The crowd moved closer. This was what they needed to hear, straight talk in tough times, and delivered like a New Yorker.

"All along, since Tesla created this generator, we have been able to produce free energy." Max paused, to allow his audience to absorb the meaning of his words. "What I'm telling you, is every month that you paid your utility bill, to keep you warm in the winter, cool in the summer, to cook your food and keep all of your gadgets running . . . it all can be supplied for free."

Max didn't wait for the helicopters to come. As long as he had their attention, he intended to use the opportunity to get his message to everyone who would listen. "We are all the victims of the Carrington Effect." He didn't pause. Delay would have left room for questions. "There are people who want you to die. They don't believe that you can survive. I believe you can. Prove me right!"

They didn't want to die, and despite their feelings of doom over the previous two weeks, they were there, not to die, but to survive. The people who chose to stay behind in the dead city had chosen to cling to the past and wither away until they were gone, or they refused to believe that the city would no longer sustain them. That group was the most dangerous; the scavengers and the gangs. If the spreading bubonic plague didn't finish them off, they would soon be killing each other for control of dwindling resources.

"The Carrington Effect is something they probably never taught you about in school," he continued. "There is a type of energy that can shut down all of our things we take for granted. It can come from the sun, but this time, it came from some bombs that did the same damage. This time, they went after you." He paused this time, hoping that his message would get through before the helos popped over the horizon.

"I need to tell you. There are people who want us to fail, who think we don't amount to a pile of garbage. These are not foreign enemies. They are Americans." Their heads were turned in the direction of his holographic image. *That's a good sign.* Max counted on his words being distributed in sound bites by the end of the day. His words needed to be heard by the nation, or he was wasting his time. While the message was being broadcast from drones, it was also being sent in a broadcast to every media outlet in the world.

The sound of large helicopters grew closer, and the effect of their appearance on the horizon was reassuring but terrifying. Six large Bell Boeing V-22 Ospreys, each capable of carrying cargo of twenty thousand pounds, rose above the distant hills like enormous black dragonflies. Their huge tilt-rotors tore through the air with their gigantic propellers until they approached the designated landing area. The crowd watched in fascination as the airplane transformed into a cargo helicopter by tilting into rotors and landing gingerly in a slow vertical descent. By the time the blades had stopped spinning, National Guard troops had already begun the process of off-loading their precious cargo.

CHAPTER 84

Lincoln spoke slowly, in deliberate, measured tones. His voice was higher in tone than Max expected, but his words riveted Max to his message. *"Politics is petty, partisan, and impotent,"* declared Lincoln. He appeared in the Oval Office at the behest of Max, who was desperately seeking a path to resolving the challenge that threatened the nation. If he couldn't win this battle, Americans would suffer, and his presidency would dissolve like dry sand in his hands. He was amazed at the book's ability to focus on his most perplexing thoughts and provide guidance by the best of his predecessors, but that was the enlightenment that made the presidency a repository of wisdom.

"You have a keen sense of the obvious, and you are destined for greatness, provided you live to steer your dreams and goals past these petty roadblocks," continued Lincoln. *"I was challenged in my time, and you are challenged in yours. Do not become so caught up in yourself that you disregard the responsibility to which you have been entrusted by the will of the people."* He had transformed from the image that had been inscribed in the national memory. The stovepipe hat was gone, along with his trademark beard. Sitting before Max was a

contemporary Abraham Lincoln, dressed in a sport shirt and jeans, with athletic shoes matching the gray of his shirt. Abe was comfortable in his clothes, and he appreciated the change. Contrary to the popular image of Lincoln, the man appeared casual.

"You know, Mr. Masterson, that there are no coincidences. You were meant to be president, as was I. That is the reason why a man with no pedigree can attain the highest office in the land. It's what sets us apart from the dictators and murderers who attain power by zealotry and blood. You will transcend the challenges that confront you, and you will do it in your own way. It is the order of life."

"It appears that in your time, I can no longer assume that a man will be president after you are gone, but a woman may be seated in your stead. Come to think of it, a woman might be better suited to the office. Women seem to be immune to the vagaries that befall the men in politics."

He blushed.

"You're blushing, Abe. I didn't think that politicians retained that quality once they attained public office," Max commented in a low voice.

Lincoln laughed heartily. *"You think I was a politician? I'm no more a politician than you are. I endured many defeats, and you endured none, but we ended up in the same place. Does that not tell you something?"*

Max thought for as long as it took Lincoln to help himself to the benefits of the liquor cabinet. *"I kept a pitcher of cool water here during my term,"* he said.

"Help yourself to anything you choose, there is the best liquor . . ."

"I abstained from those vices during my life, and I choose not to take them up during my death," Lincoln responded.

"I'm sorry, Abe, I had no idea you were a teetotaler," said Max.

"Water suits me fine. I spent much of my years observing my contemporaries being seasick on land, and acting like pure asses."

"If you look below the bar, there is a place to put your glass. If you want ice, just push the button."

"Ice, how delightful. I once dreamed of such a contrivance." Lincoln pushed the button for ice, and it complied, sending cubes bouncing across the carpet.

"I'll get the hang of it, in time," he said smiling. *"Would you like one?"*

"I don't expect anyone to wait on me, especially you," replied Max. *"I have thought about what you told me, and I'm beginning to understand that there are some people who were meant to be here."* Lincoln sat and sipped his water. He waited for Max to continue.

"If I was meant to be president, and you were, the wisdom that comes from this book will be provided from those who belonged here. I know that. What I need now is guidance. How do I deal with my enemy, and how do I turn our country toward greatness again?"

"Zealots should be killed. They will not negotiate. Those who choose to follow a path that conflicts with yours will be amenable to negotiation, but will resist surrender. Choose a path that provides them the dignity of proclaiming victory to their people. As to the rest, they are yours, and you must serve them with the same passion you reserve for your loved ones. Ignore the complainers and follow the dreamers, for they will take you to where you want to go."

"I'm beginning to realize that there are some things that a president can do in the usual way, and others . . ." Lincoln paused, deep in thought.

"When I became president of these United States, the South hated me in unison, and the nation was torn asunder. I was vilified by the very people who put me in office, and it was not safe for me anywhere. I resolved right then and there, on the day of my inauguration, that I would never cower in the Oval Office with no corner to hide. I would sneak out of the White House in disguise. My height gave me away sometimes, but it became a game of deception that I rather enjoyed.

Other times, I would travel with General Wool in broad daylight, but only at times and places where they did not expect me. You should try it."

"I have already thought of that," Max responded. *"I had some disguises prepared, and I'm driving my Secret Service to distraction."*

Lincoln chuckled with the memory of his deceptions, but immediately returned to the sober matters that he had been summoned to discuss.

"Max, learn by my mistakes, and profit from them. Never announce that you will be amongst the citizens unless you are surrounded by your protectors, but don't stay cooped up in this monument to the past. Do it in your own way. You need to be a part of this nation in the same way that a man protects his family; don't let them down, or risk failure." He sipped his ice water, looking into the glass and swirling its contents to hear the tinkle of the ice against the glass.

"The one familiar hand that we both are dealt is the threat from within. Once you step outside your world of isolation and comfort, they will pounce on you if they can find you . . ."

After a quick knock, the door to the Oval Office opened, and the glass fell. The cubes bounced across the presidential seal woven into the carpet. Lincoln was gone.

CHAPTER 85

Roger Sinclair strode into the Oval Office with authority and confidence and assessed the scene. Ice cubes and the glass lay in the center of the ornate rug, and the water had begun soaking into the seal at its center. "I never knew you to be one to throw things," he exclaimed.

"Some days I throw things, some days I don't. Today's a throwing day," Max replied without humor. "What have you got?"

"Drone pictures. When we sent the drones to New York for a flyover to assess the situation, I had one of them redirected to that location in the Hamptons that we detected from the Satellite shots in the dark zone. You know, the house that had lights when everyone else was in darkness? Well, from GPS tracking and a review of the public records, we determined that the house is owned by a one-hundred-seventy-five-year-old man who has no mortgage, has faithfully paid his property taxes on time, and drives a Bentley. This may also interest you. He served in the Civil War . . ."

"OK, are you just here for comedy relief, or do you have some nefarious purpose in messing with me? I'm sure that if I rifle through my desk, I'll be able to find something else to throw . . ." Max pulled out the center drawer and quickly scanned its contents. "Would you prefer to be impaled with a letter opener or knocked unconscious with a very ostentatious paperweight?"

"Neither, Mr. President. I'm serious. One thing about this country that most people don't realize is the records we don't keep. We keep birth records, marriage records, divorce and tax records, and death records, but we don't keep record of someone who doesn't die. What I'm saying here, Max, is that this house seems to have its own shielded power source, and is owned by the same person who has owned it since before the Civil War. Homer Francis did not die. I doubt whether he survived the Civil War, but he owns that house and has paid his taxes by check. His bank account shows a balance of over a million dollars, and the only payments are for taxes and a few for maintenance. He apparently doesn't eat, either."

Max absorbed the information with renewed interest. His conversation with Lincoln had abruptly concluded before he could get a firm grasp of the enormous task that lay before him, but Sinclair's intrusion was beginning to give him direction.

"And here is the real reason I came up here. I had some still images taken from a drone that flew over the gated compound, and instructed the CIA to give me high-resolution shots from all angles. The drone was directed out over the Atlantic, made the turn, and flew low over the large glass windows that face the water. This is what we found."

The images scrolled slowly across the iPad. They showed the scene in extreme detail that exceeded the capacity of the human eye. The digital cameras on drones were designed for military use from high altitudes, and were capable of retrieving words off a page at a distance that made their presence undetectable. With new invisibility technology, it was unlikely that the drone's presence would ever be detected by the human eye or by radar.

The compound appeared to be surrounded by a high wall. It enclosed approximately twenty-five acres of pristine coastal forest which served as a buffer from the nearest neighbors, a long walk down the rocky beach. Where most affluent homeowners open their homes to the sea to enjoy an unobstructed view, the wall fully enclosed the large modern mansion, its white walls set off with glass at rakish angles in a style that only appeared in *Architectural Digest*. This was no house lived in by a Civil War veteran, an impossibility that rational thought immediately dismissed. Max moved from interested to intrigued.

The next pics showed a series of images of the large mansion from the west, with three cars parked in the circular driveway, a Bentley, a black midsized sedan, and a minivan. The detail was so clear that Max could read a bumper sticker that read "Imagine Whirled Peas" on the minivan's rear bumper. The irony was not lost on him.

The next pic showed an overhead image of the entire compound. There was an outbuilding with no windows that added to the mystery. Explaining his theory, Sinclair added, "That building appears to be the power station, but we detected no radiation which would indicate a nuclear power plant, and no heat radiation, so we concluded that this guy has his own Tesla generator. Did I catch your attention yet?"

Max leaned forward in his chair, intent on the details. It was a mystery unfolding before him, each image creating more questions in his mind.

"I assume you saved the best for last, for true theatrical effect?"

"Oh yeah, just wait 'til you see what our little drone saw when it turned around and came at it from the east," said Roger with unrestrained enthusiasm. The drone had made a pass over land from the west, and then flew out over the open ocean before turning and making a second pass. Each successive image focused on the enormous glass windows over the large central living room, lit brightly against the evening sky. There were more than thirty images of the same room, each in more detail and closer than the previous one. There were three people in the room, standing in a triangular formation. There was a dark-haired man with his back to the windows, and a balding, middle-aged man who could be seen in profile. They both faced a third, who stood in the middle of the room facing directly to the east.

He wore a short silk bathrobe adorned with a green dragon. He appeared to be in his sixties, tall and slim, with a greasy look that made his balding black frizzy hair shine. He had familiar bulging eyes, and he held a filterless cigarette in his right hand. It was almost too much detail. His fingers bore the permanent brown and yellow stains of a lifetime smoker. His bare left arm hung to his side, adorned by a fifty-cent-piece-sized mole on his forearm. A tattoo of spider legs emerged from the mole, giving the effect that a huge tarantula had perched on his arm like a repulsive pet.

"I'll be. Adam Pryor has been right under our noses the whole time," Max proclaimed with a disgust reserved for Pryor, and Pryor alone. He knew what he had to do, and quickly.

CHAPTER 86

Max left the situation room without announcing his intentions to anyone. He quickly covered the distance to the Oval Office, and pulled the diary from its hidden place inside the desk. He was in need, and seeking direction. The book glowed, as if it sensed his desperation.

"I knew you would summon me again." It was Jefferson, still dressed in casual clothes, his red hair tied back. *"You seem to have run headlong into a dilemma."* His gaze took in the room, familiar but changed, much like his appearance.

"Yes, sir, I need your advice and counsel now more than ever," Max replied.

"I have nothing more to do in my state of repose than to sit with the president of the United States and offer what wisdom I have retained for posterity," Jefferson responded. He seemed to carry a new energy, a new sense of purpose.

"I have been reading about you, and I need to know the truth of a story that has survived to my time," Max began. *"There is a tale that you shot a traitor and left him to die on the White House lawn."* Max stood and approached the departed president, but the closer he came, the

more the image of Jefferson became translucent. He realized there would be no handshake, no physical contact at all. Their connection would be a mental connection only. Satisfied, he retreated behind his desk and placed both hands on the diary. Immediately, the image of Jefferson became brighter and opaque.

"Yes, it is true," he replied. *"There was a man who sought to sacrifice the honor of our young nation, a Tory, who had sold his soul to the British for a position in the aristocracy and financial reward. I served as his firing squad; me alone. I dispatched with the decorum of a shared execution, and after a trial by his peers, I took him out on the lawn and shot him down like the mangy beast that he was."* Max studied his calm demeanor with fascination. *He describes shooting a man to death as coldly as he might describe cleaning a fish. I need that attitude to serve me for a while.*

CHAPTER 87

The security force entered the mansion from every means of entry, breaking glass and ramming doors simultaneously. Wood and shards of crystal flew in an arc as they entered. A dozen armed drones hovered in a halo around the building, and helicopters patrolled the perimeter. The team secured each room as they entered, carefully opening closed doors until they found their quarry. Pryor stood in his glass-lined living room. He was dressed in a robe, his wiry, white, hairless legs extending below the expanse of terry cloth. He held a hefty glass of scotch, and he sipped in defiance as the well-armed force broke into the room. "You'll pay for that," he declared.

He was surrounded, and defiant, and delusional. His megalomania made him feel invincible. "You know, the legal system will determine my fate, long after your president has left office in disgrace, and my people have the resources to post whatever bail a judge in my breast pocket will impose. I'll die in luxury before you get your satisfaction in court."

"What makes you think that we are going to give you a trial?" The voice came from the mask of a uniformed commando who stood at arm's length. Unlike the others, he carried no weapons.

He was identical in appearance to the other eleven, but his voice was unmistakable.

"Masterson?"

"Yes, you sick son of a bitch."

"Well, well, aren't you ignoring protocol? I should know, I wrote the book on it," Pryor sneered. "You should be cowering in a bunker somewhere. Feeling all safe and protected. Didn't your daddy and his pretty little girlfriend teach you that? I think it's time to talk about the terms of my presidential pardon, don't you?"

"My father and Adrianna taught me a lot of things. One of the first lessons they taught me was to never negotiate with zealots and murderers, and you are both."

"Oh, that. I had Darkhorse handle all of those messy details. He has been employed by us since he was old enough to kill, and that was very young. He was taught by his father, too. You remind me of him." He downed the last of his scotch in one gulp. It was a gesture of defiance.

You tried to kill my father, but only succeeded in killing the only woman he ever loved. I don't care if you had someone else do it for you. I'm not a cold-blooded assassin, and I am nothing like this Darkhorse. Max gritted his teeth, fighting the urge to choke the evil out of the repulsive man.

"My employers have more power than you can imagine, and they control the money. This country, all of it, will soon be back in our control, and you will be history. It won't matter whether I'm gone. The plan has been implemented, and there is nothing you can do to stop it," said Pryor. Max and the cordon of commandos took a half step forward. The effect was like the tightening of a noose.

"You want me to blow his head off, Mr. President?" This time, the voice was Armstrong's.

"No, that would be way too merciful, as much as I would like for that to happen, but it makes interrogations much more difficult,

I hear," Max replied through gritted teeth. He could taste the bile that rose from his detest for the man.

"Back off, or I detonate Chicago," Pryor screeched in a shrill voice, pulling a cell phone from his pocket. He had memorized the three-digit code for each city where bombs had been concealed, and all he had to do was type in the numbers.

"Oh, we already got that one," announced Armstrong. "We think we'll just kill you and be done with it." Max had previously given specific orders that Pryor was to be taken alive and detained for the intelligence they could derive from intense interrogation, with the hope that he would reveal other members of the Society. Max was also aware that only six EMP devices had been recovered or detonated, leaving another six unaccounted for. If Pryor held that knowledge, or if he chose a city that had not been scratched off the list, he held another major disaster in his hands.

"Then it's San Francisco."

San Francisco was not on the list. Max's body language revealed that weakness. When Adam Pryor smiled, Max lunged. Pryor assumed that he would grab for the phone, and leaned away in a protective stance, fumbling for control. Max's right hand went to the back of his head, and pulled it forward, while the palm of his left hand slammed against Pryor's nose, jamming cartilage and bone into his frontal lobe. While his eyes rolled into the back of his head, Max broke his neck with a quick twist. Adam Pryor went limp and fell to the floor, his spinal cord severed at the base of his skull.

Armstrong lunged for the phone in the same motion, tossing his assault rifle to the side. Six inches from the floor, he punched the off button and cancelled the signal before he crashed to the hardwood. In one push, he brought himself back on his feet and pulled off his mask. Max did the same.

"You are a quick learner for a politician," exclaimed Armstrong, beaming with awe and pride.

"I'm not a politician, I'm . . ."

"I know, I know, you're just the president of the United States."

They turned at the sound of gunshots. Immediately, the assault team ran in that direction, leaving Max and Armstrong alone with the lifeless body of Pryor at their feet. His unblinking eyes stared, his head turned at a grotesque angle. "I wasn't sure I could do that," Max began. "You know, I thought I would feel satisfied, or relieved, or something . . ."

"The first time is the hardest, but I hope you leave that kind of work to guys like me next time," responded Armstrong, who was fixated on the cell phone. *Pryor held the fate of the nation in his hands. Now we have it back. What will Masterson do next?* He carefully removed the battery from the phone and placed it in an evidence bag for future analysis. *Our tech people can trace the preset numbers so we can track down the last of the bombs, but that won't stop them for long. Max will be fighting many more battles.*

CHAPTER 88

The sound of heavy boots pounding up stairs brought Max and Armstrong out of their deep state of contemplation and back into the present. The security force filed silently into the large room and stood in a half circle at a respectable distance. "Report! What did you find down there?" Armstrong was in total command, and his elite commandos respected his authority without question.

The chain of command required that they stand down until new orders were given, but six of them fanned out to cover the entrance doors to secure the perimeter. When they did, the telltale turquoise of their prize came into view.

"Sir, Mr. President . . . sirs," the exasperated senior SEAL began, "We found a broadcast room that looks just like the one you see on TV. Then we opened a door and heard a scream. We entered a room that looked just like a hotel room, and found this lady tied hand and foot to a bed and there was this big fat guy on top of her with his pants down around his ankles . . . and sirs, he was about to . . . you know . . . and we reacted and took him out, and then some sleazy looking woman jumped one of my men, and she had a knife, and we took her out, too."

"I think I can explain it in more concise terms," Glenda Reasoner intoned.

"These brave men rescued me."

She stood in her trademark turquoise dress, wrinkled and splattered in blood. Her hair was tousled, but she otherwise seemed unharmed. She smiled with intense relief. "I notice that you have been doing some vermin removal yourselves. Who is the man responsible for *this* act of heroism?"

"I am," Max responded.

Glenda Reasoner's eyebrows knitted together in amazement. *He's the president of the United States, and he's standing over the corpse of the most evil man in American history. He just killed Pryor with his bare hands, and he is acting like it's a part of his job description.*

"Then you are my hero, too." She approached Max with arms outstretched, and gave him a warm hug. Max gently broke the embrace and inquired. "How long have you been here?"

"Since before the lights went out in New York, but never mind that. I have so many questions, and you wouldn't expect me to pass up a chance for an exclusive interview with the president of the United States in his moment of crowning glory, would you? I have my commentary to do, and I can do it from here . . . there is so much to do . . . I look a mess."

CHAPTER 89

Max arrived at Fairlane late in the evening. A light dusting of snow glowed on the driveway under the full moon, illuminating his path toward home. It was cold and still. He chose to walk the distance from the front gate to the private entrance to clear his head, and gave strict instructions for his Secret Service detail to remain at the gate. The events of the past eight days had weighed upon his mind, and Rachel had been under lockdown as a security measure since the attack on Manhattan. They had been apart for eight long days. The only opportunity for communication was by a secure line to the house, and their conversations had been short and tense. He longed to be with her.

"Notify security at Fairlane that Rachel is not to be notified of my arrival, and I will be approaching by foot and alone. I will be entering through the private door, and I want them to leave us alone for the evening."

"Mr. President, she knows you're coming. We have been keeping her informed since the start of the crisis according to your instructions." Armstrong saw the look of dismay that his words had caused. "She knows you're OK, she knows you're coming, but she doesn't know when. She kicked my detail out of the house a few hours ago, with strict instructions that they were not to enter. My guys are holed up in the room above the garage," he said reassuringly.

"Good. Leave them there."

He turned toward the house. The only sound was the crunch of snow under his feet. He could breathe again. Max savored the moment and made his way alone, pausing only to marvel at the stars in the clear night sky that the full moon could not outshine. It was a moment in time, but his pausing provoked anxiety. He felt a longing to be home, and he missed Rachel. She was his love. No woman he had known was so right for him. She knew it, too. They both felt it. They had trust, mutual attraction, and a healthy approach to life. He had never felt this way about any of the many, and it felt comfortable. He needed Rachel in his life.

Max approached his private entrance. The technology he had ordered to be installed eliminated any chance that an intruder could enter through that door. He was scanned, and the door unlocked immediately. Forcible entry would have sealed the hallway and gassed all intruders into immediate unconsciousness, and if no antidote was administered within ten minutes, death would come quietly.

He strode quickly down the long hallway. His boots squeaked on the tile floor as he made his way toward Rachel. *She knows I'm coming. What surprise does she have in store for me?*

He entered the central part of the house, the kitchen. The four hallways all converged on the kitchen; Senator Masterson had designed it after realizing that every gathering ends up in the kitchen. There were stools and a counter that addressed each of the hallways as a welcome to anyone who entered from any part of the house. Then there was the pool; it was visible from the kitchen, too, and he saw a glow. Dozens of large candles illuminated the interior of the geodesic dome that covered the heated pool. The steam rising from the pool and the snow falling on the heated glass gave the illusion of a tropical forest inside of a huge snowball.

"Rachel! I'm home!"

There was no answer, but he was drawn to the glow like a moth to a flame.

The glass doors parted as he entered the pool enclosure. A wave of warm, humid air engulfed him. "Rachel, where are you? He stood at the edge of the pool and surveyed the effusion of tropical plants that surrounded the pool. Suddenly, he felt a blow to his butt and felt himself vaulting through the air. He flipped and landed with a splash. Max looked up, and when he had cleared the water from his vision, he saw the most erotic image he had ever seen. Rachel stood above him. She stood above him, bare, fit, and tanned. Her hands were on her hips. She was smiling, and her dimples illuminated by the flickering candles added to his delight. For a long time he said nothing, recovering from the shock and savoring the view.

"Welcome home Mr. President. How was your day?"

"Killed a bad guy with my bare hands and saved the country from certain ruin. How was yours?"

"I soloed your new plane. I'll tell you about it in the morning."

Max leaped forward and grabbed Rachel by both ankles and propelled her over his head. She spun in midair and landed feet first, facing him.

"You are vastly overdressed, my brave warrior."

Rachel reached for the zippers of Max's commando uniform and pulled. It split sideways, leaving his tank top and underwear exposed. "You're still overdressed," she said.

"OK, strip me."

Rachel reached for the wet cotton tank top with both hands and tore it from his body. She tossed the wet heap to the side of the pool. Max breathed deeply with excitement. The candles displayed his wet chest. "No fair," she sighed.

"What do you mean?"

"I'm standing in front of you, fully willing and naked, and you still have your boxer briefs on."

"Not my fault. You got me excited, and there's a hang-up."

"I'll take care of that," she replied. Rachel submerged, and stripped Max to the ankles.

"I see that you have been freed from your confines," she said, wiping hair and water from her eyes. Max pulled her into his arms and held her close. She could feel his rising excitement. *If a man could get any harder, I don't know if I could stand it. I want him.* She wrapped her legs around Max, and he entered her. She gasped, and pressed her chest to his.

Their lovemaking was hot and desperate. He was hard, and she was wet. He locked his arms around her hips and walked her from the pool to a lounger covered with a mink throw. He set her down gently, still inside her. "Oh . . . my . . . you *are* mine," he exclaimed. They writhed and became one, their bodies pumping and stroking. The passion peaked at the same moment, and they exploded in an all-encompassing mutual orgasm. They held each other, breathing hard and sweating. They kissed with more passion. He picked her up and carried her in his arms toward the bedroom. There would be no sleeping.

EPILOGUE

In the morning, Max emerged from his bedroom wrapped only in a towel. His hair was tousled, and he was exhausted, but the look of satisfaction on his face matched his mood. He was back in his environment, and for the moment, he was satisfied. He padded his way toward the kitchen, rubbing his face with his hands. He detected movement through his fingers as he emerged from the hall. Roger Sinclair sat at the large butcher-block kitchen table in the alcove, stirring honey into a cup of coffee and gazing into his iPad.

"Good morning, Mr. President. Have you recovered from your trip?"

"It's too early to tell." Max walked to the refrigerator and extracted a large bottle of his favorite morning drink, a mixture of green tea and orange juice. He dispatched with the formality of a glass, and gulped half of the contents before taking a breath.

"How did you get in here?"

"I have this annoying habit of sneaking in unannounced, but this time I came up from the tunnel. It's handy to have your own underground freeway from the White House," Sinclair replied.

"I'm assuming two things. You already know all about the demise of Pryor, and that you're not just here to congratulate me. What is it?"

"While you were out saving the country from certain anarchy, a situation erupted in the Middle East, and you need to go over there and fix it. We leave in five hours."

"At least you have a legitimate reason for interfering with my love life and my beauty sleep. Before I wake Rachel, let me ask you a question: How do you know everything that is happening before anyone else?"

"Magic," Sinclair said with an enigmatic smile.

"That response doesn't answer my question, but I'll let you slide if you tell me how that Tesla generator works." Max stood with his hands on his hips, oblivious to his relative state of undress.

"Well, Mr. President, from the best I can determine, it came from Teddy Roosevelt, and the U.S. government has kept that secret for generations. We hold the patent confidentially and retain the exclusive rights. Needless to say, the tycoons of his time would have run him out of office for destroying their dynasties in oil and transportation and power generation, so it has been bottled up all this time."

"Theodore."

"What?"

"Theodore. He preferred to be called Theodore. TR to his friends."

Sinclair acquired a puzzled look. "I suppose you won't be telling me anytime soon about how you know that interesting bit of American history."

"Not until you answer my question." Max tenaciously clung to his original inquiry.

"I'll stick with my first answer. It's magic. We know how to build them, but damned if we know how they work. We have been trying to figure that out since Mark Twain delivered them to...Theodore Roosevelt." The puzzled look on Sinclair's face was replaced with one of sincerity.

"Mark Twain? Are you toying with the President of the United

States?" Max shook his head and turned to leave. *I'll have to ask TR about that the next time I see him.*

"Are you going to tell me the answer to my question? How do you know personal details about a long-dead president," Sinclair implored.

"I have my sources," Max replied over his shoulder. *Every question does not deserve an answer.*